# SHADOWSHINE

## An Animal Adventure

D1113192

GUERNICA WORLD EDITIONS 22

# SHADOWSHINE
## AN ANIMAL ADVENTURE

Johnny Armstrong

**GUERNICA**
**World**
**EDITIONS**

TORONTO—BUFFALO—LANCASTER (U.K.)

WITHDRAWN FROM
RAPIDES PARISH LIBRARY
RAPIDES PARISH LIBRARY
Alexandria, Louisiana MC

Copyright © 2019, John Mills Armstrong III and Guernica Editions Inc.
All rights reserved. The use of any part of this publication,
reproduced, transmitted in any form or by any means, electronic,
mechanical, photocopying, recording or otherwise stored
in a retrieval system, without the prior consent of the publisher
is an infringement of the copyright law.

Michael Mirolla, editor
Cover design: Allan Jomoc Jr.
Interior layout: Jill Ronsley, suneditwrite.com
Guernica Editions Inc.
1569 Heritage Way, Oakville, (ON), Canada L6M 2Z7
2250 Military Road, Tonawanda, N.Y. 14150-6000 U.S.A.
www.guernicaeditions.com

Distributors:
University of Toronto Press Distribution,
5201 Dufferin Street, Toronto (ON), Canada M3H 5T8
Gazelle Book Services, White Cross Mills
High Town, Lancaster LA1 4XS U.K.

First edition.
Printed in Canada.

Legal Deposit—Third Quarter
Library of Congress Catalog Card Number: 2018968310
Library and Archives Canada Cataloguing in Publication
Title: Shadowshine : an animal adventure / Johnny Armstrong.
Names: Armstrong, Johnny, III, author.
Description: Series statement: Guernica world editions ; 22.
Identifiers: Canadiana (print) 20190045108 | Canadiana (ebook) 20190045116
| ISBN 9781771834605
(softcover) | ISBN 9781771834612 (EPUB) | ISBN 9781771834629 (Kindle)
Classification: LCC PS3601.R55 S53 2019 | DDC 813/.6—dc23

*To my wife, Karen, who always believed in this story.*

*To my children, Cody and Abby,*
*of whom I could not be more proud.*

*To my grandchildren, Eva, Tullie, and Bain.*

*To the memory of my beloved Doberman,*
*Stella Louise, "the Pup."*

*And finally, to the forest-folk,*
*in whose midst and boundless inspiration I dwell.*

*What we are familiar with we cease to see.*

—Anaïs Nin

# Introduction

WHAT IS SHADOWSHINE?

The expression cannot be found in any standard dictionary in English. Even so, it remains plausible to me that the little word could have been around for a long while. But, of course, nobody knows exactly how long, and nobody can say exactly who it was that first coined the term. Yet, to this explorer of deep-woods supposition, it seems reasonable that the inventor might have been some attentive character among a diverse clan known as the forest-folk, those many and varied individuals who thrived in a great living cathedral—a forest whose canopy was so tall that in some places it allowed only occasional sunbeams to reach the ground and the rolling waters of its winding, clear streams.

Those scaly and feathered and furry citizens, I believe, watched that shadowshine as it skipped across the smooth, gray skin of the butt of an ancient beech tree, and they watched it as it set off the emerald sparkle of the wet sphagnum growing on the rocky wall of a creek bank. Wherever shadowshine happened to make its appearance, the ever-vigilant forest-folk would not likely have missed the show. Who else but the forest-folk could have invented the term?

shad • ow • shine \shad' ō shīn\ *n.* [For. Folk] (Pleistocene-Holocene epoch transition) illumination, usu. in the form of moving spots in a shaded background, created by the reflection of light from ripples on the surface of water

So. Almost all of us have seen shadowshine—those ripples of light on a shady creek bank. All it takes is a walk along a stream in a forest on a sunny day. It's a commonplace phenomenon of nature.

Just as the forest-folk have, we humans have been observing shadowshine throughout the millions of years of our evolution. But why didn't we humans give it a name, like the forest-folk did? Why doesn't it rank as a noun in that massive taxonomy of the English language? If not *shadowshine*, then why not some other collection of letters of the alphabet? Something short and clever. Being that we are all so familiar with it.

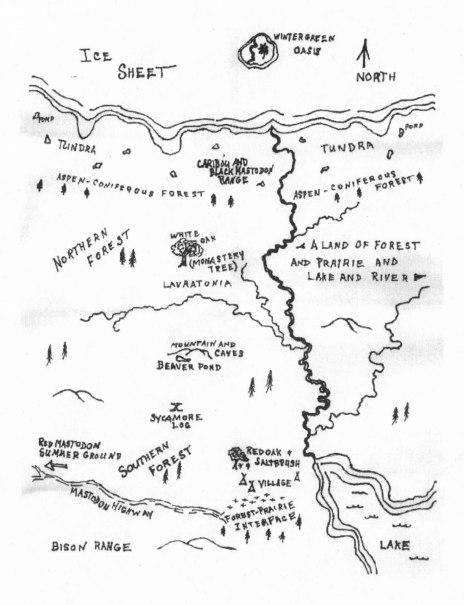

# 1

U P IN THE still, dark chill of the leafless canopy were voices of comrades in quiet chatter. Close comrades. So close, in fact, they were touching each other. Sena, a handsome, well-groomed, and rather stately bobcat, was sitting on Zak's tail. Zak was a forty-eight-year-old, twenty-nine-pound possum, considered middle-aged and slightly above the mean in weight for the species, a fairly typical specimen by most accounts. But it was a time long, long ago— a time when possums were larger, lived longer (*much* longer), had fewer teeth and more brains, liked to climb high to the top of a tall tree, could hang by their tails for extended periods, and could think and travel with greater swiftness than the possums of today.

Zak's long tail was coiled around a limb of a venerable old oak, permitting the rest of his plump fusiform being to hang in midair with a little pink piggish nose pointing straight at the ground seventy feet below. Sena was sitting erect on the limb, with his large furry feet astride the reptilian possum tail. Whenever Zak was hanging by his tail at such height, he preferred Sena to be touching it in some fashion, for he had never completely trusted it to not slip when he dozed off. The pair provided an odd silhouette in the cold moonshine about to be dissolved at the trailing edge of a late-winter night.

"Sena, do you remember what day this is? A splendid day it is for the ringtails, Nadine and Dunklin. And a splendid day, too, for a lovely little mouse couple—at least, according to the Canopy Connection."

"Zak, let's move. I want to be out of here before the banging starts."

"Of course you are talking about the ivory-billed woodpeckers, noble and novel creatures, freshly evolved, I hear. And I expect that fact puts them a notch or two up the evolutionary scale from the rest of us, including bobcats."

"You couldn't be more wrong, Zak. That's bull, as you so often like to say."

Mammalogical esoterica as it may seem, for possums, bull is always food for thought. It has a special meaning for them.

So Zak thought it over, and then he spoke. "Perhaps you are right, dear Sena. A freshly evolved species such as they represent might not yet have passed the survival-of-the-fittest test. Perhaps the clan is yet to prove itself. Bull, perhaps. And what an obnoxious amount of damage they do to the ashes and elms and pines. Bull indeed!"

"Zak, possums and bobcats are on different branches of the evolutionary tree from woodpeckers, which are no more 'freshly evolved' than we are. It's not a scale. It's a tree with lots of limbs and twigs on which the symphony of evolution plays its many lovely tunes. And while we are on the subject of trees, it's the dead ones that the ivory bills pick on, so they are not doing any damage at all to the ashes and elms and pines."

"Why not?" asked Zak.

"I just told you!"

"Incomprehensible," mumbled Zak.

If the two friends disagreed, it was usually Zak who eventually gave in, as his train of thought invariably came around to the "incomprehensible" stage, which, of course, especially if compared to bobcats, might have been due to certain possum cranial restrictions. Whether or not those restrictions were real, they certainly were of no import, since the two friends knew that in the grand scheme they were both survivors and therefore equal, more or less.

The pair climbed down from the oak and struck out along the forest floor, where they trotted side by side toward the dim easterly glow of dawn, and as they trotted, there came from above a clamorous banging and cracking and prying commotion and a shower of bits of wood and bark from high up the trunk of a dead but ancient tree. It was here that a pair of ivory bills had embarked on their morning beetle foraging. And as three fox squirrels were excitedly scurrying after one another along the living branches of the tall canopy, there also rained a mist of tiny flower parts from the earliest blossoms of impatient maples and elms. The canopy's day shift was now fully activated.

As the day progressed, Sena and Zak's long trot carried them through woodlands of oaks, gums, maples and pines and across deep ravines within which resided small running streams they had to jump. It carried them over gentle hills of mixed oak and pine and hickory and down into flat hardwood bottoms with larger streams they had to swim. It carried them through small prairies created many years before by both soil character and wildfires, and finally, it carried them on into the early evening where at last they were about to reach their destination, the edge of a prairie of more significant size than any Zak and Sena had seen during their long trek. The prairie lay to the west of a great lake whose waters were born of a river that flowed from the far north. So here was a land, a lovely land, of forest and prairie and lake and river.

As Zak and Sena soon found themselves approaching the interface between the forest and prairie, their anticipation began to rise, for here would be the designated site of a gathering of forest-folk for a wedding. Zak had to be present at all forest-folk weddings and preside over vows exchanged between groom and bride. This was because Zak, as a tiny naked baby possum, had fallen out of his upside-down sleeping mother's pouch late one night to become a helpless orphan. It was because he had not taken a firm tail-hold of the pouch's inner side wall as baby possums of that time normally did, and he just slipped free like a fat little glob of spit to land in a pile of leaves some fifty-five feet below. Finally, it was because he had been rescued and adopted by a family of gray squirrels who, like all their rodent cousins, spoke an archaic language that was strange to the rest of the forest-folk—a politely garbled and ever-so-slightly pig latin-like tongue.

It was not because Zak was a preacher or justice of the peace; it was because he was bilingual that he was called upon to attend to all forest-folk weddings. His bilinguistic ability was necessary because whoever of the forest-folk were to be married, whether it be coyote couple or cougar couple or raccoon couple and so on, there was always a romantically inclined pair of rodents who became so enraptured by the coming event that they demanded to be included, thus creating a double wedding ceremony. And so it was that there was never a single, single wedding among the forest-folk. It was always at least double.

Of course, Zak's position attracted a certain prestige for himself, which built up a certain pride that had helped him to keep up the long trot over the course of the day with his bobtailed confidant, Sena, whom he always brought along as his guest on such occasions. Zak's pride in himself had impelled him to take his position so seriously that he had reasoned he needed a title, so he had appointed himself as Poet; and further discovering a need to justify the title of Poet, he had, some time ago, thought up a little rhyme that he recited at every single forest-folk double wedding.

"Dear sir, what on earth are you doing? This is highly irregular! Incomprehensible!" said Zak, as his bobcat companion clamped spike-pointed canines onto his tail and dragged him, writhing and hissing, into the bushes and away from the well-worn path that the two had recently entered.

"Saving your life, Zak," said Sena through his teeth, but his words were drowned by a thunderous noise from the path now filled with great russet legs and trunks and ivory tusks of a moving herd of southern red mastodons. When the last of the great creatures trotted by, Zak and Sena reentered the dusty path that would lead them to the site of the wedding.

"My dear Sena, that was just a pinch too close!" said Zak. "My concentration upon the important ceremonial duties as Poet precludes any onus on my part to protect us from harm; therefore, I suggest you keep a more watchful eye and listening ear and prune your reaction time a bit. And should you be interested, which surely you should, I suppose I could impart a few of my own observations to serve as guidance toward that end, else we might be forever sealed inside the clays of Rue Mastodonia. Now follow me, sir."

"Spare me," Sena said to himself as the pair approached the site of the gathering, where the red mastodons were already waiting for them.

"Felicitations, friends," said Big Tal, a very large young mastodon bull. "But my sir!" Tal said, looking down at Zak with a serious expression. "We almost ran down a portly possum and a cat back up the trail. Poet, I hope that wasn't you and Sena."

"No, it wasn't," Sena cut in, a bit embarrassed by the affair in the path and, feline-like, not wishing to divulge any vulnerability of cat-possum travel combinations. Of course, Zak did not bother to counter, as he knew without a doubt that "portly possum" could not possibly describe him.

"Good," Tal said. "I didn't think you two would stumble into the path of moving mastodons. Well, Zak, Big Tal at your service."

"At ease, dear boy. You may remain on standby for the moment," said Zak.

Zak and Sena were able at last to relax and begin socializing with the immense congregation of creatures, all except for the rodents, politely conversing among themselves in the common language of the forest-folk. The various rodent species, of course, were just as politely jabbering in their own peculiar way.

"Zeh-Zeh-ick, Ak! Gooyon dooka azeemar?" shouted Sprunkit, who was perched on a pine root with his four wives and seventeen chipmunk children.

"Hello, Zak," said Opal, a sleek young she-bobcat sitting among a small group of feline females in the shadows of the forest's edge, who at once leaned to her long-tailed, spotted jaguar companion. "It seems the single life is agreeable with Sena. He is looking fit, don't you think?"

"Perhaps, but why must he run around with an uppity possum?" said the jaguar.

"Madam, he is our poet," said Opal.

"Ha, ZaaaaAAK!"

"Who was that?" said the startled jag, just as the previous owner of the salutation, a bobwhite quail, strutted out from between her stout legs.

And so it went: "Hello, Zak!" "Greetings, Zak," and on and on, from cats, otters, red wolves, foxes, nuthatches, thrushes, moles, and many more feathered and furry folk. Not all the forest clans were represented, however, for the reptiles and amphibians were still asleep, only to wake up a little later in the year, indignant at the news that a wedding had been held in their absence, and without the very necessary ingredient of a tree frog symphony.

"All right, Poet," said Old Ok, a respected old gray-faced black bear who served as a kind of aide-de-camp for Zak at these proceedings. "The ringtails are ready to begin, and, oh yes, there is also a pair of fulvous harvest mice who seem to wish to make it a double."

"Very well," said Zak, with all the certitude of a preeminent commander in chief. "We shall begin. Up, Tal!"

At the command, the mastodon lowered his head, and Zak climbed onto one of his great tusks, and as he was taken aloft, he quickly assumed the upside-down hanging-possum position. Zak considered this position essential because, with his blood pooled in his pointed head, he figured that his ability to remember his important ceremonial lines would become enhanced.

Indeed, it was true that he needed all the help he could get, as—with his nose pointing to the ground—the forest-folk, the wedding, the world, and the soon-to-be-wed couples were likewise upside-down, which had a distinctly bewildering effect. The handsome ringtail couple with bespectacled eyes and upright, black-and-white-banded bushy tails and the prim pair of fulvous harvest mice with their upright little naked whip tails were also bewildered, staring into the eyes of the upside-down poet swinging by his tail from a mastodon's tusk.

After Zak got his bearings, he hissed at the crowd for silence, and then he spoke. "My dear ones of our forest, herewith are we gathered in our punctilious gaiety for the hallowed funicular conjoinment of our esteemed ringtail cousins, Nadine and Dunklin, and our most faithful fulvous harvest mouse kin, Sika and Shypop. And so I ask unto you, Nadine and Dunklin and Sika and Shypop, do you four mates take your respective mates to be your respective soul mates? Do not answer that. And do you promise to love, honor, and redundantly cherish and obey her or him, whichever the case may be—respectively, of course—from this day forward and thence on into the future, too?"

At the cue of an affirmative nod from the poet, in unison, Nadine and Dunklin said, "I do," and Sika and Shypop said, "Dyoo."

"Now you shall point your noses to the sky and listen," said Zak. And after a short pause:

"O where art thou Didelphis hagge
Whose rotund belly boasteth bagge
Wherein a suckling son once clung
Thou spreadeth milk upon his tongue
And foible-tailed the naked rat
Grew to the bignesse of a cat
With sable ear and snout of swine
O Mother dear marsupid fine
Now, the brides and grooms may kiss their grooms and brides!"

At that moment, there was a low flyover of twenty-nine screaming red-tailed hawks. Everyone looked up in awe at the big birds with rusty tails spread like fans, and as their cries faded in the distance, there came from the canopy above, the eerie, mournful music of a hundred squalling gray squirrels who served as background for a melodious winter chorus of wrens, siskins, grosbeaks, kinglets, cardinals, and purple and golden finches, not merely making their usual winter season chirps but blaring forth with their full mating songs that they, as individuals, would sing on their breeding grounds later in the year.

"It's so beautiful it makes me glad to be alive just so I can be around to hear it," said Opal.

"So what about this poem, Opal?" inquired the jaguar. "Is it a statement or a question? And what does it mean? And what does it have to do with a wedding?"

"Zak says that poetry isn't really good if it makes sense to everyone and that only those forest-folk with open hearts and minds can decipher its internal rhythm."

"What do you mean 'internal rhythm'?"

"How should I know?" said the she-bobcat. "But that's what Zak says."

"I see," mumbled the dubious jag.

Sena, with a whiff of pride, watched in admiration as his possum companion's thick, gray winter coat began to glow orange in the light of the setting sun. If the marriage couples were the stars in the play, then Zak was certainly the star supporting actor.

# 2

A FEW WEEKS HAD passed since the wedding, and spring was settling on the land with what seemed a merry vengeance. There was begun a great transition of the forest's birds as many of the winter inhabitants were moving northward toward their breeding grounds. At the same time, migrants from far to the south, some from even farther south than the equator, were now entering the region to look for mates with whom to set up housekeeping. Many more from the South were only passing through to do the same farther north.

The winter days with their deathly chill were now turned to balmy, fragrant days; and in the prairies, the blue sage mint was in late bloom, the pale lobelia was in early bloom, and the new green leaves of bluestem were already five inches high. The evenings, silent a few weeks earlier except when the wind was blowing, were now filled with the romance calls of leopard frogs, spring peepers, and big whiskered brown-feathered goatsuckers in search of one of their own of the opposite sex.

For three days, an elderly upland sandpiper, whose name was Stella, had used the prairie where the wedding had been held as a stopover on her journey northward from her wintering grounds, the grassy pampas of another continent in another hemisphere. During Stella's long and traveled existence, she had become friends of forest-folk in many regions, and she had successfully raised many offspring who, themselves, had become well-known and respected uplands.

This spring marked the first time for Stella to use the prairie where the wedding was held as her migratory stopover.

One morning as she stalked through the dew-covered blue-eyed grass with her typically dignified, upright upland sandpiper posture, she was startled by a young coyote who was loping, unknowingly, straight toward her. The bird's powerful skyward takeoff surprised the pup so that he nearly fell as he switched ends and sprinted away on the same path by which he had come. The airborne sandpiper made three circles over the prairie and the moving coyote before she resumed her old northerly course toward her destination: the grassy tundra at the base of a great ice sheet where a few of her kin were already waiting to greet her.

But once while on her northward journey, Stella gazed from her flight path to the distant forest horizon, and with her large, keen eyes, she saw blue-gray plumes of smoke. And as the smoke faded into a dirty haze that was swept up by the dry atmosphere, something very peculiar happened. She sensed that the blue sky itself had become somehow unfriendly. It seemed to shimmer and flicker before her. It was so very different somehow. *Yes*, she thought, *the sky is, in some way, out of balance.* Then the shimmering aspect of the blue sky became more intense, flame-like. And Stella became frightened.

Suddenly, a bright yellow, elongate object appeared in the sky, winding, serpent-like. A meteor, perhaps. But it emitted a purity of bright yellow light that she had never seen before from any meteor. And she certainly had never seen a meteor follow a serpentine course. Then, in a blink, the gleaming object became straight, in the shape of a spear. Upon its shaft were scales resembling those of a reptile or a fish; its point resembled the head of an eel. Its eyes seemed to rove about as they peered from the brilliantly golden eel head, then they became fixed on Stella as she flew above the vast forest and prairie landscape. And Stella could see and feel the eel staring at her. It was a gaze that penetrated her eyes down to the deepest level of her being. The object remained stationary, briefly, before it shot across the blue sky like a javelin and disappeared in a silent explosion of golden sparks.

The old upland named Stella was a wise and experienced bird, and she had seen much over her long and lovely years of sandpiper existence, but she found this display deeply disturbing. The septic stare from the eel seemed to create a wound that would not heal, a sickness that she could never dispel, and never again would she look at the blue sky in the way she had prior to that day. But it remained that the best way for her to describe the event was that the sky at that moment had become simply out of balance.

# 3

THERE LIVED NOT far to the north of the prairie a small group of animals who were fairly new to the region, having apparently migrated down from the North. No one knew exactly how long they had been in the vicinity. They hunted and gathered much as the forest-folk did but possessed certain traits that seemed to indicate that their brain capacity was not well evolved. Although they had the novel ability to walk about on their hind legs, which freed up their front limbs to do other tasks, they used devices, such as long sticks with pointed rocks tied to the ends, to procure meat; they used awkward bowl-like structures in which to carry their fruits and roots and nuts and seeds; and they used stones, instead of their own teeth, to grind much of their food. To have a need for devices to survive seemed to the forest-folk rather backward and a sign of weakness.

Though the little group seemed to live in relative harmony with their surroundings, they kept to themselves, most likely it seemed, because of an almost total inability to communicate. Their strange grunts and barks to themselves and to each other were completely indecipherable to the forest-folk.

These peculiar animals were known to the community as the *sans-pelages* because they were almost completely naked except for a few patches of hair that grew in various lengths at the strangest of places on their otherwise *pelage*-less bodies. Some of the sans-pelages even wore fur clothing taken from the backs of members of the forest-folk themselves, which to the forest-folk was a source of great interest. The sans-pelages, who seemed slow and weak for their size, were not looked upon as a threat in any general way except for one habit that was always a source of concern, particularly now after a very dry winter and oncoming spring—the habit of making fires in their camps.

Sena certainly had no great respect for the sans-pelages, but he held no particular animosity either, though last winter his mate had been taken down by one of their devices and her spotted pelt was now wrapped around the shoulders of a sans-pelage female. In fact, the forest-folk did not much dwell on the subject of death, and the taking of a member of one species by a member of another for the purpose of survival was looked upon by the community seriously but with certain acceptance.

The herbivores knew that the carnivores had to do what they could to survive; and they both knew that without the carnivores, nature's equilibrium and perhaps even evolution's symphony would be out of tune. The carnivores knew and expected the risks involved in attempting to take one of the larger herbivores and that those risks were also woven into the grand scheme for the sake of the balance and, ultimately, the survival of all the species. However, there were a few occasions when the rules for the sake of the balance were, necessarily, temporarily suspended, such as when there was a forest-folk wedding or a council meeting where, except with the sans-pelages, an inviolable truce was in place.

Presently, Sena and Zak were slowly working their way northward along the western shore of the great lake that, from time to time, they could see through the trees. The lake was very wide, and as far as they could tell, there was not even a shore on the other side of it.

It was early afternoon, and they were drowsy, for they had recently had a meal—a swamp rabbit that Sena had killed and had happily shared with Zak. The entrails, of course, were Zak's favorite part, though he preferred them aged a bit. They decided to lie down for a nap in a small stand of spiderworts, and, before long, beneath the blue flowers and buzzing bees, they went to sleep and Sena began to dream. His legs twitched and his hind feet kicked, shaking the blue blossoms of the spiderworts, for he was running now, running across the prairie at night with a young she-bobcat acquaintance, Opal, who had also attended the double wedding of the harvest mice and ringtail couples.

Opal. How could he dream this way? It was the first time he had since he and his beautiful Nar had run together in the old days and nights. But now he was running with Opal, and before they ran out of breath, they stopped and faced each other in the light of the moon and the music of wolves. They wrestled and rolled in the bluestem grass and he gently bit her neck while she licked his face and ears.

Zak was not experiencing a similar bliss, for the meal had turned disagreeable, making him restless. Before long, he heard a little rustle, and before he could sit up, he was nose-to-nose with the pair of fulvous harvest mice who had been away on a honeymoon.

"Itch zaahap! AK!" said Shypop.

"Shssh!" said Zak in Rodent tongue. "What are you two doing here? Dear boy, I'm quite certain it is less than a show of brilliance for you and Sika to stumble onto sleeping bobcats and poets without a truce in place. It is indeed fortuitous that Sena and I have full bellies, or we just might have to swallow you down and punctuate your honeymoon with a full dose of gastric acid. And that may happen yet if you wake Sena."

Sena *was* awake now, but he lay still with eyes closed, listening—an old trick he'd learned from Zak.

Shypop sat back on his hind legs and tail and spoke in nervous, rapid bursts, "Foppee mem! Twee swro feezee-it!"

"What did you say? Slow down and speak quietly!" Zak hissed.

"Feezee-it! Bervad! Bervad sauteel. Eelda-com nordu. Eel fetdeh sars! Smakeemok! Wurndabwa! Wurndabwa! Chantmeh Gomunga fartasar! Wurndabwa! Soodumpit! Wee-so freh."

After Shypop had spoken, the two honeymooners made a break and scampered out of sight and sound, and in a southerly direction.

"What did he say, Zak?" asked Sena, sitting up now.

"Old boy, I thought you were asleep. It was Sika and Shypop, and they seemed quite upset."

"What did he say?"

"Say?"

"Yes, what did Shypop say? Hurry and tell me before you forget."

"Oh yes, Shypop … well, I believe he said something about his wife being upset. Something about bad sans-pelages from the North who start fires and make a bit of smoke. Something about a mungo. And that we should do something about it. The very idea. What on earth could we do?"

Sena became more curious. "Mungo. What is mungo?"

"Perhaps Mungo is the name of a sans-pelage, a very bad one who starts fires. But how can that be? The sans-pelages can't speak, so how could one have a name? Perhaps I am in error and only talking bull."

"No, maybe you're right, Zak. Maybe Mungo is a sans-pelage. Maybe it was given the name by forest-folk in another region. That could make sense."

"But why in the name of widgeon feathers would it want to burn the forest?" asked Zak. "What a dreadful habit."

# 4

Z AK AND SENA remained for a few days at the lake's edge near
the spot where they had encountered Sika and Shypop. Rabbits
were plentiful, and Sena hunted day and night between cat-
naps. While Sena was gone on his day hunts, Zak prowled around
reciting his wedding rhyme to himself, searching the available stumps
and logs for beetles and grubs, and investigating the limbs of persimmon trees for the fruit that was not yet present. This he did primarily
out of habit instead of hunger because most of his meals came from
the rabbits that Sena shared.

Just as his gray squirrel foster parents had raised him to do, Zak
slept at night. Of course, this habit was quite the opposite of the sleeping habits of the other possums of the forest, who were raised to sleep
in the day and to prowl at night. It was for this reason that Zak had
seen only a few possums in his life, which was, in part, why he had
always had difficulty comprehending the notion that he himself could
actually be a member of the species. The few times that he had been
around them, especially the females, he had noticed a strange and
embarrassing feeling run through his body, so he was quite content to
avoid the creatures altogether if possible. As far as he was concerned,
he was, at least primarily, a poet. The fact that he had never seen another poet like himself had been, for Zak, only a minor annoyance.

As the days went by, Sena became more and more preoccupied
with the conversation between Zak and Shypop. Where did Shypop
get his information? Did he and Sika actually see the sans-pelage
Mungo and the fires? Surely, as both he and Zak had suggested earlier,

this information had been relayed to the little honeymooners from rodents of another region.

"Zak, it is time to investigate."

"Investigate?"

"Yes, Zak. As you well know, there is a small sans-pelage group encamped nearby. I think it would be a good idea for us to do a bit of spying. Perhaps by studying their behavior we can find out more regarding Shypop's concerns. As soon as the sun goes down, we will be heading out."

"My dear fellow, first you speak of investigating, and then you speak of spying. It sounds quite disrespectful, but a capital idea I am certain. However, the night is the time for poets to sleep. The day, for reciting. Besides, I do not wish to risk involvement in one of their rotisserie affairs."

"When the sun goes down, we go," said Sena.

Later, in the darkness, the pair slipped quietly through the woods beneath a soft, frost-colored moonlight. It was not long before they neared the sans-pelage encampment and were about to pass by a small opening in the forest when they were startled by a strange sight in the middle of the clearing.

It was an elderly sans-pelage male who was painted white. He was not wearing any forest-folk furs and was sitting with his legs and arms crossed. His back was straight, and he was staring directly ahead in the opposite direction from Zak and Sena. There were stripes of a dark rouge stain derived from the local plant dye and ore painted on his ghostly colored skin, giving it a zebra-like appearance. He wore a headdress of moss with naked shafts of turkey feathers woven in tightly with sinew so the feather shafts stuck out from the moss in all directions like the quills of a startled porcupine.

The thorny embellishment left barely enough space for a great horned owl who was perched on his right shoulder. The owl, from time to time, leaned down and whispered into the old sans-pelage's ear hidden somewhere in the moss.

"What on earth is it doing? It could be exterminated trying to speak to a sans-pelage. The bird is far too close to the thing. It can't speak back, you know. Now that is one cheeky owl about to be plucked!"

"Quiet, Zak. Let's just watch for a while and talk about it later."

Zak and Sena sat silently for awhile, watching what seemed to be a one-way conversation between the owl and the sans-pelage, before the owl leaned forward, flapped, and glided silently across the clearing. At almost the same time, the old sans-pelage grunted, stood up, and began to walk away toward his camp.

"Dear me, Sena. Would you look at that! Have you ever known of a more bizarre morphological arrangement?"

"What, Zak? Look at what?"

"Why, of course, the crevice in its hindquarters. Vertical, too, when the creature stands and moves about on its hind legs. Do you see it as it walks away? A vertical crevice! To my knowledge, there are absolutely no forest-folk in possession of that particular affliction. Wouldn't you agree, dear boy?"

"Well, I don't know. I can't think of any at the moment, I suppose."

"No, of course not. I'm afraid that the sans-pelages quite have a monopoly on the deformity."

"Good evening, fellows. Strange creatures, aren't they?"

"Who said that? Where are you? You are spying on us!" said Zak, who was now looking up and walking around in a circle.

"I am the owl perched on a limb just over your heads, on whom you have been spying for the past good while, but just *who* said that is another matter."

"What were you telling it?" asked Sena. "Is it possible to communicate with a sans-pelage?"

"Indeed. As you should know, we great horns can read thoughts, and the sans-pelages believe that we bring them secrets from the Shadow World."

"From the Shadow World?" said Zak.

"Well, look around," said the owl. "We have a world full of shadows presently, do we not? At least that is all we should take it to mean. I do find the conversations, such as they are, entertaining, but I must admit that I'm not certain whether they understand a great deal of what I say to them. Of course, the only ones who seem to want to speak with me at all are their practitioners of their peculiar medicine. The rest of them seem to have no interest in me, as they are, on the whole, an obtuse lot."

"But what did you just tell it?" Sena asked again.

"To keep the conversation, such as it was, alive, I told it anything that I thought it wanted to hear—oh, different topics!" said the owl. "But there is almost always some kind of attachment to mysticism. They do love their mysticism. It brings about them the quality of quaintness that I so enjoy. Oh, pardon me, dear possum, I answered your question before you asked it, a dreadful habit of mine I'm afraid. Do carry on."

"Then what do you usually talk about?" inquired Zak.

"As I'd said, different topics. Is it necessary that I repeat myself?" asked the owl.

"No," said Sena. "But what exactly was the conversation about to-night? If you don't mind my asking."

"Not at all. Our medicine sans-pelage was interested in the de-tails of a very specific subject tonight. It seems that its interregional communications, such as they are, brought news about a particularly nasty sans-pelage chief in the North who leads his own flock, some-what under duress, to commit acts of violence on other sans-pelage flocks. I must say I am quite happy to be of a species that lacks a strong flocking instinct. When one is in a flock, one never knows who will pop up to lead. It could be just any old fool.

"Anyway, it said, or rather it thought, that the naughty Northern leader attacks other flocks by starting raging forest fires. When the poor panicked creatures of the other groups scurry and scuttle into the forest, he has them captured so he can take the young males and females for slaves. Of course, the older dotards are terminated handily for their uselessness, and the little ones he eats, believing this measure will help him regain his own youth and, interestingly, some sort of mysterious power, it seems.

"If only he would have asked me about that. I have been eating youthful forest-folk all my life, and it doesn't do a bit of good. But I suppose that is something else I like about the poor bald things. I am forever amazed and entertained by their thought processes. Such as they are. Anyway, tonight the medicine male was gravely concerned that the Northern villain and its egregious band might be coming to this region in the future.

"Yes," said the owl. "That's it, all right. The name is Mungo. Oh, drat! I did it again. I answered before you spoke his name aloud." He lifted his wings and sailed into the darkness.

"Zak," said Sena. "I believe we are privy to some important information not well-disseminated among the forest-folk. We must come up with a plan for the future, and we must warn the others."

"Of course," said Zak, "that is exactly what we must do. But why would this Mungo creature want to go about starting fires?"

"The owl just told you, Zak," said Sena. "Weren't you listening?"

"Incomprehensible."

# 5

ZAK AND SENA were sitting on the shore of the big lake staring out over the calm water and into a fog bank on the far horizon. The happenings of the previous evening had them in a somber mood, so they hardly noticed the large white tern who floated gracefully, like a ghostly marionette, above the water not far from shore. The top of the tern's head was coal black, and there was dark gray in its primary wing feathers and on the edges of its forked tail. In the sunlight, with the fog bank as background, its thick bill was the glossy vermilion of arterial blood.

The bird slowed to a stop and hung in the air, wings flapping, as if it were held in restraint by an invisible string. In a moment, it dove headfirst after a small fish below the surface, then it arose, arced around, hovered, and dove again. After five more similar performances, it had failed to catch a single fish. Finally, it flew over and lit on the wet sand near Sena and Zak, and began, in a manner of great concentration and seriousness, to pace back and forth while positioning the tips of its wings over its back. Its head was slightly bowed with red bill pointing downward toward the sand.

"I say, fellows," said the tern. "I do hope you are not planning to stay here much longer. Fishing is a most serious business, you understand."

"Oh, of course, I'm quite certain it is," said Zak.

"Well, I am not so certain, of course, that you are certain, or that you understand in the least," said the tern. "Not much can be expected of the intellect of those who sit around and do nothing but stare at and distract one who is engaged in the important business of fishing."

"Pardon me?" said Sena.

"No, I believe that I shan't," said the tern, "and I shall have to ask you to leave at once, as you are in my territory. No hunter of fishes appreciates this sort of annoyance, you know."

"I beg your pardon!" said Zak.

The tern lifted upward and hovered over the heads of the cat and possum. "Dear sir, are you so dimwitted as to believe that I would offer you pardon so soon after declining the same request from your bristle-nosed-bum companion? Now, go! Go! Kak! Kak!"

"Well, then, Sena, let's go," said Zak. "Indeed we do have important business to attend to, and there is precious little time for the endurance of such insolent avian invectives."

"I believe it is," said Sena, "that the fish hunters are a touchy guild."

Zak and Sena took leave of the shore of the lake with its ghostly fog bank and grumpy tern who now winged its way over the water, again in search of its prey beneath the lake's surface. The direction they chose was generally westerly, a course that would eventually lead them back to the forest-prairie interface and the site of the wedding of Sika and Shypop and Nadine and Dunklin.

As the tern continued its aerial maneuvers above the lake, the fog bank lifted, and more and more of the blue sky came within the tern's vision. But it now seemed to the bird that there was again something the matter. The blue sky seemed to shimmer and flicker with a motion that was flame-like and the tern became intensly disturbed by the sky's peculiar activity. The very blueness itself seemed unbalanced and unfriendly. *But how can the sky lose its balance?* thought the frightened tern. *And how can I possibly fly under such conditions?*

So the tern flew back to the beach and settled down on the sand to rest. It would not fly for the rest of the day. *This is not a good day for fishing*, it thought.

# 6

ATTENTIVENESS TO THE surroundings—the air, the ground, the trunks of the trees, the treetops, the very forest ambiance—was a requisite for being an astute member of the forest-folk, and over the past few days, many of those members had been able to detect a soft, gentle, high-pitched hum, born of a thousand meek voices; a sort of background concert magnitudes lower in volume than the buzz of the serenade of cicadas. This wrinkle of ambiance generally served as a beacon to the forest-folk to gather at the interface between forest and prairie where weddings and council meetings were typically carried out. Presently, due to the hum, a gathering was in place, and Sena and Zak were about to enter the picture.

"The Canopy Connection has been a-sizzle for days now, so we naturally assumed there would be a wedding or some such event and you two would be showing up at any moment," said Old Ok, with enthusiasm in his gray black-bear face. "So, welcome!"

"Well," said Sena, "there is no wedding this time, but a council meeting might be in order. Perhaps I should let Zak explain it because he was the first to receive the news."

Zak was always excited to be the one to share new gossip—gossip in his possession because of his special ability derived from his unique past-life experience as a functional component of the Canopy Connection.

The great Canopy Connection was primarily a treetop phenomenon where the squirrels broadcast and propagated information with amazing rapidity over vast distances and in all directions. But it also functioned, to a lesser degree, at ground level, where news could be whipped and driven along by the earthier members of the buck-toothed rodent clan. Likely, the Canopy Connection was the fastest, most efficient, and finest relay system of knowledge dissemination in the history of the great forest, hence its use as a beacon for gatherings. But because of the language barrier, it was not otherwise easily taken advantage of by the nonrodent forest-folk, who, usually only during times of rather extreme rodent excitement, could detect the whine from the treetops or the ground or both.

Thus, it seemed a bit of a shame that the language of the rodents was not better evolved for the rest to enjoy, but the necessity to evolve was never there; for though it was very old, it was full of vigor. There was gossip still bouncing off the twigs at the tops of trees and off the walls of gopher tunnels that was ancient and sometimes from faraway exotic places. So any suggestion that the greatest historian of ancient history who ever lived in the forest might have been an old gray-faced flying squirrel, or even a chipmunk, would have come as no particular surprise to anyone.

By the time Zak finished describing his disturbing conversation with Shypop, an audience of various forest-folk individuals had surrounded him, which was the only necessary criterion for a council meeting in progress.

"Ah. This explains the sound in the trees," said Old Ok.

"I will never be deracinated from my homeland! We shall all stay and fight," said Shinboo, a red wolf female. "We must form an army and prepare for battle!"

"Don't be ridiculous," droned the jaguar with a slightly upturned nasal tone in her voice. "This is precious little information on which to generate such a grandiose scheme. The very idea."

"Old jag, you look at the sun in summer and tell it, 'You are bothering me'; yet in the winter, you say, 'You are not doing your job.' Are you never satisfied?" said the red wolf, with her nose poked out toward the jag.

"Old! I am merely in the latter stages of the prime of life. I am not old. And if you have any doubt about it, just stick your face a little closer to me, dear."

"Please, dear jag, our truce is in place. We must not be distracted," said Zak.

"We are already distracted," said the jag. "Distracted into a gathering, a council meeting because of some foolish gossip from rodent honeymooners, passed on by a rhyming marriage-maker. Gossip passed from tree to tree, from rodent to rodent to possum. How clever of us all to find such a novel way to spend a lovely afternoon: engaging in the meticulous quantification of treetop subjectivity. Meetings are, by definition, a distraction."

"It was not only gossip from Sika and Shypop," said Sena, "but we heard essentially the same news from an owl—a sans-pelage group following a severe leader called Mungo is attacking other sans-pelage groups by method of fire. And as dry as the countryside is, fires of that sort can only mean disaster for the forest-folk."

"Why didn't you say the gossip came from an owl?" said the jag. "Now, perhaps, it is meat for thought."

"What we need now, I think, is a little leadership," said Sena, looking at the jag. "At present, no one is in charge here. Perhaps you would allow us to appoint you as chair, madam."

"Sena," said the jag, "I shall have to pass. Once exposed to the process of organizational leadership, one tends to become afflicted with a myriad of infirmities that can be quite difficult to overcome in good society. And they can have a dire effect on the digestive systems of others."

"Perhaps the mastodons and bison could form a sort of pest-patrol stampede and stomp out the sans-pelage population altogether," said a brown bat hanging from a branch above.

"I am afraid it is time for us to go to our summer grounds in the West," said Big Tal. "We have a rendezvous planned with some friends of both the southern red and northern black races who are likely wondering where we are presently. And patience among pachyderms, as you know, can run thin. Perhaps if the problem still exists in the fall we can be of some help. Of course, we mastodons are not particularly fond of fire either."

"Look at us," said Opal. "Are we not a large, diverse, multicultural society? Should we not simply embrace the sans-pelages and their strange customs? Get to know them? If only we had a way to communicate with them, I am sure we could give them new knowledge and wisdom to pass along to their offspring so they might not be such a threat to themselves or to us."

"Opal," said the jag, "though knowledge is easily transferable from one generation to the next, wisdom never survives the voyage."

"It appears to me," said one of the feathered members, "that the sans-pelages think they perceive, let us say, a certain familiarity with their surroundings."

"I've heard it said," spoke Shinboo, "that familiarity inspires certitude."

"Familiarity is a liar!" snapped the jag, clipping off the scaly tail of Shinboo's remark. "No more, and no less. A mere seductive little liar."

"Could be Opal has a point," spoke another small voice lost in the crowd. "If only we could communicate with them, maybe we could teach them to have a new perspective of themselves, which, even more important, could give them a new viewpoint of their surroundings. Perhaps that might vanquish their sense of familiarity.

"You see, what I have come to believe is that perhaps, just perhaps, mind you, many of their problems maybe arise from their vision being binocular. Yes, perhaps their whole problem is that they simply cannot see well, and so they can't come to terms with what they are and how they fit in. It makes sense, you see. At least it does to me. But I think it might help if we, or someone, could teach them to close one eye and turn the other eye inward so they can see their own noses; then, maybe they could finally learn what they are. Of course, it is only a theory."

"And it is a good theory," said a screech owl who was perched on a bison's back. "I suppose one does need to see one's own nose from time to time to keep one's thoughts on a proper course. But, mind you, there are many forest-folk who have binocular vision. And on top of that, there are some among us who cannot see their own noses even if they close an eye. Frankly, I believe it is only the end of my beak that I see instead of my proper nose." Upon saying this, the little owl swayed from side to side, contorting its face in spasms of winking one eye and then the other, an action that triggered a small outburst of sniggers, barks, and grunts from the crowd.

"Yes. I realize that," said the lost little voice. "But for the sans-pelages, it might present itself as a sort of malady that they cannot overcome. Perhaps they simply cannot fully grasp the binocular view-point without the awareness of their nasal position, which can be very self-enlightening."

"I never thought of it before," said Opal. "I think it is a splendid theory." She sat back on her haunches and looked into the night. "It must be investigated," she mumbled to herself.

As the meeting's order had degenerated into a gentle racket of squawks and growls and hisses and croaks, a spreading adder coiled near Opal's feet was the only member who caught her last comment.

"You would have to be very lucky to accomplish such a thing as an investigation, Opal," he hissed.

"Lucky?" she said. "My dear serpent, the world is an orchard of opportunity."

"Perhaps," he said. "But, of course, it remains that one must seize the plum."

"Then, in good time, my long, brown friend, I shall seize it."

"I like you, Opal," he whispered. "Just as our lives are built by chance, so may you always maintain your impeccable appreciation for the medium."

"Yes!" came a voice that rose above and briefly diminished the noise of the crowd. "This is all well and good analytically, but the question remains: What are we going to do now?"

"I move we adjourn," said the jag, "so we can think about it and decide for ourselves."

"No, wait!" said Zak. "I volunteer to go to the North. Maybe I can establish contact with the Canopy Connection in another region."

"Convenient to be elsewhere when things are getting hot around here, I suppose," said Shinboo.

"But perhaps I can find out how other forest-folk have gotten along with this problem," said Zak.

"Not a bad idea, possum," said the jag. "And I think I should consult Moksoos on the matter."

At those words, a long and silent stillness settled on the meeting. It had been a long time since anyone had heard the name brought up.

# 7

THERE BEING NO further business, the meeting was, as usual, rather abruptly terminated, but not before all present could agree that nobody would eat anybody else who was in attendance that day; at least, not until the present threat of the sans-pelage situation had passed. Of course, anyone else of the region who was not in attendance remained fair game. The balance, the symphony, had to be maintained, even though the primary goal of each individual was to avoid becoming its victim, either by starvation or by its wicked next of kin, becoming someone else's meal.

Because it was a time when decisive action by the forest-folk could commence almost before a decision was finished being made, the she-jaguar and the possum found themselves early the next morning sniffing and panting warm trail dust and the odor of mastodon dung left by the last of the great herd moving in its westward migration. The path was wide and rutted, for it had been used again and again over the course of many years. The trunks of the older trees had been rubbed smooth by the great animals, and many young saplings along the route could be found leaning low in a terminal posture.

Zak, who could move along the forest floor with impressive swiftness for possums of the day, had trouble keeping up with the jag, who seemed to show little concern. She was moving in her silent westerly trot with the purpose of a feline female, not only on a mission of altruism but also one of another sort. It had been a long time since she had seen Moksoos, and the current events had provided her with just the necessary ostensible provisions to go and look him up without causing the levitation of too many whiskered forest-folk eyebrows—or so she figured.

Moksoos was widely known throughout the great forest and its many and varied regions, for he had frequented them all quite often throughout his long existence. Further, he maintained the sort of presence that made it virtually impossible for him to be in any region for any length of time without becoming the hottest of gossip. His very uniqueness made him so—uniqueness in temperament as well as in appearance—for, as it was rumored, he may very well have been the last of his kind. He was not only startlingly unique, he was charismatic, famous and infamous, frightening, interesting, despised, and adored. But it was that cat charisma and a singular charm that made him an attraction for every single feline female of any age or species.

Even though Moksoos's name had not been of a public nature in the region for a long time, the female cats had continued to drop bits of information among themselves regarding his whereabouts and activities. The cat-female system of communication, though perhaps not as elegant as the Canopy Connection, was quite functional, at least when it came to news of Moksoos. And it had, understandably, served as a cradle of his forgiveness by the community, for the last time the forest-folk of the region had seen Moksoos, he was not on his best behavior.

"I say, madam!" Zak shouted ahead. "Perhaps we should stop and rest for a small while. Give the dust a chance to settle!"

Zak continued on, as there was no jaguar in sight. He was becoming a little tired from the pace and frustrated at being left behind. He wanted a drink, too, but that seemed out of the question. As mid-morning approached, the few birds who remained after the passage of the noisy, bustling trunk-and-ivory parade had decided to take a nap, so the only sound left for him to hear was his own scratching and scuffling required for forward progress. But on he went, following and climbing in and out of the hard ruts made by the great beasts in previous wet springs, until, finally, he came to a small creek in which ran a trickle of clear water forming little pools along the way.

After refreshing himself and clearing the grit from his throat with the cool water he began to climb the creek's bank only to be startled by the jag who was sitting motionless staring at him. It was not the first time for Zak to be struck by her looks, and he wondered how her golden coat with its shining, black rosettes had remained so slick looking and clean after such a journey as the pair had just made. He looked her over while she remained silent and fixed on him.

"Thank goodness I have finally found you!" said Zak.

"You haven't found anything at all, possum. Perhaps you should stick to your rhyming and leave the hunting to others. It is you who have been found. And I bothered to do that only to let you know that it is time for us to leave the mastodon highway. We are far enough west now. As you continue north, you should not encounter any sans-pelage encampments. You have your mission. I have mine. You go right. I go left. Do you understand?"

"Of course, madam."

"Possum, before we separate, and while we continue to have this silly council-meeting truce in place, I wonder if you would bother to explain to me the meaning of that peculiar rhyme that you recite at every wedding."

"Oh, well, you know, poetic explanations are always complex issues. I am sure I would only bore us both by my trying to explain it."

"Certainly not. Go ahead," she persisted.

"Well, madam, I suppose I am not absolutely certain where it came from, the poem. Perhaps I dreamed it. But I assure you, I offer it only as a sort of artistic ceremonial trinket in honor of romance and marriage, I suppose. It seems a kind of necessity, you know, to get the couples off to a proper beginning. And I think it is the least I can do as an opening for the magnificent squirrel-and-bird chorus."

"But what is the meaning of the poem? What about the internal rhythm, possum? What does that mean?"

"Uh, well—"

"Are you really a poet or are you merely a common possum?" she interrupted. "Do you even know what you are?"

"Madam," said Zak, looking a little pained and perplexed, "do you really think it's a good idea for you to seek out Moksoos? The last time he was in our region, as I am sure you recall, he seemed a bit cranky. Perhaps you would instead join me, as I am quite accustomed to the company of cats. You would make me a fine companion."

"On the contrary, possum, you should accompany me. I'm certain you and Moksoos would have much to talk about."

At that, the jag laughed out loud and loped off toward the south, leaving Zak alone by the little creek. Even if left by himself, it would be a relief, thought Zak, to be away from the dreary mastodon trail. So with the utmost of marsupial optimism a possum could muster, he began working his way on his mission northward, but not without feeling a little saddened and mistreated by the jag and, worse, not knowing why.

# 8

ZAK FELT BETTER going at his own pace, for it freed him up to inspect and enjoy the pristine ancient forest. He took his time to investigate the new environment that offered easier traveling than the rutted trail he had left behind, and no matter where he went or in what direction he looked, the scenery was always different, calling out for exploration.

The woods were once again full of the musical arrangements of tanagers, warblers, vireos, and little green flycatchers. He often passed giant water oaks, many of which were in possession of a resident black-and-white warbler singing its *zeezee-zeezee* song as it scooted along a vertical wall of trunk. Higher up in the tops of the branches went the *dok dok clok* of a cuckoo who, in a lazy, serpentine motion, peered down or around a branch to catch a glimpse of an insect or a mate. From time to time, a disgruntled gnatcatcher dropped down to the understory to fuss at his intrusion into her territory as he made his way through the lush green gardens of mayapple or the purple blossoms of prunella stands he found along the way.

Zak lost little time having to hunt for food, for there were plenty of grubs and insects just under the leaves and small logs; the larger hollow logs often provided him with a fine beetle selection.

One afternoon, while he was sitting by a stream studying a collection of minnows in its shallows, a gray wolf loped nearby and caught his scent. At that moment, Zak realized that he was now in another forest region with no truce in place or cat for company and protection. The wolf circled, not yet detecting his location. Zak became frightened and made a random dash through the woods, for he had no particular destination in mind for safety.

Discovering Zak's location, the wolf sprinted after the slower-moving possum, who, ever so luckily, happened onto a hole in the ground in which he could crawl for safety. The wolf snapped and clawed at the hole's entrance, but he did not enter.

Fortunately for Zak, the young wolf had had a bad experience the previous spring when he'd tried to enter just such a hole in the ground and was bitten on the lip by a copperhead. At the sound of the wolf's commotion outside, the frightened possum made his way as far as he could into the narrow passage until he came to its end, a hard, round bulge in the earth against which he rested. There, Zak remained quiet and motionless with his mouth open, looking toward the entrance. Before long, he became drowsy, and with no more sound coming from the wolf, he contemplated dropping off to sleep; but before he could, a forceful, clawed kick struck him in his ribs.

"Move over! No winter. No cold. No need snuggle."

"Who are you?" said Zak.

"Wolf gone. But he come again. Now he know my den. Now he think possum den. You go. You can go. Don't want to sleep with no possum."

"Pardon me," said Zak, "I did not know this place was occupied."

"No. You don't know. You don't ask. You come in. Wolf think possum den now. You can go."

Zak left the den of the armadillo, who was quite disturbed that the secrecy of his residence had been violated.

Zak found the outside world in busy preparation for the evening ahead. In almost any direction, he could hear the mournful calls of goatsuckers and screech owls. It was getting to be his bedtime, so he found himself a tree with a hole at its base, and, after checking for occupancy, he entered, lay down, and went to sleep.

When Zak exited the tree base, he once again discovered the lively sounds and smells and sights of a spring forest morning. He decided that, because he was now in another forest region, perhaps he should begin to consider exactly where he was going and what he should do to accomplish his mission. Where he was going, in actuality, was really no longer a consideration, as he had lost his sense of direction some time ago, so the pressure of *where* no longer exerted itself. But he could begin to try to communicate with the squirrels or other rodents to "find out about things," as he liked to say to himself.

Zak had seen a few mice along the way, but they had never spoken and seemed shyer than those of his own region. The squirrels had seemed distant, too, usually remaining high in the canopy or motionless on the lower branches when he passed. So this morning, he decided it was time to make a real effort. He set out on his journey, paying close attention to the trees and the movement of the squirrels. When he came to a playful pair of black fox squirrels leaping from branch to branch, shaking the youthful spring leaves of the lower canopy, he stopped and carefully walked underneath them.

"Icthk dah. Icthk dah!" he said.

The young pair immediately stopped in attention, frozen, staring silently at Zak.

"Ick," said Zak.

Zak stood motionless for a few moments but got no response. Then the squirrels slowly and quietly crept up the limb to higher territory. It would be like that from then on. Every time Zak tried to communicate, he got no response. He knew they understood him, but they didn't seem to care. *Perhaps*, he thought, *they simply do not wish to communicate with a poet. It must be a little strange for them, as I look so different. They have never had a nonrodent speak to them before.*

It was true. Though the Canopy Connection was powerful enough to maintain interregional communication, sometimes the passage of gossip between certain regions, excepting matters of extreme importance, would cease altogether, presumably from lack of interest in what was going on outside the community. And so it was that presently Zak found himself in a region where there was not a single Canopy Connection operator who had ever heard of a talking possum.

As time went by, little by little, Zak's optimism diminished. He knew that he was lost, and he worried about his inability to communicate with the squirrels; and the more he worried about that, the more he was nagged by the memory of the brief conversation he had had with the jag. *Am I a poet or a possum?* he wondered. A conundrum of identity was taking shape, and it was applying for residence in his thoughts.

# 9

ZAK WAS IN the habit of seeking shelter in the evenings, and hollow logs often provided him a warm, safe place in which to bed down. It was a clear and starry night that Zak found himself unable to sleep in a particularly comfortable log because of an odd racket, a thumping and moaning, from the top of the log's exterior. He tossed and squirmed in his bed. *How am I going to find out about things if I can't get any rest?* he thought. He even tried to cover his black, leathery ears with his hands, but it did no good. Finally, he could take no more.

"Who is it?" he called out.

"Who is it? Who is it?" came the source of the moaning, a small voice brimming with anxiety.

"Yes. Who is it?" Zak repeated.

"Crridit! The question must be 'Where is it?' not 'Who is it?' Oooo!"

"What do you mean?" asked Zak.

"Frrremmit! One cannot answer the frridit question of 'Who is it?' until one stands firmly on the notion of 'Where is it?' and it's driving me crridit crrazy! It's why I stand on my forelimbs!"

"Well, then, where is it?" said Zak.

"I don't know!" said the voice.

"Isn't that what you wanted me to say?" said Zak. "Then how about 'What is it?'"

"It's a skunk! A frridit skunk! And its name is Elbon."

The light of dawn was now visible at the log's end, so Zak decided to give up altogether on sleeping and go outside and investigate. When he looked up on the roof of the log, there stood two nuthatches, a redstart, a little spotted skunk, and a humming bird buzzing around the skunk's face like a pesky ground hornet. The skunk, making forlorn moans and whimpers, nervously paced upside down on his hands with his hind feet flailing in the air and his tail sticking straight ahead. He repeatedly jumped up and down on his little forelimbs making a thumping sound.

"Incomprehensible!" said Zak.

"Of course it is!" said the skunk.

"What are you doing, sir?" Zak asked.

"Oooo!"

"What is the matter? Are you nervous about something?"

"As a butterfly in a bat cave!" said the skunk in a shriveled, but emphatic, little voice.

"Why?"

"Be—cause—I—don't—know—where—I—am!" repeated the impatient skunk, making a jump and a thump at each syllable.

"Sir, you are standing on a log in the forest," said Zak. "That is where you are. Or where it is, as you seem to prefer."

"No! No! No!"

"Yes. Yes. Yes," said Zak.

"Frremmit! You don't know! All one has to do is lie upon a log at night and look up at the stars to know that one does not know where one is. Or, where it is. Or, where I am. Or, where you are. I do it every night, and it is verrry disturbing."

"Well, don't do it anymore," offered Zak.

"It's too late! Now I know nobody knows where they are. Including me! It answers naughty questions with a verrry naughty answer. You follow what I mean?"

"Oh yes," said Zak, "I can follow the incomprehensibility of it quite well. Good day. I hope you find what you are looking for."

As Zak walked away through the forest, the little hand-walking spotted skunk and his avian entourage followed. The birds flitted about the skunk like overgrown deer flies.

"Where are you going?" asked the skunk.

"Well, sir, I'm not sure. I seem to be a bit turned around," said Zak.

The skunk sniggered nervously. "You are lost, and you don't know where you are, both at the same time. Are you from this region?"

"No. I've come from far away."

"Then you must be a Southern possum. I came down from a little ways to the north of here just yesterday, and I didn't see a single possum. What brings you to these parts? Looking for a mate?"

"I am trying to establish communication with the squirrels. It is a long story."

"I should hope so," said the perplexed skunk. "Why don't you put your mind to more important matters? Like looking at the stars."

"Sir, I am on a mission. I have to find out about things."

"Have you had any luck?"

"No."

"What makes you think you can talk to squirrels?"

"I can talk to squirrels at home. I was raised by them. I know the language."

"How peculiar. So the squirrels of this region won't talk to you?"

"No. They don't seem to care about what I have to say. I really don't understand."

"You must look at the stars with me. Then maybe you can find the answer to your problem, though it can be verrry disturbing."

"Sir, do you direct all your questions to the stars?"

"Getting to be that way, I'm afraid."

Zak sped up into his usual northerly trot. Though lost, and with a bit of wandering along the way, he had always maintained a northerly course, ever since he had left the mastodon trail.

"Have you tried contacting any large rodents?" asked the skunk, now finding it somewhat difficult to keep up.

Zak stopped in his tracks. He hadn't thought of that. Perhaps it was worth a last try. But where was he going to find a large rodent?

"There's a large rodent, a beaver by the name of Quarral, who lives not far from here. A real architect, he. Builder of one really big dam."

"He built it by himself?" asked Zak.

"No, he had lots of help. He's just one good architect."

"How do you know his name?"

"Don't really," said the skunk. "That's probably not his real name. It probably came from other forest-folk."

"I must see him immediately. Please, sir. You must take me to him straight away."

"Frrremmit! I cannot, possum. The dam. Oooo! It makes me terribly nervous to be around dams."

"What for, Elbon?" asked Zak.

"Verrry dangerous. It could break, and we would drown. Even my little bird friends." All four little birds twitched nervously at the suggestion.

"Sir, you simply must. It is very important. It could mean the lives of all the forest-folk of an entire region," said Zak, perhaps exaggerating his role in the matter.

"How so?" asked the little skunk.

"I believe that I should not tell you," said Zak. "I'm afraid it would make you 'verrry' nervous."

"Verrry well, then. But we are all going to die."

"No. Certainly not. We will be fine," said Zak.

The little clan of pilgrims traveled the hills, bottoms, mountains, and valleys of Elbon's home territory. In the daytime, they chatted as they traveled, a convivial party of possum, upside-down-walking skunk and colorful, chirping little birds. But when the stars were out and a log was available, Elbon, the skunk, was a nervous wreck on the roof, ooing and thumping out his misery; and Zak thinking, *I know that I am lost without having to be told by the stars. Is it not the same thing as not knowing where one is? Or where it is? Of course it is.*

# 10

"ZAK!" ELBON CRIED out late one night, prostrate and tormented, steadfastly enduring his sentence of luminiferous retribution by ten thousand tiny suns. "You must come up on the roof. Right now! *This* is my favorite log, Zak. Oooo. Frrremmit!"

Zak, unable to sleep from the racket above his head, decided to join his skunk companion on the roof of the log. It was a massive old sycamore corpse that lay in a small forest opening. Its fragile, peeling bark had long since disappeared; the hard, woody remainder was weathered smooth, making it difficult for Zak to obtain a grip. He fell back to the ground at each of several attempts to climb the side of the great log.

"Zak! Go down to the end of the log and climb up there."

Zak followed Elbon's instructions that led him to the log's rotting base, its roots long ago dissolved by weather and the limitless hunger of the innumerable individuals of the microscopic races. Here, the climbing was much easier. When he made it to the top, he walked over to where the poor anxious skunk was lying on his back, awe and fright waging a brutal battle between his ears.

"Elbon," said Zak, "we should presently go down and seek the warmth and safety of the log's interior. I am certain you will find it much less nerve-racking, and perhaps we both can get some sleep."

"Lie down on your back, Zak. You can feel it now. Oooo!"

Zak relented and lay down on his back and looked up into the black sky filled with the tiny twinkles of light far too numerous to count.

"Do you feel the stars now, Zak?" asked Elbon, after a few moments of gazing. "We are being shone on now. Take in their tiny light. Take it into your body. But mostly take it into your eyes, Zak. Now you see. We have been shone upon by the stars. Whether or not they know it. Whether or not they care. They are powerless to take it back. They, the stars, have washed us with their soft magic. Signified our presence. Put all existence on notice of our own existence. Irretrievably, they have marked us as a part of it all. And it's verrry disturbing. But now we are. At least according to the stars. We are! Not one of those little stars will be the same again, Zak. They have shone on us. They have us firmly locked into their own pasts. They are stuck with us now. Forever. I almost feel sorry for them. But they play a dirty trick on us; they tell us we don't know where we are."

At that the little skunk, intoxicated by his prodigious marvel of heavenly matters and bursting with that peculiar combination of panic and glee, threw his hindquarters into the air, thumping out the words with his forelimbs and his voice:

"You—don't—know—where—you—are—Zak!"


After days of pleasant travel and nights of impatient thumping and impetuous cosmologizing by Elbon, Zak was beginning to wonder whether there really was a beaver called Quarral. The past few days had been, on the whole, a pleasant distraction, but it was time to find out about things. So, one day, Zak stopped in his tracks and turned to the upside-down Elbon and his singing satellites.

"I say, Elbon, birds, dear fellows, how much farther to the dam?"

Elbon had a painful expression on his face. "Oooo! I can't go any farther. I might drown."

"What do you mean?" asked Zak.

"There it is. Down the slope."

Zak looked down the gentle hillside just ahead of him. At the bottom lay a sizeable body of water nestled at the base of a mountainous ridge that curved around and cradled the pond in a cul-de-sac, wherein he saw a very large and long dam that followed a serpentine course, tying into cypress trees and knees in equidistant lengths along its sinuous way. It looked to be quite sturdy, as well as elegant in design—surely the work of amazing architectural aptitude. Its supporting structure of the logs of pine, sweet bay, hornbeam, and gum was secured from above by a mantle of the woven smaller branches of wax myrtle, witch hazel, and tupelo. But in spite of all its magnificence, no lodge could be seen.

"Rather impressive structure indeed, Elbon," said Zak, "but where is the lodge? With a dam of that magnitude, one would expect an accompanying water castle."

"Criddit! I knew this would happen. We're all going to die."

"What on earth do you mean, dear fellow?"

"Go and find Quarral. You don't need a lodge. Do you?"

"Elbon. How can I possibly find him if there is no lodge in which to seek him out?"

"I will have to show you?" asked Elbon.

"Of course you will. You do know how to find him, don't you?"

"Yeah," came back the fragile, wee voice.

Elbon in the lead, they set out to cross to the other side of the pond along the spine of the dam; the little party climbing and fluttering its way along the complicated path provided by the many small branches of the dam's mantle. Elbon had difficulty maintaining his hand-walking position, sometimes falling a short distance to the larger branches of the dam's infrastructure, necessitating his climbing out and starting anew.

Zak also worked his way along slowly and with difficulty, occasionally having to use his tail for an extra grip. The birds, of course, found no such obstacles as they twittered about the labors of their two earthbound mammalian partners. The group traveled a long distance until, finally, the dam led to the opposite shore, where it tied into a high, steep bank at the base of the mountain.

"This is it," said Elbon.

"Elbon, this is what?" said Zak.

"This is where you can find Quarral. They all live here."

"What are you talking about, Elbon? There are no beavers here."

"Yes, they are inside the mountain presently, I think."

"Inside the mountain?" said Zak, a bit downhearted by the very notion that Quarral could be so close yet locked away inside a small mountain. "How can I contact them?"

"You will have to swim to their cave. Underwater. It is an under-the-water cave that leads to their den," said Elbon.

"And just how am I going to find it underwater, Elbon?" asked Zak.

"How the crriddit should I know?" said Elbon.

Zak looked down at the little black-and-white face peering back at him. "Dear Elbon, the expression on your face might just as well be that of a baby rabbit in the clutches of a red-shouldered hawk. Cheer up, now. You know where the cave is, don't you, Elbon?"

"Yeah."

"How do you know?" asked Zak.

"From some frrremmit legend, I guess."

"Yes, Elbon, you are going to have to take me. It is quite imperative, you know."

"But it's dangerous. And my birds don't swim. We are all going to die."

"No, we won't, Elbon. You can swim ahead, and I will follow. Of course, the avian members can wait here. They will be fine."

With another mournful *oooo*, Elbon disappeared into the dark water. Zak, who hated to go into water more than any skunk ever did but was dedicated in his quest for a large rodent with whom to speak, made a hasty, awkward jump to follow Elbon. The water was cold, and Zak, though somewhat relieved to see that Elbon was swimming forward instead of backward, found it difficult to keep up. Zak was a weak underwater swimmer and soon had to surface for air. When he did, there was no more Elbon. Zak dove again and swam along the bank, but with no luck in finding cave or skunk. He surfaced again, looking about the still water.

"Frrremmitt! What are you doing?" said Elbon as he burst up from the water shaking his head, gasping for air. "I thought you were going to follow me! We are going to die!"

Elbon dove again, and Zak followed, realizing his mistake. The cave was deeper than he imagined, but he went the distance, following Elbon into the entrance and on into the mountain, where they both swam along the shaft horizontally. Then, finally, it angled upward to where air waited, impatiently, before it rushed into the mouths and noses of possum and skunk as soon as they broke the water's surface. They crawled out, gasping, onto a muddy ledge with a hundred beaver tracks on top of, and obscuring, a thousand more beneath them. Skunk and possum had almost reached their destination. It would be a beaver den extraordinaire, but, that aside, it was part of a massive, labyrinthine cavern-system inside the mountain.

After Zak and Elbon regained their breath, they began walking along the floor of the damp, dark tunnel that was only a small branch of the large and convoluted cave. The pair bumped into each other along the way as light, or even its slightest hint, was no guest at all to the present environment. They could tell that the tunnel was curving to the left as they maintained their forward progress. But soon Elbon noticed that the tunnel had abandoned its curvature and was proceeding on a straighter, rising course.

"Elbon?" said Zak, now realizing that Elbon was no longer at his side.

"Zak?" said Elbon.

Neither answered the other.

"Zak!" called Elbon.

"Elbon! Where are you?"

Neither heard the other's call, so they both turned around, simultaneously, and backtracked to discern the problem. After a small, groping distance, they wandered into each other, both jumping back, startled.

"Oooo!"

"Dear Elbon! What are you doing? We must get along now," said Zak.

"How can we get along if you can't keep up?" asked Elbon.

"Can't keep up?" asked Zak. "I had to turn back to find you. What were you doing?"

"Backtracking to find you!"

"Incomprehensible."

"Zak, feel along the wall," said Elbon, who had been blindly groping out the surroundings during the brief conversation. "I have figured it out. We had come to a fork and went separate ways."

"Well, then, which way now?" asked Zak.

"My way, of course," said the skunk without hesitation.

Zak followed Elbon closely, as his tunnel began to rise upward toward the core of the mountain. After a lengthy distance it led them to a great room in which they could hear the tinny echoes of their own noises. From the dome of the room entered enough light for them to see their own silhouettes as well as those of giant stalagmites rising to meet, and sometimes to join, similar massive stalactites drooping heavily from above. Grotesque, carbonated stony protuberances rose from the floor like great, burly, squatting beasts. When stalagmite and stalactite met and joined together, they formed tall, nacreous, wet-sugar columns that reached high to the cracked and dimly lit dome of the room.

The pair wandered about bewilderedly in the cluttered semidarkness of the chamber, having little appreciation of its roughly square shape and three additional exit tunnels, each arising from a different wall and each leading in an entirely different direction. They milled randomly about the room, confused, until they came to a tunnel at the side opposite from that which they had entered, but by now, they had no idea even where that was.

"Now we are lost," said Elbon, "and we don't know where we are. Both at the same time. We are going to die."

"Dear boy, we are only turned around a bit. It is not a sentence of death. Here, let's take this hallway; it's bigger."

So, on they went. On, once again, into the total darkness of yet another corridor, this one larger than the others—large enough for a mastodon to maneuver, though with some difficulty. It sloped downhill, making their walk seem easier, but it was longer and much more sinuous, winding like the coils of a snake, doubling back upon itself. Zak followed closely behind Elbon, his face sometimes bumping into the skunk's airborne hind feet. Zak was curious that he wasn't overwhelmed by the so-characteristic perfume of skunk, and he wondered if perhaps poor Elbon had long ago worried away all his preciously noxious secretions.

"I say, Elbon, wouldn't the gophers love this place?" asked Zak cheerily, just before the two of them blindly tumbled off a ledge and landed on something soft and warm and hairy and very large.

"I told you we are going to die!" said Elbon as they leaped off the now stirring woolly object to the floor, this time sprinting along in the blackness, bumping into each other and the tunnel's walls, Zak hissing the whole way. They could hear the beast, whatever it was, grunting angrily behind. With difficulty, they scurried along the curvy, intestinal route utilizing that wonderful energy that fear so efficiently fuels. Finally, they saw a light ahead that led them to the outside of the mountain—the side opposite from that which they had entered by swimming.

Outside in the light of day and breathing the fresh mountain air, they quickly climbed up the side of the cave's exit to a granite ledge above it. From their new perch, in careful silence, they watched a highly agitated male black bear pour out of the cave's opening, snarling and looking from side to side for his rude intruders. He continued to lope ahead, looking around, slinging gravel and small rocks from his angry gait until he disappeared down the slope and into the woods.

"My hummingbird is here!" said Elbon.

The little hummer lowered itself down in front of the two mammalian faces and hung momentarily in the air. Then it abruptly sailed upward, forming a great skyward arc that curved around and down underneath Zak and Elbon as it entered and disappeared inside the cave's door.

"I don't want to go back in there," said Elbon.

"Dear boy, the bear is in the woods. And your bird is inside the mountain," said Zak.

"Oooo!"

They climbed down off the shelf and once again entered the mountain's dark interior; and as they retraced the twisted steps of their rapid exit, they could hear the drone of the hummer's wingbeat as it circled their heads. Finally, they came to the ledge from which they had fallen earlier. Because it was higher, there being no bear for a stairway this time, Zak had to meticulously rock climb his way up to the next level, with Elbon clutching his tail with his little hands as the rest of his body dangled below.

"I say, Elbon. I do believe you could help a bit with the climbing. Your hind limbs are free to work, are they not?"

"Zak, the world has too many problems for skunks to be engaged in the mindless activities of the hind feet."

They made it to the top of the ledge, and, with hummer in tow, they slowly made their way back to the great palatial chamber filled with its many ghostly rock formations that they could see in the dim light. They walked to the left along the chamber's great wall until they found an opening to another tunnel that they entered and followed for some distance; the hummingbird, like a good scout, flew on ahead into the darkness.

Zak and Elbon proceeded to follow the hummer, but soon they heard the drone of its wings cutting the air as it passed back over their heads in the opposite direction, this time, in a beeline. They stopped and listened. Nothing. Then they heard in the distance a peculiar, high-pitched squeaking. It was the audible, lower-frequency range of the echolocation soundings of hundreds of bats fluttering down the tunnel straight for them, furious that the airspace of their own room ahead had been violated by, of all things, a hummingbird.

"They are going to kill my bird!" said Elbon.

"Elbon, this is your chance to be a hero," said Zak.

"I can't. I used it all up a long time ago."

"Concentrate, Elbon!"

Elbon dropped his hindquarters down to the floor, turning his rear toward the sound of the bats. With his tail high in the air, he lowered his nose and pressed it against the floor of the tunnel for support, closing his eyes, squeezing down as hard as he could.

"Come now, old boy, you can do it!"

He did. An impenetrable miasma of dank and deoxygenated organic molecular paralysis filled the tunnel; looming, expanding, grinningly daring the most courageous of bat to enter the effluvial fog. It was a sinister, living thing.

Zak and Elbon seized the moment to run back to the great chamber to find the hummer and a more hospitable atmosphere. There, they followed the bird to the left, again along the wall, until they came to another tunnel, which they entered. The bats had not followed, apparently having decided to retreat to their chamber and reorganize later, and, quite possibly, to rethink the importance of hummingbird transgressions. The trio followed the tunnel until it led them back to the shore of their original underwater entrance; and upon their arrival, they stopped and stood, once again, upon the eleven hundred beaver tracks, which, of course, they could not see in the darkness. Zak and Elbon sat down on the floor to rest. The hummer found a rock perch.

"Elbon," said Zak, "do you remember when we became separated today? When we went down separate tunnels? Presently, I believe we should follow the course I had begun."

So they arose, walked, and flew back up the tunnel, this time continuing on past the tunnel to the right, which they had already well explored. They progressed a few yards beyond where Zak had stopped earlier in the day, when, suddenly, they discovered a slightly pungent, castorine odor in the air.

"Beavers!" said Elbon. "They were right here all along. Why did we have to explore the whole mountain?"

"Dear sir, because you chose the other tunnel. Obviously, I shall have to lead from now on."

# 11

Now they walked, and flew, into another, smaller dimly lit chamber. And there it was. The little trio had made it to the den of the beaver whom the nonrodent forest-folk of the region called Quarral. And there he was, too, curiously staring at them.

He was not difficult to pick out from the many beavers in the room, but aside from being a bit smaller, he was not anatomically different from the others. His feet and broad, scaly tail were black; his pelage was composed of a gray underfur overlaid by long guard hairs, giving his glossy coat, as with all healthy beavers, that characteristic durable vitality necessary to joyfully take duty head-on into whatever extremes water or weather presented.

Like all his kin, he was well constructed; a trait he understood, for behind those shiny little eyes of his bubbled a thick, brown gumbo of all the appurtenances of artistry in construction, such as design, arrangement, form, rearrangement, overlaying, dovetailing, under-girding, pulling, cutting, pushing, production, and transport—each one of these building partners having as its ultimate goal: monument.

But all these partners shared their hot flavors under command of a simmering, dark, rich roux named Innovation. Thus, all monument was uniquely Quarral. His signature innovation made certain of it. And anyone who was in Quarral's presence knew it. It was what made him stand out among the other beavers. He was a creator—and he never stopped creating. He was the chef du jour. Bon appétit!

But as soon as Zak, Elbon, and the hummer entered the room, all Quarral's attention became fixated on Zak's tail, whereupon the little beaver, with wrinkled concentration in his face, walked straight over to it and lifted it, and with mounting ferocious curiosity, studied it, gently working it, bending it, shaking it back and forth, putting his ear to it, smelling it, calculating its mechanical possibilities, with Zak all the while looking on with curious concern.

Finally, Quarral gently placed it back down on the floor, and, rising, he folded his arms on his chest and put his right hand to his cheek. Then he looked about the room, winked and raised his eyebrows. A soft eclectic laughter spread among all the beavers. They knew exactly what Quarral was thinking: that somehow, sometime in the future, somewhere, someone was going to come along and find some use for this thing in the construction business.

He turned around, making a broad, imperious hand-sweeping gesture, and faced the trio, and said, "Darponneh. Vee-ibenoo."

Zak was taken aback by the beaver's thickness of dialect. He had never heard it before. The famous beaver's expression of welcome had an audibly aromatic, romantic quality about it.

"Are you the architect, sir?" asked Zak in the language of Rodent but thinking in the parlance of possum: *This was not a brilliant question.*

"Seeibure."

"Certainly, sir, of course. I reasoned you must have, uh, been the one," said Zak, nervously stammering, not certain whether he was getting his point across in his own Rodent dialect. "Well, I must say, it is very beautiful—your structure—your dam, sir."

"Aweh! Saermee."

There was a short, awkward silence, as Quarral stubbornly continued to probe Zak's tail with focused radiation of inquisitive thought. After a moment, he turned to fix his regard on the upside-down skunk. "Oat-vamee. Pagueschlinil?" he asked Zak.

"No. He doesn't have a foul odor at all, sir," responded Zak truthfully, but not wishing to inject the conversation with his knowledge of Elbon's newly discovered unlimited potential.

"Beh soe," said Quarral in his mesmerizingly gentle tone, now regarding the hummer delicately hanging in the air, producing its own soft, romantic flutter-drone and showing no apparent appreciation at all for that which the ground dwellers knew as gravity. He peered into the face of the little bird, then stepped back with his arms folded. "Vasseyeh-oo!"

Obeying, Zak and all the beavers sat down, more relaxed now; but Elbon would not give up his handstand posture. The hummer followed Zak's cue and lit on one of Elbon's hind feet.

"Nehsze mehsza laypar ecva crune uittiair vom coo," said Quarral. "Beh zeebar, soo vaseh?"

"Yes, of course," said Zak. "I realize it is a bit strange. You see, I am from another region, and I met my friends here—"

"Weh-ee?" interrupted Quarral, intrigued that Zak was from other lands—an exotic. "Meetdwa, onmoni. Vescaoo vaveheu deh mattibau castor som-ka?" he asked, casting an arm in the direction of his dam.

"Oh no! Of course not," said Zak with earnest excitement in his voice. "The dams of my region do not approach the magnificence of what you have erected here. I have never seen anything like it!"

Quarral looked back over his shoulder at the other beavers, who were all nodding in modest affirmation of that which they already knew. He tried desperately to keep a smile tucked away and safely out of sight. "Qoorpwa veteu see see? Pweesze euvadeh? Vescaoo vaeh swibes ter draval?"

"Oh no. Thank you," said Zak. "A capital idea, certainly, but we are not looking for work. You see, sir, I have a bit of a problem."

Zak proceeded to recount to Quarral the story of the present sans-pelage threat to his own region, his inability to communicate with the squirrels, and his whole life history as he knew it, finishing the story with the account of his time spent with Elbon and the birds, their trek across the dam and their experiences inside the mountain. Quarral, throughout the long process, kindly listened and thoughtfully raised concerned eyebrows from time to time, thinking, studying the situation intently in his mind as it all unfolded. By the time Zak was finished, the other beavers were sound asleep, Elbon was on his back as if he were stargazing, and the hummingbird was in a semitorpid state having moved his perch only as far as the end of Elbon's big toe.

"Sze vwah," said Quarral after a short period of contemplative silence.

"So you see," said Zak, "I must presently ask you, sir: Have you heard of any such sans-pelage acts?"

"Nawh."

Quarral continued to look at Zak with concern. Then, gathering all the skills of diplomacy in his possession, he said, "Sze per na oucorepas praucom qoorpwa euvetsik."

"Well," said Zak, looking forlorn and slightly embarrassed, "presently, I must admit that I am not at all certain why I am here either."

"Deh siffyseel," said Quarral, utilizing all the best of the voice of castorine compassion.

So Zak, realizing that his rodent quest was at its terminus, asked Quarral how he and his party could exit the mountain without swimming, as that would have been impossible for the hummer; and Quarral gave him directions. The kindly beaver optimistically suggested that perhaps Zak might have better luck with his information hunt in another region and that he would, of course, notify the local Canopy Connection that there was a "friendly, talking possum roving the countryside, seeking information." Zak thanked the bright beaver profusely for his listening and helpful concern as his little party began to gather themselves to once again enter the darkness of the tunnel so they could find their way out of the mountain.

"Ba ee-eyetoe. Ick," said Quarral.

"Ick," said Zak.

Now the trio backtracked up the old tunnel in which Elbon had been the leader earlier in the day. They bumped around in the darkness until they again entered the dimly lit chamber with its squatting, calcareous, burly beasts, and sugary columns, patiently standing their ground—waiting for what, they could not know. With Zak in the lead this time, they at once were stopped in their tracks by the great room's chilly, damp atmosphere and its gleaming, ghostly silhouettes.

"Zak," said Elbon, "this is the room that leads to the frremmit bears and bats! I hope you know where we are going."

"He said to go to the left when we reach the great chamber," said Zak.

"What else did he tell you, Zak? Did you find out what you wanted to know?"

"Oh, of course. He was a great help indeed, Elbon."

"I'm verrry happy to hear that!"

They followed the wall to the left until they reached and entered the corridor that Quarral said would lead them out. They continued along its long route, which from time to time forked to the left. Each time they tried a pathway to the left, it sloped downward and led them to water, and they had to go back up to the original pathway and turn left again. They finally came to realize that the tunnel that Quarral had told them to take was coursing around the watery cul-de-sac created by the dam and heading toward the opposite side of the great pond. Eventually they saw light, and soon afterward, they exited the mountain at almost the same spot they were at when they had first come to the pond earlier in the day.

"Would you look at this," said Elbon. "We are not lost anymore but merely don't know where we are."

"There, dear boy," said Zak, "it's not so bad, is it? All things are relative."

"I must gather my birds!" said Elbon. "You will come with us, Zak? We can stay at my sycamore log. And we can spend many nights studying those disturbing stars."

"I'm afraid I must continue my mission, Elbon," said Zak, downhearted and wanting to be alone to collect his thoughts.

Elbon, with a blush of disappointment on his face, looked up at his possum friend and said, "Good luck, Zak."

"I say, Elbon, I don't suppose you could give me directions, could you?"

"How can I give directions if I don't know where the crridit I am?" asked Elbon.

"Yes, I suppose you have a point there."

"I am sorry I cannot help you, Zak. I know that I am not in very good form, but we can take some comfort in the knowledge that I know what I am. At least, I think I do. So you see? There is hope for me yet."

"Yes. Of course there is, dear Elbon. Always," said Zak.

Zak turned and walked a distance through the leaves and the comfort of the lighted woods while, at the same time, feeling an old familiar but ill-understood demon bumping about inside of the walls and attic of his mind. He stopped and thought for a moment: *Just because Elbon doesn't know where he is doesn't mean he can't give directions.*

"Elbon! You said you were not lost!"

But Elbon and the hummingbird were already down the hill and working their way along the top of the dam to greet the waiting red-start and nuthatches on the other side of the pond.

With the unwitting directional consistency of a compass needle, Zak again turned and faced north to continue his trek through the forest. He walked, trotted, walked, and then broke into his long, steady trotting march that so well maintained his old course. Certainly, he had no idea which direction he was going, for he was lost, but he thought that if he did not keep moving, he would never find his way back to his region—so, northward ho!

It was late in the day, but Zak continued with his unremittingly productive trot. He felt distraught that he had traveled so far only to become lost and that he had not even gained any useful information to show for it. He had even been too embarrassed to tell Elbon that neither he nor the brilliant architect called Quarral could determine why a possum would leave his troubled home and travel so far to simply converse with rodents. Zak felt spiritless and impetuous and ridiculous, and he wanted badly to go home.

As the blue of the sky was fading fast, the waning light transformed his dark thoughts into overgrown shadows. He was tired, but he continued into the night until he came upon a great log. Rather than investigate it, he decided to lie down in the leaves next to its hollow end. The night was warm and fragrant. He looked up at the stars, Elbon's stars. "If we can ever determine where we are," Elbon had seemed to say, "then, perhaps, we can begin to work on who we are. At least we know what we are. Surely that is a beginning." This seemed to be Elbon's message, thought Zak, now overcome by fatigue from lack of sleep and philosophical overload from his neurotically hyperactive spotted friend.

Whos, wheres, and whats fluttered about like vicious moths in his drowsy semiconsciousness—his early stage of creeping sleep. He could see their colorfully ghoulish, little faces, popping out of and back into the somnolent blackness behind his closed eyes. They were bothersome and nightmarish. One of them was bigger than the others and had a grotesquely exaggerated mouth and tooth structure of an angry cat, hungry and gnawing, as if it wanted to devour him, but he did not know why.

His sleep progressed and became profound, transporting him into the great chamber of the mountain that he and Elbon had visited, already, four times. He drifted from a mean, goblin-populated phantasm into a hellish nightmare, for the burly, stationary stalagmite sugar-beasts now arose as great white glistening bears dripping thick strands and globs of honey. They stood up and prowled about the room, hungry, and angry at giant, fanged, and grinning foul-smelling bats with pointed ears. The bats flapped about the bears' heads while making painful, piercing high-pitched sounds.

Zak had to dodge among the great white feet and legs of the distraught and furious bears to keep from being crushed or discovered. He saw one of the bears leap up and slap a huge bat to the floor, whereupon there was a mad rush of bears to the mortally wounded creature. As the bears began fighting over the putrid, quivering bat, the great room began to vibrate from the melee, quaking in a pandemonium of the roars and snarls of the bears and the screaming rage of the monstrous bats that now were fearlessly swooping on the bears, biting their ears and noses and sucking blood from balls of honey in their fur.

Hundreds of stalactites became dislodged from the shaking ceiling and rained down as great cone-shaped spears upon the thunderous vermination, skewering and pinning to the earthen floor bats and bears alike into their bloody ponds. The sound of the snarls and screams intensified and unified into the sickening continuum of some horrific laryngeal gag. The fur of each bear corpse became a shimmering swarm of maggots cloaking the deteriorating bear shape beneath it. The hide of each dead and dying bat quivered and swelled with edematous undulations, creating cracks and holes from which foul purple fluid gurgled to the surface and ran onto the floor.

Zak tried to work his way to the tunnel that had earlier led him and Elbon and the hummer to safety, but the evil stench in the room had become oppressive and overpowering, causing his head to split from pain. He thought he saw his black bear friend from home, Old Ok, lying in the dirt, still and bloody.

Zak awoke with a mournful hiss and the realization that it was all a bad dream. He shook his head. It did not hurt anymore. He closed his eyes and slept for the rest of the night.

# 12

GRUNTING AND SNORTING to the rhythm of his gait, the old plains bison noisily rattled his way through a dry, brushy, cane-filled brake. Fatigued and dazed and on the verge of stumbling, his large open mouth, swinging from side to side, slung cords of thick saliva in an arc above and outward and to the ground. Cut out from the herd and followed for much of the day, he struggled to continue forward, alone; it would not be long before he would have to give in or collapse. Finally, he decided to stop and make his stand. He would not run anymore. He stood in a tiny, brushy clearing within the canebrake, his legs slightly spread, rocking back and forth in time with his repetitive gasps for air.

The tall, black, green-eyed predator that stalked him was sitting peacefully not far behind like a mere observer, licking its raven-hued chest and forelimbs, checking out the surroundings as if perhaps seeking easier, more palatable dining. It had been following the bison herd for weeks, occasionally cutting out a tender calf for a meal. But every so often, it liked to indulge itself with a little game, that of separating out an older, larger animal and tormenting it. It seemed to derive great pleasure in contemplating what the old bison was thinking—that this day would be his last.

And indeed, the old bull was thinking just that as he stood alone, waiting, waiting to greet his own personal predator-executioner. Waiting to become just another lost, insignificant link in the great food chain. Thinking, *My, it all went by too quickly.*

Then unexpectedly, in the distance ahead, a slight movement with no sound attached signaled the bison's weary eyes, and he realized he was staring into the face of a robust female jaguar, who likewise was startled to see him standing before her. With her body low to the ground, she began to creep toward the bull. And as she approached, he lunged forward, shaking his woolly head and worn, black horns, grunting and pawing.

With her fangs showing and her ears laid back flat against her head, she began to circle slowly around him. He turned around, following her movement, and shook his head and pawed again. She circled back in the opposite direction as if yet unsure of her route and method of attack. He again turned on her cue. She began to creep in a little closer, every muscle on tense, yet confidently serene, alert, ready to be summoned to sudden, lethal motion. She leaned back slightly, about to charge, when, suddenly, she felt the end of her tail slammed, mashed fast, to the ground; whereupon she whipped around, snarling loudly with wild, glaring eyes staring into the face of a gray-whiskered black cat of at least her own weight, but taller, panther-like and green-eyed. His head was thrown back with large ivory fangs protruding far forward, his body somewhat off balance from his uncontrolled laughter.

"Moksoos! You piss of a bitch coyote!" snapped the angry and embarrassed jag.

"Hello, Swrogah, it's been too long," he said smiling, releasing his paw from the bloody tip of her tail and turning slightly to watch the bull seize his opportunity to exit the scene and teeter back in the direction of his herd. "Surely, my dear, you weren't planning to make a meal out of that old piece of leather."

"What do you think you were doing, scaring me like that?" she asked, blinking her teary eyes.

"Oh, dear Swrogah. Look at you. Still the most beautiful feline ever to grace the countryside."

"So why were you stalking that bull if you weren't going to make a kill?"

"I was only playing with him," he said. "The old bag of snot needs his memory prodded from time to time—needs to remember he is still alive. Only when he thinks he's about to die does he recall. What a pleasure seeing the old thing suddenly wake up and decide, once again, that life is worth living. Now he is going back to the herd with an important message, and he, himself, will be important today. And he will know it."

"Moksoos, you are still as savage as an angry wolverine."

"I'm not savage, Swrogah. You know very well that one needs to deliver a vital message, so to speak, every now and then. My, you do look wonderful. You just never age. Come now, love, you know I'm not savage."

"Well, tell that to the populace at home. Tell them how it is my black, long-fanged friend with green eyes is not wicked. Explain to them why you took out a cougar, two jackrabbits, and a marmot right in the middle of a council meeting."

"Oh yes, that. Well, someone must break the rules sometimes, you know. I volunteered. Probably nobody else felt any responsibility to break rules for the rest of the day. So, you see, I took the pressure off. Besides, I didn't like the way the cat was looking at you, dear. The others, well, I guess they were unfortunately involved in that old dangerous business of wrong positioning and wrong timing. Yes. You are right, Swrogah, I'm afraid I completely lost my temper. You do forgive me, don't you, love?"

The jag made a disgusted eye roll and bent down to lick the blood off the end of her tail.

"No harm done, eh, Swrogah? What a thrill it is that you have come. I've got this herd of bison. How fortunate that I now have you to share it with. We have days and days of happy hunting ahead. This is a dream come true. I've missed you, jag. You were always my favorite, you know."

"Moksoos, how is it that you are always so contented?" said Swrogah with a look of slight disgust.

"And why not? What more can an old cat ask for?"

"You are not old. You never will be, I think."

"Of course I'm old. But unlike that old bull, I don't need to be reminded that life is still good."

"How do you know he needs to be reminded?"

"I like to give him the benefit of doubt."

"So Moksoos," said the jag with a change of subject, "do you still have your owl friend who likes to go around trying to speak with the sans-pelages?"

"Of course. In fact, fairly recently he was snooping on one of them in your region."

While the sunny days that followed were filled with joyous romance mixed with the thrill of the hunt, their evenings were often spent in curiously witty conversation with an old friend of Moksoos, a great horned owl whose favorite perch was a branch in a buckthorn bush. Here, at the edge of the clearing in the canebrake where Swrogah had encountered the old bull bison, they would sit for hours in the dim glow of the moon or the Milky Way, catching up on the local gossip, sharing their feelings on the interregional politics, and simply celebrating the beauty and mystery of the natural setting around them, a setting of which they felt thankful to be a part. But, at times, the conversations between Moksoos and the owl were, at least in part, of the nature of thought-reading and without much use of the spoken word.

Swrogah found these silent conversations between the owl and Moksoos to be interesting and titillating even though she was not privy to the discourse. That Moksoos could read the owl's thoughts was, to her, a mysterious and an admirable quality possessed by her old friend. In fact, for the jag, such a secretive state of affairs between Moksoos and the owl was a welcome dash of enigma.

Moksoos had been correct from the beginning—the pair made a first-rate couple as they spent their daylight hours playing and chasing each other, swimming together in the streams, climbing the hills and small mountains of the region, and terrorizing the bison to remind them that life was sweet. It was the perfect vacation.

# 13

INDEED, AS THE great horned owl had informed Sena and Zak, the
sans-pelages were a species that seemed to carry the business of
mysticism and mythologizing to a near-limitless spring tide. To
that end, evil spirits lurked and buzzed about the invisible world, pes-
tering, maiming, and sucking the blood of their victims like the fat,
nasty flies of a herd of Pleistocene equines in early summer.

Apparently, at least in the notion of the sans-pelages, there were
not any nice spirits. But what good is a spirit if one doesn't have to
worry about it? Who is going to remember the spirit who would never
withhold needed sunshine or moisture, or prevent the birth of an adequate number of hunters and warriors, or foul the water source with
death, or whimsically cast the paralyzed body, weeping of festering
sores, to an eternity of pecking by a thousand red-eyed, bald-headed
vultures? Any spirit of consequence had to supply a certain degree of
terror to receive its nourishment of love and humble supplication; to
be the stimulus for the creation of the bonfires, dances, and chants;
to be the very reason, beyond feeding and mating and sleeping, for
sans-pelage existence.

According to legend, the spirits usually did their vile business, as
well as their more spiritually mundane daily and nightly routines, in
a dark place known as the Shadow World, which could not, of course,
be breached by any living sans-pelage but from which information
could be derived via communication with owls. And it seemed to the
sans-pelages that it was only the medicine males who had the ability

to send and receive both the silent and the voice messages of those peculiar birds.

Occasionally, however, a particularly evil spirit might decide to manifest itself in the world of the sans-pelages, where it could move about in the form of a creature of the forest at night or of the dark depths of a large body of water or even become embodied within the plasma of the campfire flames. Thus believed the sans-pelages.

And they believed that one such spirit had roamed the great forests and plains for many years, wearing the cloak of a tall, sinister-looking black cat with green eyes and severely overgrown ivory canines. Though over the course of the years there were only rare sightings, its bizarre and wicked appearance had made it a great source of sans-pelage fear and anxiety for a very long time. Never a sans-pelage hunter wandered away from his camp without the ever-present, dark disquietude that the infamous fanged black-cat spirit might be watching.

But on a particular late evening in spring, a naked, zebra-striped medicine male, who wore only a headdress of moss and sinew and turkey feather shafts, spoke to the chief and elders of his small village. He informed them that their worst suspicions, born of news and gossip gathered from non–Shadow World sources, were corroborated. For he proceeded to lay out the details in characteristic rudimentary sans-pelage vocalizations, of bad news delivered to him by a great horned owl. This time the news was not that of any vendetta of an angry spirit. Instead, it was about the odious carryings-on of a beast of another sort—Mungo.

Though only a mortal sans-pelage male, Mungo was so wicked, had such a contemptible reputation for meanness, that he almost ranked high enough with the sans-pelages to merit spirit status. For years, he had been known to go from region to region plundering, committing murder, rape, arson, acts of torture, slavery, and cannibalism. What more could one do to earn their highest spiritual praise?

# 14

"I BEG YOUR PARDON, sir. You really must move along now."

Zak, startled by the voice, jerked his head up, rudely awakened after a long and peaceful sleep, at least after his nightmare. But there, standing by the opening into the great log just next to him, was a most dignified-appearing gentlemale, seemingly endowed with the full raiment of possum aristocracy, including its burdensome airs.

"Hello," said Zak. "You are a possum."

"Please, sir, you must be going now. This is not a shelter for vagrants."

"Who is it, Grumley?" came a raucous voice from far inside the log.

"Uh, what is your name, sir?" asked the imperious possum.

"Zak."

"A Mr. Zak to see you, sir," said Grumley, glancing down at Zak with a leveling look and muttering, "Another sad prototype of the diminutive Southern stratum, by my estimation."

"What? Who?" barked the voice from the log again.

"A Mr. Zak to see you, sir."

"I did not come to see anyone," said Zak.

"Send him in! Send him in!"

"You shall see someone now, sir. Please enter."

"Come in! Come in, my boy!" said the voice.

Zak was led through the dark interior of the log and into a chamber with a hole in the roof that allowed some of the early morning light to enter. There sat a plump elderly possum with his likewise chubby wife and pretty young daughter to whom Zak felt an immediate strong, and strange, attraction.

"I dreamed it, my boy!" said the portly elder male of the household. "And now you have come! There is something mysteriously wonderful about dreams, isn't there, my boy? Indeed it is! And look at you. You will make a fine son-in-law. Won't he, Mother dear?" He glanced over at his silent wife whose face bore no particular expression. "Sure you will," he said. "Now tell us all about yourself. My, what a fine specimen you are. Now, what is your name again? What's his name again, Grumley?"

"A Mr. Zak, sir."

"And what a fine specimen he is! Very good, Grumley; yes, that's it. Look, Mother! Now really, dear boy, you must tell us about yourself. Where are you from?"

"All I can say," said Zak, "is that I am a poet, and from what I have heard, I must be from the South."

"For your capital sins, I am certain," mumbled Grumley to himself while staring frigidly out beyond the end of his pink snout.

"What was that, Grumley? Thank you, Grumley, that will be all for now," said the elder male.

"Yes, Master."

"From the South!" shouted the elder. "I knew it! I knew it! It was in my dream! Of course, I dream of my daughter's suitors coming from other regions, too, but never mind that. It all fits! It all fits quite well, doesn't it, Mother? Of course it does! Now tell me about yourself, about your family. You look like you come from a family of very high standing in the community. Look, Mother, what a fine specimen he is! I know of some didelphic clans in the South; now, which order are you from? Come, my boy, I am patiently waiting."

"Didelphic clans? I don't think I understand, sir," said Zak.

"Really now, dear boy," said the elder, "we must get on with the business of your heritage if you are to be married to our Prissy. You must tell us about your family. Your parents! Your parents! Do carry on."

"My parents are gray squirrels, I think, but since my dietary requirements are different from theirs, I'm afraid I have little contact with them."

"Grumley! He says he's a squirrel!" exclaimed the startled elder. "Well, my dear boy, you so look like a possum! Doesn't he, Mother? Prissy? Doesn't he so look like a possum? Grumley! And what a fine specimen at that! Well, dear boy, I know you are a busy one, whatever you are. Have important things to do, don't you? So you really must be going now, mustn't you? Grumley! What a shame you can't stay longer. Grumley! Where are you? Please lead Mr. … what's his name, Grumley?"

"A Mr. Zak, sir."

"Uh—to the door! What a shame, eh, Mother? What a shame he can't visit longer, but he says he's got important matters to attend; a rare thing these days, eh, Prissy? Indeed it is; now snap it up, Grumley. Do snap it up a bit. Don't keep Mr. … what's his name again, Grumley?"

"A Mr. Zak, sir."

"Uh—waiting! Snap! Snap! Grumley!"

"Yes, Master."

When Grumley led Zak down the hollow log back to the entrance, Zak pulled him to the side.

"I beg your pardon, sir," said Grumley.

"Mr. Grumley, your master used a term that I seem to be most intimate with in some fashion, but I don't exactly recall its meaning."

"Really, sir?" said the haughty Grumley.

"'Didelphic.' What does it mean, Grumley?'"

"Dear sir, have you bumped your head? Pray, what kind of bullish question is that?"

"Please, Grumley, just answer me," said Zak.

"*Didelphis* is your genus. Good day, sir."

"Genus? Genus for what?" asked Zak.

"Really, sir."

"For what, Grumley?"

"Look at your feet, sir."

Zak sat back and held them up in the air.

"Look at them, sir. As you can see, you have no claw on the big toe of either foot."

Zak looked at his feet again. "What does it mean, Grumley?"

"It means you are didelphid, sir. A possum!" said Grumley as he disappeared into the log, shaking his head in disgust, his notions regarding Southern possums summarily reaffirmed.

Zak strolled out away from the log and into the sunshine, relieved to be away from the quarters and questions of the log's interior. He again continued his meandering northerly course, but before he was out of hearing range of the log, he heard, "A Mr. Bump to see you, sir."

"Bump! The answer to my dreams, Grumley! Send him in! Send him in!"

In some ways, of course, Zak had always known he was a possum, but the notion had never before taken enough form to really sprout and establish that part of his identity. But now—now he was a possum. He had been told. It had been explained, even if, ironically, by that rather contemptuous example of didelphic flatulence, Grumley. But Grumley had done it—had done what no one else before had done—he had, even if quite by accident, helped Zak across the barrier. He had even shown Zak. And should it ever slip his mind in the future, all Zak had to do was look at his feet, for a naturally clawless big toe is proof positive possum in all marsupial circles—the ultimate possum passport. All he had ever really needed was to be simply briefed in the matter. Now, finally, he knew what he was. Amazing.

As time passed, Zak trudged on enjoying the balmy air and exploring the new territory of a brand-new sense of himself, for revelation now percolated inside his head. It felt good, and he thought that he could think more clearly now; for now, he was classified, speciated, validated. Even his tail felt more trustworthy.

"And my poem!" he said aloud to himself. "'Whose rotund belly boasteth bagge.' Yes. It came from my brothers and sisters when we lived inside our mother's pouch—'O where art thou Didelphis hagge.' Indeed, how could we ever know where our mother was when we were tucked away? The poem must have brought us comfort. My brothers and sisters are all poets. And I just added on new verses to fit my own predicament. Perhaps *all* possums are poets. Like the old possum in the log said: 'It all fits! It all fits quite well, doesn't it, Mother?'"

As evening approached, Zak continued over the hills and across their gullies with their small creeks. He was trotting now and so lost in thought that he hardly noticed a frightened little gray squirrel that scurried across his path with his tail pulled up over his head and ears.

"Cormastum! Ick! Ick!" shouted the little squirrel.

When Zak reached the bottom of what was to be the last hill for a long while, he found himself in a swampy bottomland forest that he had to cross if he was to continue in the mistaken direction he had chosen. The moist air was ripe with the scent of the damp soil, and he wondered how this country could be so damp when his own land, apparently somewhere far to the south, needed rain so badly. For a while, he continued to maintain his progress, enjoying the smells and dodging the great vines and roots in his way.

But, as the gray squirrel had predicted, the waning, muggy daytime soon became drastically shortened by a dense accumulation of black and gray-green clouds moving down upon the bottomland in which Zak was now well embedded. The lower, smaller clouds of the lurking squall line slowly swirled and moved in and out of the darkness of the parent cloud in peristaltic waves, suggesting the sluggish, methodical breathing of some atmosphere-starved monster hidden in the black background. It was of no great consequence that Zak continued to meander on his northerly course toward the heart of the storm system, for no matter what direction he might have tried now, there was no escape.

The leaves began to blow down on him and around him and onto the now-darkened floor of the swamp, and as the hum of the wind gained pitch in the branches above, he could hear the crack of limbs and trees breaking in the distance like bones being crushed in the jaws of something hungry and powerful. The rain began abruptly and became an incessant cascade roaring down from the ebony mountains of the storm. Zak could hardly see, and he became frightened.

*I must go forward,* he thought. *All is water and storm, but I would be no better off if I merely held my position. What would be gained by doing that?*

So onward he went, sloshing into the great wet and windy wall that seemed to be trying to obstruct his path. Finally, in the pitch-darkness, he could go no more, for he had come upon a stream of significant size with its banks already overflowing and its channel waters spinning rapidly downstream carrying rafts of leaves and debris.

He found a small hornbeam and climbed up its stout, muscular trunk to the first limb he could find. He climbed aboard the limb, and wrapping his tail tightly around it, he lowered himself upside down and began to rock back and forth in the wind. The lightning now came so repetitively that it created a strobe effect, holding, frame by frame, Zak's fusiform shape in its different positions of angular motion as he swayed beneath the limb. He closed his eyes and tried to keep his mind off the storm and sleep—an impossibility. He began to think about his friends: Old Ok, Sena, Opal, and the jag.

*Yes, the jag is my friend, too,* he thought. *There is something about that old female that I like, some solidity of character hard to find. And brave Sena, and Opal surely at his side. Perhaps they are engaged in battle at this moment, slashing and clawing the throat of a loathsome, murderous sans-pelage whose ghastly fires surround them in their deadly struggle. Old Ok, my faithful black bear friend, where are you? Could it be that my friends are in a worse predicament than I am presently?*

Suddenly, the stout little hornbeam was snapped in two, crushed by the weight of a massive water oak whose roots had given way to the wind and the erosion of the rushing waters of the stream. Zak was jerked far beneath the surface of the stream to the depth of its channel, where he tumbled and rolled along the bottom, writhing without direction, disoriented in the new dark world into which he was plunged. He badly needed a drink of air, but there was none to be found.

Finally, after a while, he gave up and breathed the muddy water, and painful and shocking as it was, he soon began to acclimate and accept his surroundings that now had a bizarre appeal, reminiscent of something like the mother he had lost so long ago. The lightning again flashed, framing the swamp's green treetops and the dun floodwaters beneath the trees, but Zak was no longer in the scene.

By morning, the swollen waters had shrunken into the confines of the banks of the stream. A newly sculpted sandbar had made its appearance beneath the clear sky whose clouds had been routed by the sun and a heavy, blustery atmosphere. On the edge of the sandbar lay the body of Zak, whose once-vibrant fur was now plastered with leaves and tiny sticks and the scum that is born of such floods as had occurred on the previous eve. Two raccoons gingerly walked out onto the sandbar. They stood upright as if it helped them to get a better view of the corpse.

"I believe that it is feasting at the grand table with the master," said one of the raccoons.

"Or," said the other raccoon, "perhaps it is merely playing that which only the members of its clan can play so well."

# 15

S CREAMING ITS ANCIENT chants in the repetitive high-pitched, jay-like calls of its species soared a red-shouldered hawk, apprised by its keen vision of a vast unbroken wilderness stretching in all directions to the blue-green crystal horizon. What sprawled below the bird was the great mat of green life that blanketed the red and gray surface clay and ore and stone and seepage of a massive swath of continent.

And in that mat of green dwelled the many thousands of earthly displays, innocent in their splendor, acknowledged by the very young, and forgotten and fouled by the self-centered idiocy of dying youth. They were the vital scenes of clear brook and shaded sandy bank, of great hollow tree trunk, of lush fern grove, of velvet, rolling-grass prairie, of lichened rocky ledge, of blue, glass-clear pond, of flower and seed pod, of beak and claw and bone and tooth and horn, of fossilized sediment, of dew and mist on deep-green moss—each, a part of the fragile harmony of evolution's grand symphony.

Below the hawk, iridescent-blue swallows soared over a grassy clearing next to a pond, dipping and dodging, unencumbered by gravity or inertia. In the woods near the pond and the grassy clearing, two stately beings lay upon a bed of leaves fallen from the previous autumn. Leaves upon leaves and soil from ten thousand previous autumns; the ancient forest, annually, little by little, constructing its own geology, the bed-ground garden of its nourishment; the old forest itself a thriving individual being as surely as a cat.

The day had come when Swrogah decided it was necessary to bring up the subject of the happenings in her home region. She had rather dreaded it. She did not know how Moksoos would react. What could he do anyway? He was a powerful, well-known figure to be sure, but what could he do about a group of sans-pelage arsonists? Eat them? She knew Moksoos did not ordinarily kill what he didn't eat, and all carnivores knew that the sans-pelages ranked very low on the scale for cuisine.

But it was important to her what was happening in her region, and if Moksoos received the information with his characteristic disinterest in such matters, she knew that it would not be long before she would have to make the journey home alone, thus ending their time of enchanted contentedness together. She now found herself badly in need of a perfect world.

She lay awake in the leaves and in dread at the end of another successful hunt and meal and long nap. She nudged him so he would awaken, but he was already awake.

"I suppose I should tell you something," she said.

"Speak to me, my spotted gold," he said. Then Moksoos looked up and began to stare at the sky with great curiosity.

"There is, or might be, a problem in my region—Moksoos! Are you listening? Why are you staring at the sky?"

"Yes?" he said as his attention returned to her.

"Do you remember Zak? The possum? The one who does our weddings? Who attends to the ceremonial matters?"

"Oh, the possum," said Moksoos, with the raised-eyebrowed expression of remembrance of something peculiar. "The possum who thinks he's a poet. Isn't that right? He thinks he's a poet? Yes, I do recall the little beast."

"Well, he and I left the region together."

"You left your region together? You? Swrogah? You have been traveling with a possum? You have a possum traveling companion? Ha! I can't believe it!"

"Moksoos, he's not such a bad fellow. Loquacious, but rather bright for a possum. Of course, I would never want him to know I said that."

"Oh, of course not! Not you, Swrogah."

"What do you mean by that?"

"Do you hear the chipmunks, dear?" asked Moksoos, with his ears perked, now looking across the forest floor. "They are busy in their chatter. I believe it is time for us to go to a council meeting."

"Must we?" she asked. She had dreaded this, too.

The mere presence of Moksoos, in whatever region he happened to be, often caused a stir with the Canopy Connection, which, in turn, often precipitated a meeting of forest-folk. In his travels, he sometimes left a trail of council meetings behind him, gatherings of members who had no idea of their meeting's purpose. During such times, the more outspoken would often try to find some sort of justification for the assemblage. Moksoos, who always tried to attend the meetings, was, like the others, oblivious to his causation.

Swrogah would have preferred to have Moksoos to herself. Their hunting and playing and sleeping in blissful solitude was a precious experience not to be disrupted. At the same time, she felt a certain discomfort going to a meeting, the guest of the great Moksoos, in a new region where she would, no doubt, be the object of judgmental stares and whisperings by a pack of jealous cat-females.

But on they went, and they did not have far to travel before they reached the gathering. Together, they entered it, with the large waiting huddled array of species parting, giving the pair a wide path as if receiving royalty. And just as surely as Swrogah could already see it coming, Moksoos led her straight to a group of she-cats near the center of the assembly. The pair sat down, her leaning against Moksoos's ribs, him gazing and smiling in flirtation at the feline females.

Mazee, a handsome, plump, middle-aged she-lynx flirted right back at him. "Hello, Moksoos. Where have you been, dear? Why don't you come around?"

"My dear Mazee. You know very well where I've been. With the bison, of course." He smiled. Swrogah was already irritated.

"And when are you going to take me bison hunting?" asked the lynx boldly as she moved in close to Moksoos while rudely staring at Swrogah.

The other cats laughed softly in thrilled anticipation and amazement at Mazee's urbane flirtatious aggression. They pressed forward, slightly, toward the gate that was swung open by their heroine.

Swrogah's ears went back.

"Since when does a lynx hunt bison, my little one?" said Moksoos in a tender tone.

"Where did you get your jaguar friend?" she asked a little too arrogantly.

"My dear, this is Swrogah," he said. "Swrogah comes from another region far to the north."

"Faaah to the north," the lynx repeated in a slow, mocking monotone, keeping her ugly stare on the jag. She half yawned.

"Yes. There is some trouble in her region, dear, and she … well, she and this very bright possum left it to seek out some kind of solution. Uh. I believe. Something like that. Is that right, dear Swrogah?" he asked, flustered by the gravity of his slip of tongue and hoping, ironically, that she would rescue him from the quicksand folly of having just tossed her into the scarlet flame of public humiliation.

The she-lynx smiled deeply and looked again at Swrogah.

"Is that true, dear? How very quaint that you should travel with a possum."

"I assure you," said Moksoos, guardedly cutting in, "it was completely necessary. There is presently a serious threat to her region."

"That is the most ridiculous thing I have ever heard, dear," said the lynx, haughtily watching Swrogah's eyes while moving in to rub her head against Moksoos's chest. Mazee was now only inches from Swrogah's face.

The other she-cats sniggered.

"What was your diet, dearest? Blackberries and beetle dung?"

In a powerful split-second motion of snarling acrobatics, the lynx found herself lying on her back gasping for the breath that had been slammed from her lungs while Swrogah stood atop with one forepaw at her throat and a very well-positioned, well-clawed hind foot buried in the lynx's soft belly skin, ready, in another split second, to rip and disembowel. The other she-cats backed away aghast.

"I want to see your liver, Mazee dear!" snapped Swrogah, her nose pressed between the eyes of the dazed and panicked cat. "And I want you to see it with me, Mazee. We will dine on it together. Would you believe that lynx liver is a possum staple where I come from? Here, my *deah-est*, would you like a small taste of the possum's dish for an appetizer?"

The lynx howled in pain and fear as Swrogah's toes flexed, driving their long talons farther into her soft belly skin. Her pathetic wailing made everyone, including Moksoos, turn their heads away with gritted teeth.

"I am getting out of here," said Swrogah as she arose angrily and walked away, leaving the embarrassed and frightened lynx to skulk back to the mercy of the other shocked and disgusted she-cats.

Moksoos followed Swrogah. The party was breaking up anyway.

# 16

LOST SOMEWHERE INSIDE the dark little cranial chamber of the poor unconscious and half-drowned body of Zak were the stirrings of a vague realization of a presence—a presence of something identifiable as self—and the self further discovered the presence of something it identified as nonself. The self felt a great discomfort with its own existence, so it would have been happy to simply vanish or go to sleep; but it couldn't because the nonself, formless as it was, seemed to be thriving and creating a disturbance. The self had no choice but to follow the course of the proceedings so that the inchoate plasma of nonself could take shape, which it soon did in the form of sound—the sound of polite, reverent chatter. At this point, the self decided to make a bold move; by connections most mysterious, it made light enter the picture.

"Oh, look, Brother, it has opened its eyes!"

"Welcome back, Brother Possum. We were afraid you had left our world. Here, we have brought you these grubs and dewberries."

Zak raised his head and awkwardly rolled over on his belly and elbows with his hind legs sticking straight out behind. He shook his head and began to nibble on the meal.

"You must rest here in the sun, Brother Possum. You have had a very close brush with death; apparently, you almost drowned. Now my brother and I must leave you for a little while, as we must attend to our field study. When you finish your meal, you must take a nap; you will hardly notice our absence."

The raccoons bowed their heads reverently to Zak, dropped to all fours, and bounded off into the forest, leaving him with the grubs and berries for which he had a growing appreciation. As soon as he finished the meal, Zak, as advised, took a long and peaceful nap.

Later, when Zak awoke, there, standing on their hind feet with hands clasped at their chests as if praying, were the two raccoons.

"Feeling better now, Brother Possum?"

"Yes," said Zak, "quite better. I believe you have saved my life."

"Only the deity can do that, Brother Possum."

"Whatever the case, I am indebted to you. And introductions are manifestly in order. I am Zak, a didelphid with nakedly nail-less big toes. So, who might you masked pilgrims be?"

The two raccoons looked at each other with puzzled expressions and broke into a soft reserved chuckle.

"Perhaps, Brother Zak, what you really would like to know is that I am Brother Xyan-with-an-X, and this is Brother Zyan-with-a-Z, but who we are is the chief point for which we devote so much of our time to study."

"Study?" said Zak, "How peculiar, or how interesting, I should say. And I notice that when you come around me you walk upright on your hind limbs with your hands folded."

"It is the custom of our religion that we do so," said Brother Zyan-with-a-Z. "You see, Brother Zak, we are monks."

"Incomprehensible. I thought you were raccoons," said Zak.

Once again, the raccoons broke into their reverent chuckle.

"Indeed, we are also raccoons," said Brother Xyan-with-an-X.

"So you are religious raccoons?" asked Zak.

"Indeed we are, and quite symprodically," said Brother Zyan-with-a-Z.

"I don't understand," said Zak. "What does that word mean?"

"Your lack of understanding is quite understandable," said the pious raccoon. "That word you just heard is newly discovered and you, Brother Zak, and Brother Xyan-with-an-X here, are the first to hear it, for it has lain dormant, as a virgin, so to speak, for eons. You see, we are practitioners of Lavratonianism."

"How fascinating," said Zak, with a high level of hidden disbelief.

"Of course, Brother Zak," said Brother Xyan-with-an-X. "In short, our chief method of praising our deity is by the mining of different areas of the countryside for undiscovered words. In fact, we are just finishing up a rather fruitful excavation of this region of the forest. We believe, Brother Zak, that this work is of extreme importance. And if we do not continue to make new discoveries on our study sites to add to our collection, then who we are, if it is ever to be determined, just might possibly erode away into a state of withered pracrineal fruductulation."

"We most certainly realize," said Brother Zyan-with-a-Z, "that to the layman, like yourself, the practice might seem a bit scridprifi-cal, but I do believe that Brother Xyan-with-an-X has summed it up rather nicely, so to speak, in a mussel shell."

"Interesting," said Zak, still wrestling with the concept, but over-taken by curiosity. "Would it be possible for me to briefly accompany you to one of your study sites?"

"Certainly we would be honored by your presence, Brother Zak," said Brother Xyan-with-an-X, "but I'm afraid we are all through with our prospecting for the day. Perhaps we can discuss it in the morning."

The next day, Zak again awoke to the two raccoons standing piously at his side. Before him was a pile of sun dried minnows.

"Thank you for your kindness, brothers. And it must soon be time for us to go prospecting."

"I'm afraid, Brother Zak," said Brother Xyan-with-an-X, "I must tell you that we finished up with our study site earlier while you were sleeping. We had a rather fitful night contemplating the question of your accompaniment and finally decided that, since you are not a member of our order at present, we should apply for consultation on the matter from the Hierarchy. Indeed, the time has come for us to report to our monastery and render our offering of field marvels. So, in that regard, we invite you to accompany us. It is only a few days' travel, and you will find our monastery quite lovely, as it is a great hollowed white oak—one of the largest in all the forest."

"Thank you again for your kindness, but I cannot spare a few days," said Zak. "I'm afraid I must try to rejoin my colleagues, who, I am sad to say, are in a dire fix. If it were not such a pressing matter—"

"Dear brother," said Brother Xyan-with-an-X, wearing the expression of deep raccoon concern, "what could possibly be the cause of your perturbation?"

"I am afraid that the forest-folk of my region, which I suspect is a long way from here, are at great risk of becoming victimized by a band of terribly evil sans-pelages."

"Stop!" said Brother Zyan-with-a-Z. "That is very strong language. It burns our ears. Please be careful."

"What burns your ears? *Sans-pelages?*" asked Zak.

"No, dear brother, the other word," said Brother Xyan-with-an-X.

"*Evil?*" asked Zak.

"Please don't say that!" repeated Brother Zyan-with-a-Z, clearly upset.

"Brother Zak," said Brother Xyan-with-an-X, "that hideous word you just said, twice, is of small use in our vocabulary. In fact, there has been little attempt to analyze it from the Lavratonistical Perspective. Indeed, we believe that the word has no validity except as a vehicle of mean-spiritedness by its users."

"Surely," said Brother Zyan-with-a-Z, "the sans-pelages are not deserving of such a lotudinous label, for it could portend serious implications for us all."

"Now, Brother Zak," said Brother Xyan-with-an-X, "what my brother with a Z means is that whether or not one regards the sans-pelages as contributing members of society, we must admit our kinship, for they, I'm afraid, are truly our brothers and sisters, and therefore a part of us. As you know, everyone's pedigree eventually leads back to the world's greatest inventor and pioneer, that very first humble, miniscule mite of matter who decided one day to split into two miniscule creatures, who themselves decided so courageously to take up the cause. So you see, then, we are all of the same rock—or slime, at least."

"Therefore, we must try to consider the poor sans-pelages in a light of kindness and respect," said Brother Zyan-with-a-Z. "Their obscure way may not be of them. Perhaps it merely represents some locus of defection in their religion. Of course, that is only a theory of mine. What do you think about it, Brother Xyan-with-an-X?"

"I always considered it to be the result of a locus of defection in their evolution as well."

"Ah," said Brother Zyan-with-a-Z, "that is most riducative on your part, Brother Xyan-with-an-X."

"Thank you, Brother Zyan-with-a-Z."

With their collection of imagined gems and Zs in tow, the raccoons began the walk to their monastery tree. In the end, Zak felt inclined to follow them, at least for some distance. Why not? After all, they were going in the same direction that he was going.

The little raccoon-possum procession rapidly moved northward, occasionally taking side trips so one of the raccoons could scout for new word sources while the other remained with Zak to keep him company and to make sure that there would be no possum breach of purity of a potential epithetic excavation.

When they finally arrived, Zak stood before the magnificent old oak that shaded him from any hint of direct sunlight. The ground beneath it was covered thickly by the acorn shells of the previous fall and the rotted shells of many and many a fall before. It was ancient. Its massive crown could support, and probably did support, its own miniature Canopy Connection. Over the course of its many years, it must have been the home, the Mother Tree, to a million forest-folk—squirrels, mice, raccoons, skunks, possums, bobcats, bats, birds, beetles, and bears. Its hollow entrance at the base was vast and led into a ponderous, cavernous blackness. Its trunk of scaling, gray bark rose up like a great granite wall of a towering cliff side.

Zak was asked to wait outside while the two brothers piously entered the tree to render their offering and try to establish contact with the one they called the Hierarchy.

As Zak waited, he noticed from time to time other piously behaving, hand-folded raccoons, often strolling in pairs or threesomes, entering and leaving the tree's great opening. After a time too long of watching the comings and goings of the peculiar environment, he noticed the two brothers, X and Z, stroll out into the light of day and toward him.

"Ah, Brother Zak," said Brother Zyan-with-a-Z. "Thank you for your patience."

"Yes. Yes," said Brother Xyan-with-an-X. "What do you think, Brother Zak, of the Great Monastery Tree of the Hierarchy?"

"It is lovely; impressive indeed!" said Zak in earnest enthusiasm.

The three stood silently for a while, which proceeded to transform itself into a long and awkward while. They gazed about, faking interest in the surroundings, looking down at their feet, each taking care to not make eye contact with the other two. Finally: "Well, Brother Zak," said Brother Xyan-with-an-X, "I must apologize, as I am afraid our effort to see the Hierarchy today met with failure. Upon our application, I am sorry to tell you, we were informed that no such request as that with which we came would be heard at all."

"Oh. Well," said Zak, feeling the raccoons' embarrassment, "that's quite all right. Perhaps it might be worth trying again later."

Again, the raccoons fell into an awkward silence.

"Well," said Zak, "on second thought, perhaps I should be getting along. Have to find out about things, you know."

"Of course, Brother Zak," said Brother Zyan-with-a-Z.

"Look, brothers! His Presence!" came a meek voice from a large assembly of raccoons, now standing around the great tree's entrance but leaving a respectable distance between themselves and the being who revealed himself to the shaded light of day.

At the great entrance loomed a tall, almost totally white but yellow-stained and overweight raccoon. His posture was bowed slightly. He had thick folds of fur-covered fat around his neck that made his head appear small compared to the rest of his large frame. His eyes were barely detectable behind the tight squint of his puffy little face, causing his lips to raise slightly to reveal a far-less-than-full set of brown and broken teeth. His tail, its rings long ago faded, was an orange-yellowish, damp mop somewhat resembling a most unusual overgrowth of hair on the top of his head that draped over his ears and forehead in matted tangles. He might just as well have been a member of another species.

The old raccoon remained at the entrance for a small time, standing quietly; all the while, slowly and deliberately moving his head from side to side to regard his reverently silent audience. He raised his right hand slowly in a frail wave, turned around, and then tottered back into his hollow darkness.

There was a great hushed excitement among the members of the raccoon audience as each individual felt touched by the glory of having actually seen the Hierarchy reveal himself to them and acknowledge their presence by his wave of hand.

"We are most fortunate indeed, Brother Zak," said Brother Xyan-with-an-X.

"Indeed!" said Brother Zyan-with-a-Z. "It is a truly rare event for the Hierarchy to be seen in public. You are extremely lucky to have been with us today and be bathed in his presence, Brother Zak."

Zak nodded in ostensive amazement, thinking that it seemed to him that it was the Hierarchy who needed the bathing. "I say, brothers," said Zak, "would it be possible for you to give me some direction, as I'm afraid I lost my way some time ago? To get back to my friends, I have come to believe that I must go south; but, if I am at all illustrative of my clan, evolution was most miserly with possums regarding the knowledge of position and bearings."

"Of course," said Brother Zyan-with-a-Z. "We would be delighted to direct you. Let's see, the South, well, one has only to go forth descomdantly, and that's about it, wouldn't you agree, Brother Xyan-with-an-X?"

"Yes, I believe so, but perhaps with just a touch of unularial angulation."

"Oh, I completely forgot about that," said Brother Zyan-with-a-Z.

"Wait!" said Zak. "Perhaps if you would merely point in the direction I should go."

"Oh no, Brother Zak. Pointing is forbidden," said Brother Xyan-with-an-X, "but I'm certain that the directions we have given are quite adequate."

"Well, then, thank you. You have been most helpful," said Zak, thinking, *Helpful, yes, in many ways indeed; but not at all helpful regarding the business of guidance.*

"You are welcome, brother," said the raccoons as they walked away, leaving Zak alone in the peculiar religious-raccoon environment.

He began walking away from the community that stirred in and around the ancient white oak, and he wondered if perhaps the old tree looked forward to a time in the future when the occupants of its hollow chamber would be traded for another species. As he walked along once again in the solitude of the deep forest, he thought about the old raccoon called the Hierarchy. It made him feel thankful to be a possum.

Zak ventured a small distance, then stopped. He decided to sit down and think and try to recollect his sense of direction that had vanished so long ago. He looked up at the sky for a few moments, and then he closed his eyes and thought, *I may not have the means for accuracy, but I shall be consistent. I shall choose a direction and never veer from it until it leads me home.*

With that, he stood up, walked around in a small circle, and set his course; but it was merely his old course, only now more precise, for, if it could be maintained long enough, it would ultimately lead directly to the hearth of the center-most fires of Polaris.

# 17

ALMOST AS SOON as Zak and Swrogah had left the region on their quests to the North and the South, Sena and Opal had become bobcat mates, as well as close pals and hunting partners. They spent much of their time prowling the forest near the large lake that lay to the east of the forest-prairie interface where Sika and Shypop and Nadine and Dunklin had been matrimonially tethered by Zak, the possum-poet.

Early one morning, Opal and Sena walked out on the gray sand near the lake's edge. The horizon to the east blazed in the soft hues of dawn as blades of orange and pink light fanned out over the purple clouds that lay as great somnolent bodies at the intersection of sky and water, for no distant shore of mountain range or tree line could be seen.

The sky over the glassy, purple water, and the water, too, were fairly well populated by black cormorants and very well populated by gray-and-white gulls barking their rowdy calls and laughs as if in a boisterous revelry over the birth of the new day. A large buff-brown sandpiper with a very long, narrow, downward-curving bill stood at the lake's edge and made its watery *curleeeeyew* trill as if some being of similar strange morphology might actually be within range to hear it. One was.

Another smaller, brown-backed sandpiper species, with a spotted breast and forward-bent posture, teetered past the larger bird. Then it broke skyward with stiff, shallow wingbeats that swiftly carried it only a small distance down the beach, where it went into a smooth short descending glide to the water's edge.

A pair of crested ducks in a synchronous duet of strong and purposeful direct flight split the air overhead; the elegant gray female made excited *ooooo-ik, ooooo-ik, ooooo-ik* squeals. They slowed and glided into the trees where they found a limb for a perch. A pair of dark swifts, chattering to one another, sailed far above in another stratum.

"Zak and I were here earlier in the spring," said Sena. "We were rudely asked to leave the premises by a tern."

"Well, did you leave?" asked Opal.

"Well, yes. It said we were interfering with its fishing."

"A possum and a bobcat driven away by a pretty little seabird," she said, smiling at the thought.

"We had to get back with the news from Sika and Shypop. Besides, the bird wasn't that small."

"I wonder how Zak is doing," she said.

"I am worried," said Sena. "I'm afraid he will get lost. I know him. He'll wander around reciting his poem to himself and lose his sense of direction. I've seen him do it before. I shouldn't have let him leave by himself."

"Why did you?"

"Would you have wanted me to go with him?"

"Not without me."

"There is no reason presently for us to go to another region, Opal. Nothing bad is happening here."

"Do you think the jag will come back with Moksoos?"

"I don't know," he said. "But what could Moksoos do about a herd of crazed sans-pelages?"

They gradually worked their way northwesterly, skirting the small sans-pelage encampment of the region, looking for any sign of a disturbance. They smelled no smoke and saw no evidence of an invasion of the territory by Mungo and his march of burning sans-pelage pestilence.

They hunted the small grassy meadows created many years ago by wildfires started by lightning strikes. Such locations were a good source of small rodent and bird prey. They found a small species of rabbit to be plentiful in the wooded hillsides, and in the bottomlands, larger rabbits and birds. They usually hunted separately by method of stalking to procure their food source. It involved the artful combination of the ancient skills of cats: those of patient waiting, of listening with keenly sensitive ears for long periods to gather the data of forest sound and process it into the knowledge of sharp reconnaissance, of creeping with ghostly stealth, and, finally, of striking with great lethal swiftness.

After a few days, they worked their way back south until they came to the great mastodon trail. As they walked along the large and rutted path, Sena stopped to listen. Then, in the next moment, he left Opal's side and began to creep slowly in the direction of a little rustling sound that came from a grove of dewberries and yucca. As he slowly and silently moved forward, he lost the sound. He waited, crouched, and stared ahead patiently for some length of time, but the sound did not return. He arose and walked back to the trail where he thought Opal would be waiting. She was gone. He stood and waited, staring again at the forest. She must, too, be tracking a sound. He hoped she would have better luck with the prey.

Sena sat down to listen to the forest, his light buff-yellow ears with their large posterior white spots and their tips ending in sharp black points were forward, alert. He patiently held his position for a long while, but he heard no sounds save those of an Opal-less forest. He decided to move. He continued to track along the mastodon trail toward the east in the direction of the prairie that was quite a distance away. There was no Opal. He had lost her scent completely. She was gone.

\* \* \* \* \*

Now, Opal hunted her mouse and bird and rabbit prey alone, secretively, while remaining vigilant in avoiding detection by the dangerous sans-pelage beasts in whose community she now resided. It had been several days since she had deserted Sena's side to mollify her undeniable yearning to acquaint herself with the habits of the sans-pelages. She had not wished to expose Sena to such risks, and she supposed he would have thought it foolish and dangerous, though she was sure he would have followed her anyway had he known where to follow. *Besides*, she thought, *I can accomplish this mission more efficiently alone.* She was right.

For several days now, she had waited at dawn in a willow and witch hazel thicket next to a stream that ran close to the little sans-pelage encampment of her region. The object of her fascination and study was a very young sans-pelage male who made morning treks to the stream's sandy shore while its mother was still sleeping.

In the dwarf delta of the stream, not far from the shore, was a still pool where irises and cattails and green, feathery mosses grew among hundreds of frogs' eggs and their black and brown tadpole products. Here, the little sans-pelage beast happily occupied his time trying to catch a few of the many tiny frogs and toads that had arisen from their near-stagnant, green water-world to discover the new frontier of dry land. When he caught one of the little frogs, he carefully held it in his hand and studied it, turning it over on its back before repositioning the frog and pointing it in the direction he thought the little creature wanted to go as he released it to its own life duties.

His mind was astute in its cloak of youth, for he heard, acutely, the sounds of the insects and birds in the easy breeze. With his skin and his nostrils and even his taste buds, he touched the air that touched him. He took in the shades of green in his presence and somehow, on some level of his consciousness, he realized the significance of that color and the importance of its well-being on his own well-being. He smelled the balmy, musty odor of the mud at the edge of the little pool, and he sensed its connotation of adventure and its connection with the fragile transparent dragonfly wings that clattered among the green blades of cattail; and he sensed that odor's connection with all else that was reflected in the still water's surface on those mornings as Opal watched.

He waded into the little pool, carefully, so not to disturb the mushy bottom. He squatted down and watched the tiny tadpoles make their underwater voyages across the miniature oceans that spanned from one mossy outpost to another. He saw in the clear depths the diminutive forms of mosquito larvae as they leaped and climbed with wormy strides as if in some peculiar medium other than a liquid. He saw and touched and smelled and listened, and, he beheld, with his immense power to behold such things, this little vital, undisturbed and innocent scene so wealthy in the life it harbored. He touched it with all his senses, and it touched him back. It was all so very real to him, and yet so mysterious.

Over the course of a few days, Opal had patiently, and very gradually, crept out from her cover so that she could be seen sitting quietly as she stared without threat. She was careful not to frighten him, and it did not take long for him to become accustomed to her presence. She had obviously won his acceptance, for, after a while, it seemed to her that the little beast came to the shore of the stream in those early mornings to greet her rather than chase the tiny frogs and toads or curiously study the cattail pool.

Over time, they became comfortable enough with each other that she could rub her head against his head and he would reach out his hand and touch her. The first time he touched her head, he looked into her eyes and made a strange sound from its throat, a *pishiu* sound. They became friends. But she could not, for anything, figure out how she was going to get him to close one eye—let alone, close one eye and, at the same time, turn his other eye inward to view his nose.

* * * * *

"Why are we here?" came a voice in the crowd.

"Well, I'm not at all certain," said Old Ok, looking somewhat downcast. "Why are we here? I seem to have forgotten. In its progress of erasing all things, time first erases memory, it seems."

"You didn't forget, old bear," said Opal. "You simply heard the buzz in the trees like the rest of us. I do wonder what the excitement is about. None of us except the squirrels know why we're gathered."

"Perhaps Zak is coming back with some astounding news," said Shinboo, the red she-wolf, with the old sarcasm in her voice.

"Zak isn't coming back," said Sena, his eyes blushed with melancholy. "It has been too long now. I should never have allowed him to leave this region. He must be hopelessly lost. I know he is. Besides, I don't know what use news from rodents of other regions would be to us anyway. I don't even know why he left."

Shinboo nodded in disgusted agreement.

"Mungo is not coming here either," said Opal. "At least, not today."

All eyes turned on her.

"How do you know that?" asked Sena. "And where have you been? I haven't seen you for days."

"I have a friend," she said.

"What do you mean?" said Sena.

"I mean that I have a friend who I am going to teach to close one eye and turn the other eye in to see his nose."

"Opal! What on earth!" said Old Ok.

Sena was speechless.

"They will kill you!" said Shinboo.

"Sena, I wonder if the owls could teach me the sounds of the sanspelage," said Opal. "My friend made a sound like *pishiu* the first time he touched my head. That is the name I have given him now. Pishiu."

"You let it touch you?" asked Old Ok.

"Yes, Old Ok. It is only a baby."

"Oh, please, no," said Sena.

# 18

ZAK'S BOREAL ROUTE had remained unbroken, so by now, there was a great distance of countryside that sprawled between him and the east-west-running mastodon trail to the south. Time, as well as many miles, had passed, for early summer was entering the Northern forest with its languorous, indolent strides.

Ever since Zak left Lavratonia and the pious raccoons, he had made very good time, and now he was seeing the character of the landscape gradually changing before his eyes. The forest was becoming more and more populated with aspens and conifers, and as he began to reach higher latitudes, he could tell that the aspens were growing smaller. The spruce trees were becoming spindly and withered, because their tap roots could now enter the soil only a small distance before being turned away by a solid and impenetrable foundation of permafrost. Finally, it came to be that, except for the small willow bushes that grew with the grasses in the thin layer of tundra earth, the trees were only a memory.

One day, he came upon an elderly upland sandpiper female and her four half-raised chicks. The upland's name was Stella. It was the same Stella within whom festered a dark memory for which there was no cure. The dark memory of the vivid realization that even the blue sky itself can never be trusted.

Upon his entrance into her territory, she quickly hustled the chicks into the tall grass and willows to keep them out of sight. She then hopped upon a rock where she stood, elegantly, with her large dark eyes fixed with keen suspicion.

"I say, madam, I mean no harm," said Zak, "but could you please tell me how far it is to the South?"

"Which part of the South?" Stella gently asked.

"I come from a region in the South; that is all I can say. Is it far, do you think?"

"To get here, did you see the ocean?"

"No, I have never seen an ocean, only small rivers and streams and ponds."

"To get here, did you cross smoking volcanoes and mountains with rocky peaks covered with snow?"

"No," said Zak. "Perhaps a small mountain here and there, but mostly hills, valleys, and flatlands, and certainly no snow."

"How about deserts with forests of yucca?"

"No."

"Tropical cloud forests?"

"No, madam."

"Then you are almost home. It is no distance at all to your South," said the elegant upland.

Zak thanked her and continued northward while she watched him, curiously, until he disappeared into the horizon, which, with those eyes, Stella could see very well.

The news that his Southern region was near elevated Zak's spirits, but, things being relative, he had failed to consider that distance to him and distance to a bird who flies almost half the length of planetary circumnavigation twice a year might be two very different notions of geographic scope.

Many days more he traveled northward, and he noticed patches of ice and compacted snow, which he would stop to smell and lick for the novelty. Over the course of more miles and time, the patches grew larger and larger, until, finally, ice was all there was, for he had come aboard a great ice sheet.

On days when the sun was shining, the ice was wet and slick, and his feet often slipped, making his walking tiresome. At night, the stars, when they were out, shone with a peculiar brilliance that he had never noticed before, and in spite of his weariness, he spent hours studying them and wondering what they were about.

He thought of Elbon. *Is he presently watching them with me?* Zak tried to soak up the shine with his eyes as the little skunk had suggested. "Take it into your body," Elbon had said. "But mostly take it into your eyes, Zak. Whether or not they know it. Whether or not they care. They are powerless to take it back. They have marked us as a part of it all. They have us now firmly locked in their own pasts. But—they tell us we don't know where we are. You—don't—know—where—you—are—Zak!" He could almost hear the little thudding drumbeat on the roof of Elbon's favorite log.

"Yes, Elbon," Zak muttered out loud to himself, "I am lost, and I don't know where I am, both at the same time."

When morning came after such clear, illuminating nights, he awoke only to discover that his feet and belly and tail were stuck to the frozen melt of the previous day, and he had to painfully pry himself up to start walking again. There were often days when he was completely fogged in, and he never saw the sun at all. When the fog was thick, his path was dark and the air was cold, but when the fog layers thinned above him, the air became pleasant and warm. It was during these latter times, however, that it became difficult to tell up from down, for all was a blinding white glare.

Zak had had no significant nourishment for many days, and he knew he must soon find food. An agonizing acute hunger had plagued him a few days earlier, but now it was dulled, partially replaced by the worrisome realization that he was starving. Of late, he had lost some of his strength, which necessitated his stopping at times to take short naps.

It was on such an occasion, when he lay on the ice trying to arouse himself to continue, that he opened his eyes and noticed before him a worm that had risen up from its icy burrow as if to inspect the new anomaly of landscape. Zak, seizing his opportunity for nutrition, quickly shoved his snout forward and ate the worm.

Encouraged by the little meal, he arose and continued the journey. *Why would a worm want to live on the face of a great glacier?* he thought. But as time went by, he found more worms, and, though they became a monotonous cuisine, they sustained him. He became adept at knowing their whereabouts and habits—that they could be found only when the sun had made the surface of the ice wet from melt. He often came across shallow pools of water, and around such pools, he learned that the ice worms were gathered in abundance.

With his new diet, and his strength rejuvenated, he quickened his pace, thus increasing his speed in the wrong direction. So on he went, and the farther he distanced himself onto the ice, the lonelier he became, isolated from all living things except the silent worms who were his only source of company as well as his only source of food.

As time went by, the fog began to give Zak the false impression of some improvement in his lot, for it eased his fearsome awareness of the vast, nacreous, frozen ocean around him and the feeling of being so profoundly lost. When enveloped by the mist, he sometimes imagined that behind the next bank of damp cloud, there might be Old Ok waiting to greet him and ask him to chair a double wedding. Indeed, once while almost asleep on his feet, he thought he saw the jag, who actually seemed happy to greet him: *Hello, possum. Where have you been? We've missed you.*

*Hello, madam, I was lost, and now I've come for you to take me home. Is it possible for a possum to keep up with a jaguar on the ice?*

With no reply, she silently disappeared into the mist. This sad state of affairs was less troubling, however, than the forlorn loneliness Zak felt when the fog lifted and he had to really stare into the broad, cruel, barren face of his interminable situation.

Finally, late one afternoon at the end of an unusually cold and dishearteningly clear day, he saw another fog bank ahead, and feeling the strange attraction that fog banks now provided, he broke into a trot. *At least it is some place to hide*, he thought.

When he reached the cloud, he continued until it grew so dark he could hardly see. He decided to stop and rest, but when he tried to slow down, he noticed his forward motion continued, for he was in a downhill slide. He dug his claws into the wet ice, and though it helped to slow him some, he continued downward. He became afraid and spread his arms and legs out wide to grip the ice. He tried to use his tail for a brake, but it was no use, for now the angle of the slope had become more acute and his speed increased. Having completely lost all sense of orientation, Zak began to spin around and around out of control in the darkness where he felt as if he were falling through space, but this time without the poignant stars to light the way.

Eventually, after what seemed to Zak an eternity, the incline became gentle, and he gradually slowed to a stop. In the dark and eerie silence, Zak was afraid to move for fear of going into another slide, so he rested a bit. When he finally did walk forward a few steps, he realized he had stepped off the ice and was standing in soft grass and smelling a new warm, lush fragrance in the air. In the darkness, he soon discovered a rocky fissure that led to a small cave. It was the warmest place he had found in a very long time, so, out of weariness, he crawled inside and went to sleep.

# 19

I T WAS LATE at night, and Moksoos sat in the small brushy clearing
next to the canebrake, the exact spot where he had snuck up on
the jag weeks earlier to pin her tail to the ground just as she was
about to attack the old bull bison.

The time they had spent together had been the happiest time
he had ever known. He thought she was the perfect mate. He liked
the way her mind worked. He thought that she was both elegant and
pragmatic. He liked her humor and the synergism expressed by their
combined humors. He liked her slight unpredictability, the way she
stood up for herself, the way she let him know what was expected
of him, the way she always came through with what he expected of
her, and the way she could gently steer him away from his own self-
centeredness. He liked the way she hunted. The way she slept. The
way she played. It brought him great pleasure to make her happy. He
thought that she was luxurious. Sensual. And he respected her. And
he liked the way she cared.

He had told her that there was nothing he could do for her. That
he could not prevent sans-pelages gone wild from setting fires to her
region. That it would all pass eventually. And that in the meantime,
she should stay with him. That it might be dangerous for her to leave
his side and the safety of the bison range. He knew she would not stay.
She was too determined. Too hardheaded. Foolish. After all, she traveled with possums. He missed her badly.

He simply did not want to interfere. He was a cat. What could a
cat do?

"You are one confused head of ivory."

"Leave it be," spoke Moksoos to his old friend, the great horned owl perched in the nearby buckthorn bush.

"Well, well. Poor Moksoos. He knows his problem will not go away."

Moksoos remained silent as he spoke with his thoughts. The owl read them and spoke out loud.

*Things eventually take care of themselves, owl.*

"No, no. This problem will not resolve itself. It will not," said the great-horn. "There are times when one must take a stand."

*Do not be concerned. It is merely a sans-pelage.*

"But this sans-pelage chief, such as it is, has been around for a long and tiresome time. And this business of going from one very dry region to another, setting fires, will not do, I say. It will not! And it appears now it wants to become a member of the Shadow World, a spirit, because it eats the flesh of the little ones of its species. And it thinks a member of the Shadow World behind the flame will perform the conversion! From where come its foolish notions, Moksoos?"

*I told you, it won't last forever. Their life spans are attenuated. Fortunately.*

"No, you are right. It will not live forever, but if it sets a viable precedent among them—"

*Let us change the subject, owl.*

"Do not interrupt me, Moksoos. And why are you looking up at the sky?"

*Well, perhaps they will all simply do themselves in.* Moksoos turned his attention back to the owl. *Then my bird friend will be satisfied.*

"No. You are wrong. It would not be particularly advantageous for them to kill themselves off. They are as valid a species as any other, though I must admit that the only decent thing they ever do, in my estimation, is leave their bones behind. But presently, they have a malevolently effective leader. Why this flocking instinct one sees in some species?"

*Part of the balance, owl.*

"Part of the balance? Seems to me to be a mishap of evolution bound to destroy the balance. You obviously do not flock."

*I seem to be atypical, since the other members remain in union for the most part. And they do not seem to appreciate me not remaining in union with them.*

"The other Shadow World members? The other members do not approve of your 'catting around' outside? Or inside? Now, which is it? And just how many other members of the Shadow World are there? Perhaps it is one of *them* who is meddling with the atmosphere."

*So many questions tonight.*

"But I ask only because I am curious. And it seems that only rarely do they come out. I know that is none of my affair. But I am curious."

*You are an owl. Act like one.*

"I am an owl? So owls are not supposed to learn about the ins and outs of their world? You sound a bit sanctimonious for one who wishes to be a member of the forest-folk. Well, I do know this: There are no other members of the Shadow World who are like you, Moksoos."

*And how would you know such a thing?*

"You care. I know you do. I can see it in your old feline face. Such as it is."

*Do you honestly believe I would dispatch your sans-pelage creature simply because it wants to be a spirit and because you wish it were exterminated?*

"I know you have never harmed a single sans-pelage, but this might be a different situation. Have you thought of that?"

*It will not happen, owl.*

"I live here, too. I have a family. I do not wish interference with the balance. But a bad precedent could eventually … Stop looking up. Pay attention to me!"

Moksoos again returned his attention from the sky to the owl. *So it will make you feel better, I will tell you this: The one course I shall take is to more closely follow its actions at the times it wishes to communicate with some particular spirit in the flame. It is a bit ridiculous, though, since no such being exists!*

"Well, you must do something. Or something bad will happen to her region, too. And you wouldn't want that. Will you allow me to accompany you as you go about spying on Mungo and his medicine males?"

*I expect she is on to better things now.*

"No. Of course not. She is mad about you. Such as that is."

# 20

THOUGH ZAK WAS tired after the long journey and slide down the glacier, his rest inside the tiny cave was fitful. It was barely wide enough for him to turn around in, and it was no longer than two lengths of his tail. He slept for only short periods before being awakened by bothersome dreams.

Finally, he fell into a deep sleep and had a terrible nightmare. He dreamed that his cave was being visited by a large wrinkled and hairy serpent with a flat face revealing two round dark holes for eyes and two fingerlike projections, one arising from the top of its forehead and the other from its chin. It made vulgar snorts at his belly, between his legs, and in his ears, and finally, it coiled itself around his tail and began dragging him from his place of restlessness. Zak awoke only to find that his exit in reverse was actually even more rapid than it was in his bad dream.

Once outside the cave and in the light of day, he found himself dangling upside-down in front of the massive head of a northern black mastodon. It was a bull with large, peculiar-looking floppy ears. A pair of monstrous tusks, more mammoth-like than mastodon, arose from his upper jaw and gracefully curled, snail-like, downward, then upward and then backward to end almost on level with the source of the thick, black, and hairy trunk that was holding the irate possum by its tail.

"Please, sir! Put me down immediately. This is most irregular! How rude, sir!"

"My word!" said the mastodon. "A possum! Where did you come from? I imagined I was the only contemporary beast in this valley."

"Off the ice, sir. Now put me down immediately!"

It was about seven feet to the ground, so Zak made a loud thump before he wobbled to his feet to catch his breath.

"Why on earth did you do that?" demanded Zak. "What a sorry excuse for a host you are! Do you treat all your guests so horridly? You are disgracefully bereft of manners and taste."

"Bereft?" roared the mastodon. "Certainly not! I assure you that I have a plenitude of manners and taste, a virtual treasure of the pearls of climactic social evolution. An eclectic collection, so to speak. That's it. A vast selection of eclectables. Surely you get the picture."

"Who are you, sir?" asked Zak. "What is your name?"

"Sark is the name. And since you seem to be so fond of saying *sir*, it is *Sir* Sark to you. But who I am could be a rather tedious question."

"Well, Sir Sark, I get the picture, and it isn't a bit comely. And I am most impressed with the way you have your facts confused regarding the business of manners."

"Little fellow, I regard facts as sinister creatures to be avoided at all cost. They remind me of brides."

"You are certainly accomplished at one thing," said Zak, "speaking bull."

"Dear possum, haven't you noticed? I *am* a bull. You should at least expect me to be familiar with the language."

"Good heavens! Are you trying to confuse me? And what for, may I ask?"

"For the sake of conversation, possum. The chief target of good conversation is complexity. Whether or not it makes any sense is quite inconsequential. What one says is of no matter so long as one confounds. I like to think of it as a sort of proper pedantical progression. Indeed, I predict that at some time in the future, there will be a great demand for eloquent speakers who say nothing of any substance."

"Incomprehensible!" said Zak.

"Bull's-eye! If I may pardon my expression."

"You really are quite illogical," said Zak.

"You, little fellow, are the ruination of logic. You soundly bludgeon the poor, insubstantial frailty and leave it writhing on the ground."

"So what do facts have to do with brides, may I ask?"

"They are both horrid obturations in the path to pleasantry!"

"Then I suppose you are not married."

"Of course not," said the mastodon. "Why should I marry when I have a whole herd of female consorts? I dearly love them, but they are why I sometimes come to this valley. It is my retreat to solitude. Poor marriage, cloaked with its heavy burden of righteous pretense, is merely a suspended state of holy acrimony. I can assure you that nothing spoils a honeymoon more than involving it with marriage."

"You seem a bit unscrupulous to me, Sir Sark. Have you no virtue? Just what do you say about virtue?"

"Which one?"

"Try kindness, to start with."

"Kindly."

"Charity?"

"Charitable."

"Sense of duty?"

"Dutiful."

"Loyalty?

"Loyal."

"Honesty?"

"Not a virtue! It is based on Truth and, therefore, it is pure idealism. Nothing more."

"Idealism?"

"The property of youth and certainly not a virtue."

"I did not say it was a virtue," said Zak. "I simply restated the word in the form of a question."

"Then I shall restate my answer in the form of yet another answer: Mere childish foolishness."

"Those are the words of a cynic," said Zak.

"Thank you. Cynicism is a virtue of utmost charm."

"You do seem a mysterious fellow, Sir Sark. You think you are wise, but—"

"I assure you that wisdom is no virtue, but mystery certainly is. Thank you again."

"I'm tired of this," said Zak.

"And I am thirsty of this. I think I shall go to the river for a drink and a bath. You are welcome to follow, but you don't appear to me to be the sort who would fancy a bath, though it is obviously badly needed."

With that, the big mastodon turned and moved away in a slow trot. A deep thunderous puff erupted from beneath his tail, leaving Zak in the heavy, gaseous cloud of large-bestial deprecation.

Because he certainly had no place else to go, Zak followed Sark to the river.

*What river?* thought Zak. *What kind of place is this? This is not just a valley but a beautiful emerald-green oasis inside a monstrous sinkhole in the ice. How warm and pleasant the weather. How strikingly lovely it all is!*

*This valley must be what a tropical rain forest is like. Trees with iridescent green and purple trunks! I shall have to climb one. Great vines the size of tree trunks growing up the trunks of trees with leaves as big as I! And so many amazing flowers growing from both the trees and the ground. They must be like the exotic, spectacular flowers of distant southern regions that the squirrels described so long ago. Yes. Their Canopy Connection serves them quite well. The messages and legends it brought them from the South must be the truth. Ah, there is that word again. Truth. Did he say Honesty is merely an idealistic notion because it is based on the vision of Truth? This "Sir Sark" is a most opinionated fellow indeed.*

The air was balmy and ripe, flourished with the odors of germination and spermy richness of a tropical rain forest. Trotting along behind, Zak could hardly keep up with the large mastodon. From time to time, he had to stop to climb over or around the great roots and vines of the dark and damp, lush jungle environment. The long journey that went into the late afternoon carried them through dewy, green fields where they had to cross clear streams with colorful, rocky bottoms. The depths of some of the streams were strewn with moss-covered boulders from which long, green, feathery streamers wagged in the current.

When Zak and Sark reached the black-sand beach of the river, Sark broke into a fast trot and plunged into the glassy water. The tidal wave that resulted from the splash sent Zak scampering back up the beach to the edge of the jungle where he sat and watched the mastodon swimming gracefully in the depths like a great otter.

After what seemed to be a time too long, the big pachyderm surfaced with a great fountain of water rising straight up from the end of his trunk. He then maneuvered quickly into backstroke position and began blowing the stream into his ears and under his elbows and between his legs, all the while his great tusks were swishing back and forth like giant scythes. He then slowly rolled and began treading water.

"Well, my little boreal boor, you might as well come in for your bath. I am sure the river will eventually heal the wound of your pollution."

"I think I should pass, Sir Sark. I am afraid I would freeze to death. I have found that clear rivers are always cold."

"Cold! Of course it isn't! The earth beneath this valley is amid a sort of prolonged hot flash that keeps the river pleasantly warm. See the steam rising?"

Among the long and leaning shadows of the approach of evening, Zak slowly walked along the dark, sandy beach down to the water's edge. He waded in no farther than ankle deep. Making sure to keep his tail high and dry, he washed his hands and whiskers and walked back up the beach to sit down. Sark came out of the water and sat down beside him. They both stared across the river at a vertical aqua-blue wall of ice rising hundreds of feet to the great frozen prairie above.

"Well, you certainly chose the correct entrance into the valley," said Sark. "Had you come from that direction, I fear you might have had a rough landing. But tell me, what do you think of my wintergreen oasis?"

"It is quite beautiful. But I am very tired."

"What is this? The marsupial megrims of a pugnacious possum? I'll tell you what. Tomorrow I shall take you on a grand tour of your newly found vacationland. I shall wake you at breakfast. Dear boy, it occurs to me that perhaps you are off your schedule. Possums do not usually sleep at night, do they? Or are you some sort of an opposite possum? Perhaps I should call you O. Possum?"

"Sir Sark, it is a rather long story. I shall have to tell you about it some other time. Good night."

"Good night, O. Possum."

# 21

THE MILKY RICOCHET light of the full moon shone upon the dark side of the great sphere, illuminating softly all things on its sombrous surface, including a great continent of forest. And from the perspective of the forest's ground dwellers, the sky thus was filled with a tangled, branching arboreal silhouette where both slept and prowled a large portion of the forest-folk population, some of them were themselves silhouetted in the shaded pearl environment. A great horned owl was perched on a limb against the light. Its feathered ear tufts created the impression of small horns. Its large yellow-rimmed pupils were expanded to gather a generous helping of the soft ricochet that was in its vicinity.

Swrogah sat still in the milky predawn moonlight of the great mastodon highway. There was precious little dew to settle the dust that any small disturbance easily set adrift. She had had in the early evening of yesterday a swim and a bath in one of the sizable streams of the area, but it had not been that refreshing because the water in the stream was so low that it was warm—almost stagnant. The countryside was as dry and brittle as it was when she had left it earlier in the year. More so, she thought, for now there was the added component of increased warmth and length of day.

She was disappointed, deeply, that Moksoos had not come with her. She mulled and ruminated and finally explained to herself that there was nothing much he could do about the sans-pelages, except, perhaps, frighten a few of them, for it was rumored that they feared him as a sort of supernatural being. She realized that such an attempt on his part would eventually be reasoned out by the beasts and he would, in the end, lose his spirit appeal, which she assumed he thoroughly treasured. As much as Moksoos liked to frighten and torment, she figured that it would be a sad prospect indeed for him to be reduced to the level of mere cat in the eyes of the sans-pelages.

It was easy enough to understand why they had thought of him as something other than a tall black cat with green eyes and oversized canines—he was different from anything they had ever seen—and he had been spotted by them only on rare occasions in the past. That was fuel of the highest volatility for their rumor and legend-making; the stuff to be spoken of by their old and wise ones, the gurus; that was the soil from which imagination could sprout and send runners of root and stem, to blossom, pollinate, divide and multiply, and become a rich and magnificent garden of lore.

And it was what the young ones would hear about and accept as cold fact that, for better or for worse, this was the world in which they lived—a world inhabited by a cat spirit, an evil one at that (even though he had never harmed a single sans-pelage in his entire life). She knew very well that "the great Moksoos" wanted that garden to remain lush and fruit-bearing and to never be disturbed. But he could have at least come with her, she thought. She would not have asked him to take, in any way, an active role in whatever events should take place. The selfish old fool. She missed him.

"You did all you could, Swrogah. All you could. Such as it was."

She glanced at the horned shadow perched on the limb, and, without acknowledging it, she got up and walked along the trail to the east.

* * * * *

"Opal," said Shinboo, looking up at the trees, "you should petition the owls to teach you the language of Rodent instead of Sans-pelage. What is it about now?"

"Here we all are gathered again. Why?" said Old Ok, in wonderment. "I wish Zak were here to tell us."

It was evening, and yet another gathering was called forth by the buzz from the ground and above. The ground at the interface of prairie and woods where meetings and weddings occurred, cultivated by the feet and claws and belly scales of the forest-folk, was becoming in some ways like the mastodon trail, trenched and dusty from recurrent gatherings called by excited squirrels, as well as by the more earth-bound rodent clans.

"Perhaps it is because company has arrived," came an old familiar voice in the darkness.

"Who is that?" asked a bat.

When the source of the voice stepped out from the shadows, Opal and Sena froze; Old Ok crouched, snarling; and all the rest of the forest-folk, except a few cat females, burst away in a fearful commotion of fright, running into each other and anything else that stood between them and somewhere that was a great distance from the meeting place.

Sena and Opal looked at each other and could hardly contain their laughter.

"It is all right," said the jag. "He did not come back with me."

Old Ok grinned and shook his head. "I'm sorry about that. I guess we are still a little touchy. Welcome home, madam."

# 22

"O. POSSUM! BREAKFAST time! Arise!"

Zak awoke awkwardly from the deepest of somnolent depths, his eyes slowly wandering up a great serpentine trunk that led to the face of Sir Sark. When Zak got to his feet, he teetered slightly.

"Are you quite all right, O. Possum? I hope you are well rested. We have much to see today."

"Quite all right, Sir Sark. Don't worry about me."

"I never worry over details, O. Possum."

When Zak got his bearings, he realized that he was feeling hungry, rested, and ready to explore. In no time at all, Zak and Sark were grubbing and browsing the jungle for breakfast. Zak found the jungle floor to be in good supply of peculiar-looking, but tasty, grubs, and the roots of the ginger were a most pleasant surprise.

Suddenly, Zak was startled by a loud trumpeting sound that came from Sark.

"Ah, Truth!" he said. "Oh yes! Glory! That is the fun one, O. Possum. Not only is it as idealistic as Honesty is, but it is as slippery as a salamander. If Truth were actually real, it would be a terrible debauchery. As it is, you see Truth one way and I another, and we both see it differently depending on from what angle we view it or whether or not we close one eye. What a scintillating object of Nature! A sort of fairy princess of myriad form who comes and goes of her own caprice. I am quite certain poor Honesty would dearly love to be a virtue, but how can she with Truth running about behaving so charmingly?"

Sark bowed his head slightly and extended his trunk to the ground so Zak could climb aboard. He was then lifted many feet into the air and placed on the hairy top of the mastodon.

"Very good, Sir Sark," said Zak, choosing for the moment not to pursue the mastodon's sentiments on what obviously was a well-nurtured subject of his. "What a fine view it is! Do carry on."

"My life would surely be a tragic waste if I could not improve upon the point of view of possums."

With Zak gently swaying from side to side atop Sark's head, the pair began their tour of the last island of an archipelago long lost in an ice sea. The valley scenery was, to Zak, of a most impressive character and grandeur, for there were many hills with small craters giving off warmth in the forms of smoke and steam. On the little hillsides grew magnificent conifers of a variety Zak had never seen. Almost everywhere there were clear blue brooks and pools of water. Some of them were hot, giving off large curling plumes of steam, and some were only warm. Within the latter swam iridescent green catfish among violet algae-covered rocks.

When the clouds and fog allowed the sunlight in, it sparkled on the rolling brooks and was reflected into the shade, creating shadowshine that danced across the dripping wet fronds of palms and grand tree ferns and onto the leaves of tree limbs that grew out over both the waters and the ground from massive gnarled trunks. From the limbs grew aerial roots that extended into the ground to form new trunks to support the limbs.

The air was always heavy with the tantalizingly sweet esters that streamed constantly and invisibly from the flowers. The whole of the valley seemed but one shimmering, living being nestled in a vast white blanket of packed ice.

They followed the streams along their tour. Some of them led into the jungle and up the hillsides to tall, splashing waterfalls. Others led them through the green meadows with their innumerable and variously colored flower species. The pair climbed to the tops of some of the hills, where they peered into the pits and cracks in the earth from which columns of steam and sulfurous emissions arose. From the tallest hilltops, they saw the vast panorama of the landscape, always bordered on the distant circular horizon by the blue ice that arose and shimmered in the sunlight.

Later in the day, Sark stopped to rest on a knoll that overlooked a clearing in the valley. He sat down on his legs and huge elbows. Like a good tour guide, he had given Zak a full accounting of the valley as he envisioned it along their journey.

"Sir Sark, this has been a most excellent tour. For that, I consider you a decent host, after all."

"Oh, dear possum, why must you take on this drab, maudlin spirit? I was pleasantly taken in by your boldness yesterday, for there are few things I enjoy more than scurvious repartee. Come now, do not be such a pitiable conversationalist. Malign me, you furtive-faced marsupial runt!"

"Indeed, yesterday I was tempted to do just that," said Zak, slightly irritated by the prod, "but I was hardly able to get in a word with your constant rattling of horribly peculiar ideas and your lurid and lewd sensualistic philosophical abstractions, something that would never foul the pristine air that breathe the finer forest-folk citizenry of my region. I can well assure you of that, sir."

"Now there's a prissily pretentious presentation of possum bull. Bravo! You deserve an award … Lurid and lewd, you say?"

"Lucidly!" said Zak.

"How so, may I ask?"

"I have, myself, conducted marriage ceremonies, and I happen to believe in the sanctity of the institution. Indeed, I hope to be married someday myself."

"A personal problem with which you shall have to deal on your own, I fear," said Sark.

"But yesterday, you said you dearly loved a whole herd of females, and yet you do not wish to be married. Do you really love them—each and every one? You seem to use the term loosely."

"Well, it is true what I said. That I love them each and every one, however, is not something I am particularly proud of. In sad fact, I see it as more of an admission of guilt, for love is a rather noxious form of primitive instinctual aggression. Once it arises, it is then tidied up with a series of intellectual cosmetics. But I can also say that I am fond of them all, and fondness is an emotion of far greater dignity than love is."

"I do not wish to malign you, Sir Sark, or engage in your scurrilous chatter, but I suppose your carryings-on could make sense on some kind of infirm and primal level. Or perhaps your fairy princess, Truth, is playing her chameleon act on the both of us. But please, tell me more about this beautiful island valley."

They sat silently for a few moments, enjoying the scenery of the green clearing sporting its steaming blue ponds.

"This is a very old place, possum," said Sark. "I do not know how old it is, but there seems to be a timelessness about it. I suspect that it represents the remains of an ancient forest that was here long before the ice."

"Are there no forest-folk here?"

"Only a few—birds, lizards, a few snakes, and smaller creatures, like the grubs you had for breakfast."

"Do they speak?"

"Yes. But I have never been able to decipher a single word of their language. It is bound to be archaic. It seems to be an anachronism, like they are."

"I have noticed the grubs are odd fellows, but why would you say that about the reptiles and birds?"

"Because they are odd fellows, too. For instance, there is a species of bird that reminds me of a lizard. It has a head like a lizard and claws on its wings. Of course, it has feathers, so I know it is a bird. But it is weak in its character of flight. In fact, it seems to be better at climbing than at flying. And there are lizards who remind me of birds. One particular lizard sort stands on its hind legs and struts about like a partridge while plucking little things off the ground, chiefly smaller lizards that look more lizard-like than it does."

"What on earth does it do with them?" asked Zak.

"It eats them, of course."

"Poor things. Life is so short."

"On the contrary, O. Possum, life is ancient and stands a good chance of outstaying all else that exists. It is like foam forever riding the crest of a wave. Of course, the individual bubbles in the foam do not last long. They must make room for replacements. But the great wave ambles along continuously in an ocean of time."

"Tell me, Sir Sark, how long have you been coming here?"

"About three hundred years."

"No. How old are you?"

"About eight hundred, more or less."

"How long do you mastodons live?"

"Well over a thousand years, barring complications. How long do possums live?"

"Well, I'm not certain. Perhaps a hundred years or so. I've never given it much thought. So you are an elderly mastodon?"

"Obviously it would do no good to say, because you can have no concept of age. You possums don't live long enough to attain it. For you, I am certain it would be utterly incomprehensible."

"Sir Sark, you attain a degree of disagreeability that is most amazing!" said Zak.

"That is better."

"What is better? I only wish to say that I, too, have a sense for living and aging and their implications."

"Tell me about them, O. Possum."

"The implications?'

"Yes."

"Well, there must be many, but the ultimate implication of living and aging, I suppose, is dying."

"I knew you wouldn't understand, O. Possum. Life and aging and their implications have little to do with death. Old age and death are merely a part of the progress of life from the viewpoint of the individual bubble inside the foam on the great wave. And that view can be described as a floating awareness on a river of time. It can peer up and down and out both sides and backward, but it cannot see forward.

"You see, possum, it seems that in one's youth, one is floating in a broad river that moves so slowly it looks as though it is almost stagnant. Though the river itself is attractive, one might say gorgeous, for some reason the scenery on the shore doesn't quite meet the river's standard, so one's attention is drawn to one's self and to the water and to how to get it to move along faster.

"But eventually one looks around and notices that the river really has begun to speed up its flow. And strangely, the shore is now quite beautiful and so fascinating that one wonders why one had not studied it more early on and what one must have been missing while studying one's self and the water.

"As a little more time goes by, the river begins to move quite rapidly and is becoming narrow and the shore is becoming more and more interesting. The objects on the shore are becoming so attractive that one reaches out to touch them, but it is difficult because the river is moving swiftly as if in a narrow canyon, so the objects get left behind. Objects now so beautiful that they have stolen one's heart go right by and are gone forever. And as faster and faster rolls the river, more and more objects come up into view that are now alive and have become dear friends and a part of one's own life, but they are so quickly ripped away that a part of one's own life goes with them.

"Now as narrower and faster yet goes the river, more and more precious become the friends on the shore. At this point, they are going by so rapidly that one hardly has time to focus before they are gone. And if one so much as even tries to focus on a friend as it goes by, then a whole row of friends who come after it will be, ever so painfully, completely overlooked!

"It is all quite confusing and frustrating, but I suppose one has to accept one's lot. It could be worse. One could be a possum and miss it all but perhaps a little stagnant water and flotsam."

At that moment, the mastodon threw back his head and trumpeted a laugh that echoed off the nearest glacier, but the wrinkles around his old eyes were glistening.

"In short, the price we pay for precious time is to become its victim."

# 23

I T WAS EARLY evening, and Mungo and a few of his generals sat in a semicircle under a large wooden lean-to, the only structure that remained of what had been a small village that morning. Under its bulky roof of palmetto leaves, the large chief presided over his warriors; all were engaged in a procession of primitive grunts and laughs. In their peculiar language, they passed stories among themselves about the vicious attack they had made upon the village that day. They did much bragging among themselves, for they had many spoils from their brazenly cruel, plundering charge that had destroyed the little village and its inhabitants, as well as a large portion of the ominously dry countryside, which, even at that moment, continued to burn.

In the early morning of the attack, there had been a gusty wind from the west, so they had started their fires to the west of the encampment. Some of Mungo's warriors had marched into the smoldering village behind the rapidly moving inferno, but many of them had stealthily surrounded its perimeters to surprise, capture, or dispatch the fleeing victims.

Early in the melee, Mungo had strolled through the chaotic village scene, enjoying the sounds and sights and smells of the terror that had been fomented by his own orders and by his own hands. The chief, who was large and powerful in every sense, stood at least a head taller than any other sans-pelage who was on scene that day.

As he moved along in his relaxed pace, he had noticed one of his generals dragging a young mother by her hair. She was crying and fighting to hold in her arms her small boy who was likewise terrorized.

Upon seeing that the general seemed distracted by the female when a battle raged, Mungo had quickly marched over to the general and, with one hand, had powerfully gripped him by the skin and flesh of his left chest, lifting him in the air and slamming him to the earth on his back. Her hair still held in the grasp of the general, the female was brought to her knees.

The breathless general looked up in terror to see Mungo's wicked face as he reached behind his back to unsheathe a jagged, swordlike flint dagger. Mungo then slowly lowered the knife down to the nose of the terrified warrior, inserting its tip into his left nostril, all the while staring into his eyes with a bitter, disgusted stare that seemed to say, *This is your warning. There will be no more.* And in one light-ning-quick rotation of his body, Mungo lunged, driving the dagger completely through the lower midbelly of the kneeling young sans-pelage mother. Inward the knife coursed to extend through the skin of her back, then backward to exit again through the front of her belly.

It was finished in less than a moment. She doubled over but never made a sound. With her mouth open wide, gasping, she stared at the ground, now just inches from her face. In her state of shock, she was just able to notice a red ant moving busily about in its daily routine. She watched it as it chemotactically probed, with both quickness and purpose, its environment—a fine-sandy environment that, to the ant, must have been a large rock field. She watched it until it disappeared into its dark little tunnel, about to be flooded with her blood.

Knowing that presently the general should no longer be dis-tracted, that the dying female and her child would not go far, and that the child would be picked up later for slaughter and hide removal, Mungo, with his dagger resheathed, quickly left the scene to continue his morning stroll through the noisy, riotous mayhem he so enjoyed.

As early evening approached, Mungo, by now, had already par-taken of the meat—pieces of the young sans-pelage taken from its dead mother's side—to rob the bloody remains of its youthful powers. A frightened medicine sans-pelage, who was forced to accompany Mungo as he sat with his generals, declared that the chief was looking quite fit and already showing positive effects from the youthful meal.

The poor medicine male, who was subjected to the constant threat of death, had to always proceed with great diplomacy and be certain that whatever news he delivered to his odious boss, it was not unpleasant.

Indeed, it was this medicine male who had that very afternoon reported to his chief a celestial event that must have been of the greatest significance. For he had seen the blue sky flicker and shimmer before his eyes as if it were somehow unhinged. The eerie scene had frightened him terribly, but he reasoned that surely this peculiar atmospheric spectacle was a sign—a sign that a spirit from the Shadow World wanted to communicate with his powerful leader. And because the blue sky had moved about much as did the flames of a bonfire, he reasoned that, *indeed*, it must be the spirit of the flame, the Fire Spirit. It was the Fire Spirit who would convert his chief into a genuine deity of the Shadow World.

But of course, the celestial spectacle witnessed by the medicine male was far less revealing of its true nature than that which an elderly upland sandpiper named Stella had been witness to. She had seen the unabridged version—the eye of the storm.

Mungo, over the course of time and particularly with each devastating raid against his species, felt himself growing more fearless and powerful. Of late, he had decided that it was time for the spirits of the Shadow World to consider him as an equal, a great conqueror of the day who would thrive for eternity on his youthful gluttony. So the task fell to the medicine male to solicit, by whatever means he could utilize, this bestowal of merit from the spirits for his chief who now so briskly demanded it.

The bonfire roared outside the shelter, where members of the army danced around the blaze in celebration of their chief and the spirits, and of the plunder and slave booty of which almost all of them had partaken in some cruel fashion.

Another medicine male in the group, wearing only a headband of bison rawhide, danced in a frenzied trance before falling to the ground, writhing in supplication directly to the Shadow World to bestow spirit status upon his chief. For he, too, was in great danger of losing his life if Mungo's demands were not met, a prospect so catastrophic that it could very well prompt Mungo to not only dispatch and replace his medicine males but to attempt to wage a war with the Shadow World itself, if only he could figure out just how to accomplish such a deed. He was becoming jealous and resentful of the spirits for not coming forth with what he commanded.

To be sure, there had been much brutality and suffering in the world of the sans-pelages because of Mungo's march, but there were other victims. Many members of the forest-folk had lost their homes or their lives, or both, that day. And even still, the fires raged—roaring, cracking, exploding the crowns of trees, devouring the life of the forest with all the momentum of a prowling, hungry dragon. The bright orange beast's tall curtain of smoke turned the setting sun to dark purple and the air into an unbreathable, toxic mix of gas and soot. Its splintered tongue licked upward in fierce, twisting red columns swiping down birds, bats, and flying squirrels in flight. It could not get enough to eat, it was always starving for more, relentlessly hunting and taking.

\* \* \* \* \*

In another little sans-pelage village, far away to the south, blazed another, smaller bonfire around which sat some females who had gathered a pile of roots and tubers that they were grinding into a good-medicine potion. Some of the males were removing from an intestinal sack the meat from a deer they had taken by their devices the day before. Several of them smeared themselves with blood from the meat in honor of the animal from which it came. They passed helpings of the meat around to themselves and to the females and to the young ones who sat in the glow of the fire. A female passed out handfuls of beetles that she had just toasted in the ashes.

An elderly female was sitting with those who were grinding the roots and tubers in a bowl. She whimpered in pain and sadness for the joints of her hands and legs that were swollen and tender and red. Finally, she gave up her sitting position and lay down on the warm ground in the hope that it would give her some kind of comfort.

When the females were finished with their grinding, the old ze-bra-striped medicine male who wore only a headdress of moss and sinew and turkey feather shafts walked over to the females and took from the grinding bowl two handfuls of the powdered-root-and-tu-ber mix and placed it on the head and hands and legs of the naked, outstretched female elder. He squatted down over her as he briskly rubbed the potion onto her body, massaging it in, front and back.

When he finished, he arose and began dancing. Some of the males joined him in dance while the females clapped and sang chants. Then the medicine male broke into a frenzied dance of rapid motion, twirl-ing around with a twisted, freakish expression, eyes glazed in a deep trance. He began to chant loudly, imploring, in his altered conscious-ness, the spirits of the Shadow World to aid him in his medicine making so the old female might get relief.

He began leaping and spinning around faster and faster. He then ran back to the bowl of medicine and grabbed two more handfuls of the medicine powder and twirled himself back to the fire and threw it into the blaze, causing an explosion of sparks and smoke. Then he leaped into the fire, screaming, before he jumped back out and ran to the stream, where he could be heard by all as he continued his wild chanting. Soon he reentered the scene around the fire, yelling and howling and dancing, before he fell to the ground in a silent, de-formed heap of trembling sans-pelage.

"I can see now why its turkey feathers have only their shafts re-maining. Poor thing!" cracked Swrogah, fighting herself to keep from laughing out loud.

"They are very peculiar," whispered Sena, who was also smiling.

"Do you suppose it's some sort of council meeting they're hav-ing?" asked Old Ok.

"Well, Opal dear," said the jag, "you have gotten us this far. Are you going to show us your little friend?"

"I see him!" whispered Opal. "There, next to the female who was grinding something. It is Pishiu, all right."

As the three cats and the bear continued to watch the strange scene from their shadowy locale of the forest, one by one they began to yawn. But before they dozed off, they saw the old leader of the small camp walk over and kneel beside the medicine male. He then tried to coax him up from the ground so he might enjoy his venison and now-cold beetles.

# 24

S OME WEEKS HAD passed, and Zak and Sark had covered almost
every straight, curved, and crooked cranny of the great tropical
oasis of the Northern ice sheet—a grand expedition of which Sark
had never grown tired even though he had made it many times before.
As a thrilled and observant tourist, Zak had taken it all in, including a
few lucky, but brief, sightings of the lizards that looked like birds and
the birds that looked like lizards. And once, late at night, Sark had gently awakened Zak and had taken him to the top of a knoll so that he
could watch a most beautiful light display in the northern sky—shimmering undulations of pink and emerald beneath the glittering stars.

One morning as the pair was browsing for breakfast, Sark over-
heard Zak making chattering sounds to himself while foraging under
the foliage in search of a particular larval delicacy.

"Possum! What on earth are you saying? 'Sable ear, snout of swine,
Mother dear, marsupid fine'? What are you talking about? Do you of-
ten go about speaking to yourself? Oh, that is peculiar, O. Possum.
Very peculiar."

"Yes, Sir Sark. I am a poet. A possum-poet, to be exact. Though
the notion might not cross your mind daily, I can assure you that it is
not a bit peculiar. It is what I am. And, I daresay, it is also who I am."

"Indeed?" said Sir Sark, taken back a bit and eyeing Zak with curious suspicion. "So you think you know who you are?"

"Perhaps I do," said Zak with a rather delicately balanced tone of
superiority. "Actually, though, it was only recently that I learned what
I am."

"I can well accept that one knows what one is, but the who?" asked Sark.

"Indeed, I have a spotted skunk friend by the name of Elbon who believes that there might be a way for us all to find out *who* we are if we can ever determine *where* we are."

"Now this is getting confusing," said Sark. "I am sure I would like to meet the spotted little fellow, but, for now, back to the who, please."

"What about the who?" asked Zak.

"The who! You just said that you know who you are. How?" asked Sark. "How on earth can one know who one is when any possibility whatsoever of learning it is taken away at the beginning of life?

"Anyone should know that the only time one has a chance of knowing such a thing is at the very moment of one's birth or one's hatching. And unfortunately, one's poor little brain is not well enough ripened at that tender age to appreciate it.

"You know very well that at the next moment society rushes in to extinguish the little who and replace it with who knows what? Eh, perhaps a poor choice of words there. Allow me to rephrase it.

"Like a naughty ghost, possum, the chance summation of custom, circumstance, weather condition, and mere whimsy, of whatever sort happens to be in the particular vicinity at the time, invades the little being, snuffs out the who, and substitutes it completely—which is, of course, why nobody really knows who they are. It is quite academic. And there is not a single thing we can do about it. Are you with me, O. Possum?"

"Not exactly," said Zak.

"What is your problem, O. Possum? Have you been eating mind-altering grubs?"

"You see, Sir Sark, I was not exactly a possum when I was young."

"Oh my," said Sark. "Perhaps you should spend the day in one of the hot pools to soak the poison out."

"What I mean to say is that, though I was born a possum, I was orphaned shortly after I entered the world. Soon, I was taken in by gray squirrel parents. Of course, I grew up to realize that I was not a squirrel, but I also had some difficulties with the concept of my being a possum. It was only just recently when my own notions of possum-hood were confirmed. So, you see, for a very long time, I did not know *what* I was; and, by not knowing that, perhaps I knew *who* I was."

"An interesting story, O. Possum," said Sark. "Now I can see why you like to sleep at night and prowl during the day. But am I now to believe that if one has problems with one's own identity, then one knows who one is? That is, if one knows *what* one is, then one cannot know *who* one is? And, conversely, if one does *not* know *what* one is, then one is somehow privy to knowledge of the little *who*? Well, that is indeed a stretch, possum. I shall have to think about it. Now tell me again, straight, O. Possum. Are you really certain you know who you are?"

"I only said 'perhaps,' Sir Sark. I have no particularly firm notions at present."

"Yes. Well, perhaps that is the healthier point of view, O. Possum. But while we are on the subject of *whos*, *whats*, and *wheres*, I suppose I should inquire if you have considered any propositions on the subjects of *when* and *why*."

"Why, no," said Zak.

"I believe that you have made an excellent decision, O. Possum."


By the end of the day, they had worked their way back to the river where Sark had another bath and a swim in its warm, clear depths, blue-green tinted by the reflection of the great cliff of blue ice and the lush moss and algae that grew in the river's opulent submarine environment. The river was very deep, and from Zak's perch on a large boulder, his mastodon friend appeared as a small frog gracefully swimming around in circles just above the rocky bottom.

Finally, Sark glided back up to breach the river's surface, spewing in all directions a large column of water from the end of his trunk. He then swam to the shore and sat down on the dark sand. Zak climbed down from the boulder to join him, where, again, they gathered in the jungle scenery as well as that of the aqua wall of ice that arose so high from the opposite bank to meet with the vast ice prairie above them. Downstream they could see the river disappear at the base of the blue wall with twisting clouds of steam rising at its exit. There, the waters swirled around in a massive and loudly sucking vortex that followed its course on beneath the broad face of the glacial rampart.

"Sir Sark," said Zak, "could you tell me which way south is?"

"That way, O. Possum. The way the river is flowing."

"Does it continue to flow south for a very long distance?"

"Indeed it does, possum. Why do you ask?"

"I have been trying for a very long time to get back to my region in the South."

"What, then, are you doing here?"

"I am lost, Sir Sark."

"My word. I thought perhaps you were some sort of possum explorer on a Northern excursion. How long have you been trying to get back to your region?"

"For a very long time, I'm afraid. Actually, ever since only a short time after I left home. My jaguar companion and I went west on our local mastodon highway. After we traveled awhile, she went to the left and I, as instructed, went to the right. Could it be that I had been going north all that time?"

"Possum, I think you should consider the possibility that you have a magnet in your head. What on earth were you thinking to have wandered onto the ice as you did?"

"It was all strange territory to me, Sir Sark," said Zak.

"That should have told you something."

Zak proceeded to explain to his mastodon companion all the details of Mungo and the sans-pelage situation and its potential consequences for his forest region and its residents, the friends he had at home and those he found on his journey northward while lost, his bilingual ceremonial duties as resident poet of his region, and, finally, the intention of the jag to find Moksoos.

"I have met Moksoos," said Sark. "It was a long time ago. Strange fellow. Last of his kind, they say. And I have seen sans-pelages, too.

Indeed, I understand that their population is expanding to the north. After what you have just told me about this Mungo fellow, it is not a prospect that I behold with fond anticipation."

"Sir Sark, do you think there is any chance that I will ever find my way back home?"

"Of course! We shall leave first thing after tomorrow morning's breakfast," said the mastodon.

"Do you mean to say we can go together? That you are ready to take leave of your wintergreen oasis?" asked Zak.

"Of course. I myself am presently ready to go back to my poor, lonely females. I am certain that they must be quite distraught by my long absence," said the mastodon, with a hint of smiling anticipation in his wrinkled face.

"This is most excellent news," said Zak, feeling more elated than he had in a very long time. "Perhaps when we reach the location of your females, you could give me some direction as to how I might maintain a southerly course to my own region."

"It won't be necessary, O. Possum. We all will be going to your region. You and I and my fifty females will simply follow the course of the river."

"Really, Sir Sark?" asked Zak, thinking that at last he would have something to show for his long absence, and something big at that.

"Indeed, possum. Perhaps I could see Moksoos again. I have a few questions to ask him. And I would like to have a word, so to speak, with this Mungo character, too."

"So ... Moksoos. You said you have met him?" said Zak, slightly dubious.

"Yes, and under rather peculiar circumstances. It was many seasons ago. I was by myself, or thought I was, right here at our tropical oasis, possum. Well, one day, I'm afraid I rather absentmindedly blundered off a rocky ledge and fell into one of those hot pools of water."

"Yes. Like one of those you suggested I have a soak in," said Zak.

"Precisely. Well, when I hit that wicked water, it paralyzed me. I sank to the bottom like a boulder."

"But you are such a good swimmer."

"It did me no good. I could not move at all. I lay there on the sterile boiling bottom of the pool thinking that in the next moment I was going to melt into a million little pieces and parts. Then I totally lost consciousness. After that, I really have no idea what happened, for when I awoke, I was lying in the shaded grass under a palm tree in perfectly good health, except for my ears, I'm afraid. They have been bent ever since. The heat must have melted the cartilage. Of course, my females find the deformity quite attractive. But there, sitting on the grass staring at me, was Moksoos. He somehow knew my name and introduced himself. Before I could get any words out of my mouth, I blinked and he was gone. Haven't seen him since. Quite strange, possum. I feel like he somehow saved my life. But if that is true. Then how?"

"I have heard Moksoos has been in all the regions, but I never thought of him coming this far north," said Zak.

"He must get around quite a bit, possum."

The next morning, the pair slowly worked their way through the jungle, Sark snatching massive trunkfuls of greenery from the ground and the trees while Zak dined on berries and beetles.

"Eat well, possum. We have a big day ahead of us."

"Sir Sark, how long do you suppose it will take us to find your females? I should think it will take us the rest of this day just to climb back onto the ice."

"O. Possum, the roof of the ice sheet is the way one enters the valley. The cellar is the way one exits."

"What on earth do you mean?"

"Follow me, possum, and do what I say. That is all you have to remember."

The pair walked back to the river, Sark in the lead. They made their way downstream along the bank to near the spot where the river disappeared abruptly under the ice wall, making its threatening, siphoning noise.

"Dear sir, why have we come back to the river?"

"Which direction do we want to go, O. Possum?"

"Why, sir, you know fully well that we must go south."

"And which direction does the river flow, O. Possum?"

The most appropriate words that Zak could think of at that moment were those of an Elbon paraphrase, "Oooo! Sir Sark, we are going to die!"

"Have a little faith, O. Possum."

"Have you ever gone in there before?"

"Yes, of course. Many times. It is the exit from this valley."

"Well, it cannot be the only one," said Zak.

"It is the best one, possum. It's quicker this way."

"I am sure it is. How did you discover it?"

"That is a story of adventure, possum. It was a long time ago. I was standing in the river's shallows when I felt the ground quiver. Little waves danced on the water's surface. At the next moment, I heard a deep muffled thunder that seemed to echo and bounce around somewhere under the ice. After that I heard the sound again. But the next sound I heard was that of a wall of floodwater roaring down the river straight for me. Well, it took me quite by surprise, and I soon had to face the realization that I had been effectively flushed down the tube. It was a bit of a scare, but there were air pockets here and there along the way, and with some serious swimming on my part, it eventually carried me home. But normally, barring any hiccup from under the ice, of course, it is a most pleasant journey. Another wonderful sightseeing tour. You will be impressed."

"Sir Sark, I have watched you swim. I am quite certain that I cannot hold my breath so long under the water as you do."

Sark extended his trunk down to Zak's level.

"It is not a problem, possum. Climb aboard and find an ear. You will have a generous air space inside to sustain you until we reach a place along the river where we can both breathe."

Zak climbed up the trunk to his old perch and carefully worked his way down to the mastodon's large and deformed right ear. As Sark began walking into the shallows toward the center of the river, Zak crawled, twisting his way underneath the hairy, leathery flap of broken and collapsed pinna until he found the dark little cave of the ear canal. He turned around and backed against the opening, reaching with his tail to grasp a few hairs that arose from the floor. Suddenly, in an instant of jolting, convulsive rotation, Zak found himself catapulted through the air, flipping end over end until he landed on his back with a splash. When he swam back up to the river's surface and regained his bearings, he began swimming his way slowly back to the mastodon. He looked bewilderedly at Sark.

"O. Possum, are you all right?"

"What on earth did you do that for? Now that you have spat me from your ear, do you really expect me to accompany you on such a dangerous expedition? Really, sir."

"You must have touched something sensitive, possum. Don't worry. We won't make that mistake again. Now climb aboard and let's go. You wish to get back to your region, do you not?"

Zak, dripping wet, tried to shake the water out of his fur and ears as he climbed back up onto Sark's head. He again entered the ear, careful this time to not disturb any canal hairs with his tail.

"Are you ready, possum?"

"Sir Sark, do you really wish me to answer that question?"

"Well, hang on!"

With Zak well hidden inside his ear, Sark dove deeply to the bottom and began swimming downstream toward the draining vortex. As soon as they entered the whirlpool, they felt themselves go into a rapid spin like satellites around some powerful, invisible gravity source. With his tail and both of his arms and legs Zak held fast to the large, knobby tragus of Sark's ear. The mastodon had been correct, for the broken ear provided Zak with an ample air supply, and he was able to hold his head above the level of the water that now raced past him.

After a while the spinning water led them into an immense and completely dark and water-filled tubular chamber surrounded on three sides by glacial ice worn smooth by the river's current. Here, their circular motion abated as they swiftly continued forward, Sark gliding along making only enough swimming strokes to remain parallel with the flow. Zak wondered how long his mastodon friend could hold his breath, but soon the current slowed and Sark broke the water's surface of the first pocket of air. He then slowly swam to the shore and sat down on the narrow, rocky bank bordered by the wall of ice.

"Sir Sark," said Zak toward the ear canal, "do you wish me to stay here or climb out?"

"You can stay where you are. I am only catching my breath before we continue."

"It is dark in here," said Zak.

"And it is dark out here, too."

"I thought you said I would be impressed."

"You are not yet impressed?"

"With a sightseeing tour?"

Sark once again entered the submarine blackness to swim with the current, from time to time rising to the surface to breathe as they reached other air spaces along the way. The river continued to move them downstream with great swiftness, and by the end of the day, they had traveled a very far distance from the tropical outpost they had so enjoyed over the previous weeks. For the second time, Sark found a narrow, rocky shore between the water and the ice wall and stopped.

"It will soon be night, O. Possum."

"It has been night all day long, Sir Sark. Why did we stop?"

"For a change of scenery, possum."

"Yes, of course. I should have known. Are you tired?"

"Not at all, O. Possum. The river does all the work. We will continue on our way through the night. I will be able to doze a little as we go through the air pockets. I suggest you get some sleep."

The mastodon once again plunged into the water's depths.

"How much farther do we have to go?" Zak asked the ear cave. But his only response from the mastodon was that of garbled bubble sounds.

# 25

THE NEXT DAY, too, was a day of darkness for Zak and Sark. They continued their rapid transit toward the South with only infrequent stopping for a chat and a chance for Zak to get his mastodon's earful of fresh air.

"Tomorrow morning there will be scenery, possum, for we will finally have some light from above."

"Well, a little light should at least afford me the opportunity to take in the full lesson of anatomy of the thermally rearranged mastodon ear."

"That won't be necessary, O. Possum. Tomorrow, the water level will be lower and the river's cave much larger. There will be no more need for submarine travel. You will be able to take your old perch again, so you will not miss a bit of the show."

After the passage of the next evening, their journey had carried them a great distance south of the wintergreen oasis, and the farther south they went, the thinner the ice sheet became. Now, near its southern limits, sunlight was able to penetrate it, dimly, down to the level of the river. As they approached the southern edge of the ice sheet, the river became wider and its corridor transformed into a great, dark, gray-blue cavern of smoothly sculpted ice. The river now moved at a gentler pace, and the water was becoming cold. There were thick banks of fog along the way that prompted Zak to recall the fog banks he had visited while on his previous long northward journey that had stretched somewhere on top of the great white roof above his head.

They drifted slowly and quietly now, taking in the bizarre, glassy shapes that the river had carved in the walls and ceiling, odd icy protrusions alternating with intricate scalloped designs. The water was smooth, and there were no sounds other than those of the gentle, sloshing movement of Sark in the water and the occasional tinny echoes of splashes created by the drops that emanated from the slow melt of the massive ceiling; and there were no signs of life, save their own, in the stillness and eerie blue-gray light. As they drifted onward, the river became wider, and they began to take notice of broad pillars of ice that arose skyward from the still water to support massive archways beneath the great vaulted, blue-gray dome above their heads.

"Look at them, possum," whispered Sark. "How they just stand about, still and silent, as if on duty. Aqua stanchions holding at bay the chaos of collapse."

Sark decided to detour to the narrow, rocky shore of the river's right bank. When he reached it, he stepped onto the beach and extended his trunk for Zak to scramble down. The moment seemed to call for silence, so they kept their thoughts to themselves. Zak began walking down the shoreline, inspecting the red and gray pebbles and egg-shaped rocks and great discoid boulders, all water-worn over the course of time to become smooth and edgeless conformers to their river environment. There was not a hint of green anywhere to suggest that the water had been born of such an extreme of tropical flourish as it indeed had.

Then something caught their attention. They did not feel the ground shake, but they did hear the ice around them groan as more drops of water from above hit the river's surface like that of a light passing rain shower. And then they heard the deep faraway sound of thunder that seemed to come from the direction from which they, themselves, had come—the direction of the wintergreen oasis.

"We are going to get wet, O. Possum."

Zak required no explanation from his friend as he scurried up the mastodon's trunk to take his perch.

"We shall take to mid-river and move slowly downstream," said Sark in a new, serious tone. "It will give us our best advantage of maneuverability when the surge hits. There is no great hurry, as it won't be here for quite a while."

"Surely, Sir Sark," said Zak in a speech more rapid than usual, "it would be to our best advantage to be moving along. And at a quite speedy pace, I should think, what with earthquakes and great surges of water roaming about. Really, sir."

"It doesn't matter, possum. The southern edge of the ice is much too far away. We will simply enjoy a quicker exit than I had originally planned. But I cannot outswim the river's surge, and there is nothing to be gained by my using up all my energy reserves trying to do so."

"Dear sir," said Zak, in the most coaxing style of diplomacy he could muster, "I steadfastly remain of the opinion that expeditious forward progress is our best policy."

At great relief to Zak, and without saying a word, Sir Sark arose and waded back into the water to continue the journey south. For both of them, a sense of dread had replaced that of euphoric anticipation and awe.

They continued to drift slowly along in the chilled silence of their pale-blue setting of river and ice. The farther south they went, the more ice columns came into view. It came to be that the great pillars and arches were everywhere and in all directions; and they became the central theme of the voyage, as the channel itself became no longer recognizable and the shores of the river no longer in view. On occasion, Sark had to dive and feel his way along the bottom to seek out the channel that had become lost to his vision as well as to his memory.

During one such dive, Zak, as usual, was left behind to drift slowly and to carefully attempt to retain his position so he would not become lost to his mastodon companion when he resurfaced. As the icy pillars passed by, Zak felt as if he were floating in the cold slow-moving floodwaters of a vast swamp of gigantic cypress trees and tupelos. He was reminded of the sugar columns and beasts in the dank cave that he and Elbon had explored and which he had, by himself, re-explored in his most disquieting nightmare.

Then, once again, Sark surfaced in a splashing disruption of the great swamp's silence. And again, Zak climbed aboard the top of the mastodon's head. They continued drifting southward following the rediscovered but invisible river channel. Zak wondered whether there might be bats living in the great blue cavern of the river. He hoped he would not at some point in the future have a nightmare about the present experience.

"Sir Sark, I certainly hope that you have no plans for us to traverse any waterfalls along the way," said Zak.

"Not a single one, possum. Why do you ask?"

"Actually, I am quite certain that I hear one ahead presently. How could you forget such a thing as a waterfall? I assure you that I remain quite uncertain that this course was our best prospect for removing us from the ice. Rather incomprehensible, actually. And I must ask again, Sir Sark, how on earth could your memory of our route have deleted the presence of a cataract? You do not hear it?"

Sark stopped his slow swimming and listened forward. He made a full revolution in the water. "It is an echo, possum."

"An echo? Of what?"

"It is an echo bouncing off the ice in front of us. The sound is from upstream, and I must say, it has come quicker than I expected. It is time for you to take a tight grip."

The sound behind them and the echo in front soon became a single continuous, ominous roar coming from all directions. Sark felt a new, strong current in the water pushing him forward and upward. It quickly grew into an overwhelming force that seemed to exponentially gain in strength, moment by moment, beneath them. The icy pillars, now with crushing, downstream wakes of wave and spray, raced past them as the mastodon put all his strength into swimming to avoid a collision. Unless by gift of fortune or goodwill of the river, there was no more hope of their remaining in the channel, as both possum and mastodon were, save Sark's expert swimming, mere victims of the flood.

As time went by, both they and the river rose rapidly toward the arches and ceiling of the great cavern, and as they continued their quickening forward movement, Sark noticed that the water was becoming warm as Zak, too, noticed the air in the cave warming up.

Water now fell from the roof as a heavy, cold rain from the melt above. At the highest level of the chamber, the sun shone through the ice brightly, and as more time and distance went by, the ice above became thinner. As the water continued to rise, Zak sometimes had to duck his head to avoid crashing into one of the arches that arose from an icy column to span upward toward the ceiling of the cavern before it pitched over to join another, remote column lost in the ice forest.

Outside on the roof, the ice was quickly melting because of the great expanse of warm rushing water beneath it. Holes and cracks were beginning to appear from which burst forth springs and geysers. Rivulets of the warm water ran down the ice roof, melting it now from above.

As Sark continued to fight the current, threading his way between the glassy pillars, Zak looked up at the bright ice above his head, and from time to time, he saw the movement of dark shadows. Shortly he came to realize that they were herds of large animals in frightened stampedes, fleeing from the noisy, forbidding vibration of the rushing and eroding river beneath their feet.

"Sir Sark, look up!" said Zak.

"I can't look up!" yelled the mastodon. "You must watch the ceiling and tell me if I should dive so you won't be crushed. Perhaps you should think about moving into the ear again. Would that be possible?"

"What did you say, Sir Sark? I cannot hear you!"

"Never mind! It is not that much farther until we are out of this mess."

"I cannot hear you, Sir Sark!"

In the next moment, a giant slab of ice fell from the highest part of the bright dome, turning slowly in the air, reflecting the glare from above. A part of it broke loose and winged away from the main body only to land on the bridge of Sark's nose. It exploded into innumerable glittering shards in front of Zak. The force of the jolt was strong enough to drive them both underwater for a short distance before Sark, dazed and in pain from the blow to his face, was able to regain his bearings and swim back up to the surface.

Zak remained flat on his belly, his hands, toes, and tail tightly grasping the coarse hairs of the mastodon's head. In the raging waters and pouring rain from the ceiling, they could now see brown beastly shadows falling helplessly from the light above the now partially gaping roof. Seemingly hundreds of the brown bodies fell, end over end, splashing into the water around them that Sark was so painstakingly trying to navigate.

"Sir Sark, are you all right?" yelled Zak. "Dear boy, you took a nasty blow to your nose!"

"What is it?" yelled Sark.

"It was the ice! You were clobbered on your nose by a block of ice. Did you not see it?"

"What is it?" the mastodon yelled again.

"What do you mean, Sir Sark?" said Zak, thinking that perhaps his ride and traveling companion had been rendered temporarily senseless.

"On my back! What is it, possum?"

Zak turned around to look. There, plastered flat with legs spread, clutching the mastodon's back, somewhat in Zak's own fashion, was a new passenger—a caribou bull.

The caribou's eyes were closed, and his nose was pressed tightly against Sark's hairy, thick hide, as if, out of fear, seeking something warm and reminiscent of the living. His large, palmate, mahogany antlers were cast forward, a tine only inches from Zak's nose.

Zak made a frightened, drooling hiss.

"Sir Sark!" yelled Zak as he continued to stare at the closed-eyed, likewise frightened caribou, frozen in his own life-clinging disposition.

In the next moment, Zak felt Sark's head again rocked downward as if bow-sunken by another shock from some large icy object. Both the stern of the mastodon and the caribou rose into the air above Zak's eye level. In dread of what new catastrophe might have occurred on Sark's head, Zak turned around to look forward. There, sitting above Sark's sore nose bridge, and looking him straight in the eye, was a very large, bewildered, and irate grizzly bear.

Now feeling a sudden, strong proclivity for antler climbing, Zak quickly climbed aboard those so conveniently offered by the caribou.

"Up, sir!" shouted Zak.

The caribou, now alert to his surroundings and wild-eyed at the snapping and snarling scene on Sark's bow, leaped, with his possum boarder, straight up, and fell over backward into the water. The bear angrily stood up on the mastodon's head and roared loudly.

"What is going on, possum?" said Sark as he reached his trunk above his head and crammed it up the crotch of the bear, who immediately jumped skyward, only to fall, belly first, upon the hard, spinal ridge of the mastodon's back.

At that point, the bear, now more fully understanding his own predicament, remained flattened and still, in much the same manner as his predecessors had done aboard the *Great Ship Sark.*

The caribou, with his large, round hooves, was an excellent swimmer, and, by now, was reoriented and swimming not far behind Sark and the bear. Zak was swinging back and forth by his tail, which was tightly twisted around an antler beam above the back of his new mode of transportation.

Suddenly, there was a dramatic increase in the water's turbulence. The river rose rapidly toward the ceiling. The caribou and Zak were thrown against Sark's rump, causing them to be almost nose-to-nose with the annoyed grizzly. The frightened caribou then decided to dive just as Sark seemed to be about to have a collision with the icy roof. Zak, still clinging to his beam, felt himself snatched deeply under the water as the caribou, to avoid further distraction of the bear, tried to furiously swim beyond the great mass of mastodon above his head.

In the next moment, the force of the current slammed Sark against the ceiling with such power that he and the bear smashed through the dome and onto the outside of its icy roof. Here, they slid, spinning round and round on their backs in their newly created rivulet upon the surface of the great ice sheet.

With no more great beast above his head to concern him, the caribou casually swam toward the river's surface, where he and Zak emerged at a point far beyond where Sark and the bear had made their crash exit from the cave's roof. When caribou and possum broke the water's surface, they could see that the river was rapidly carrying them toward the light of day; they could even see the tundra in the distance.

# 26

A S THE RIVER swiftly carried the caribou and his hanging-
possum antler ornament out of the great ice cavern and into
the warm sunshine, Zak was able to see many other caribou
swimming gracefully downstream among the river's muddy gray rap-
ids. Some of them were exiting the water to stroll calmly on the right
and left banks of the river as if they had arrived—in singles, pairs, or
more—at their designated stops along the way. They were the brown
shadows that had fallen into the river around Zak and Sark when
the roof had collapsed upon the mastodon, shortly before he and the
grizzly bear had made their own breach in the ice and had exited to
the outside of the cave's roof.

The river was wide, having filled its delta completely with the
milky-gray flood that surged from under the ice sheet; but, in the
distance, Zak could see the rust and red and yellowish hues of the
late-summer tundra flora. He looked around for Sark and wondered
to where he could have possibly disappeared. One of the other caribou in the water swam up alongside and spoke.

"Eh, Durzey! Z'vaz bad, no? Me thootz vez finizhed vhen ze beer
a'fallowz uz doon ze big ice 'ole. I could na beliv ze brute fallowed uz
on ze ice in ze fierzt plaze. Vyat beer can catch a carib on ze ice? None
be noon ta me. But next thin ya noo 'ez in ze ice 'ole! No controol thar.
Iz doongeruz fer a carib."

"And no beer can catch a carib in ze varter neither," spoke the
caribou, Durzey, in whose horns Zak rode. "But thiz unz a'ridin' ze

back of a blik maztodoon! Never zeed thet befoor, I can tell ya. And I can alzo tell ya I frittened thet beer alf ta deeath."

"Ya frittened ze beer, Durzey? 'Ow'd a carib fritten a beer, vood ya tell me?"

"Vhen 'ez a'ztandin on ze back o ze maztodoon, I frittened im. I zvimz up behind im and 'e joompz an fallz on ze maztodoon'z back a'hidden iz faze. Thetz 'ow a carib frittenz a beer, Zfevvy. And vherez ze brute now? Can ya zee 'im?"

"No. 'E'll proobly be a'climbin up betwin yer laygz in ze nickzt mooment. An ya zay 'e vaz a'ridin ze back of a maztodoon? Vood 'e be Zark, I vonder? 'Iz femalz av been a'vaitin 'im by ze river fer dayz."

"Donnoo. Coulda been," said Durzey. "Couldna zee much of 'iz faze in ze ice 'ole. 'Iz femalz a'vaitin im, eh? Vy couldn't I be zo lucky, Zfevvy? And 'im a'runnin off ta 'iz retrit an leavin em behind fer veekz and veekz. 'E'z a ztrange caze, 'e iz."

"Not meanin ta be poorznal, Durzey, but yer vife I'm afraid'z goin ta be takin ya apart. Tiz vell noon zhe don't lak ya runnin vid ze 'erd thiz dayz. Vell, vyat iz thet? Ya bringin 'er a trinket?"

"Vyat ya mean, Zfevvy?"

"Thet thin yer a'packin in yer hantlerz. Iz it alive?"

Durzey looked up at Zak. "Eh! Yooo! 'Aven't zeed zvinzycroot lak ya befoor. Vyat spezeez iz ya? And vy ya ztayin on me 'ornz? Z'bad on ze balanz, ya noo. A'danklin lak thet."

Zak wasn't sure what to say or whether he should say anything at all, thinking that in any moment Sir Sark would appear and rescue him from these peculiar-looking deer, so he and his big black friend could resume their journey to the South.

"Durzey," said Zfevvy, "I don't thin et can 'eer ya. Lookz ta me lak zoom zorta parazyt. Meeby a foonguz. Vhen ve be gettin ta zhore ya can zcrip et off."

"Iz not a foonguz, Zfevvy. Et vaz talkin in ze cave. I 'eered et. Et zpoke ta me an ze maztodoon. Eh! Yooo! I 'eered ya in ze cave. Eered ya zay 'Zir Zark.' Vaz et Zark ta oom ya vaz a'zpickin?"

"Look. Thar they iz. All lined up along ze riverbink a'vaiten. Lak overgroon blik zheepz. Tiz a pity 'e don't tend ta'em better. Yer right, Durzey. 'E'z a ztrange caze, 'e iz."

As the two caribou continued to swim with the current, Zak looked to the river's right bank with great anticipation, for there in a large and long black line, waiting, were the fifty female black mastodons. He searched their longing faces. Like them, he wondered where the old bull mastodon known as Sark could possibly be.

"I say, fellows, perhaps we could put to shore with the mastodons. I must meet with Sir Sark," said Zak, finally breaking his silence.

"Eh! Did ya 'eer et, Zfevvy? Ya zee now? Et'z not a foonguz a'tal."

"I 'eered et, Durzey."

The pair of caribou continued swimming with apparent purpose, seemingly oblivious to Zak's request.

"Eh, yooo!" hollered Zfevvy as if under the assumption that Zak was hard of hearing. "Ere ya von o' them cridderz from ze North I've 'eered aboot? Von o' them joongle cridderz from Zark'z retrit?"

"Ezk 'im iffen e'z a leeazard, Zfevvy."

"Eh! Yooo!" yelled Zfevvy. "Ere ya von o' them leeazardz ve've 'eered aboot?"

"Sir, I am a possum," said Zak. "I came down the river with Sir Sark, and I must rejoin him presently. And I am quite certain that my best chance of doing so rests on the side of the river with the mastodons."

"'E keepz a'zayin Zir Zark, Zfevvy," said Durzey. "Do ya zpooz et'z ze zame maztodoon?" Durzey looked up. "Vood ya be zpickin o' ze maztodoon Zark?"

The two caribou left the midriver current and swam toward the left bank.

"Please, sirs, if you would kindly drop me over on the other side," Zak continued pleadingly but futilely.

When they reached the eastern shore, the caribou shook themselves. Zak rattled in his mahogany cage with Durzey's motion. Durzey then quickly and unexpectedly dropped his nose to the ground and began furiously pawing and probing his large round hooves at his horn rack to rid himself of his passenger. Zak's perch was luckily far enough forward for him to be missed by the dangerous prodding hooves.

"I say, sir," said Zak, astonished by the caribou's rude behavior, "now that you have established that I am not your fungus, it appears that you wish to kill me anyway. Why didn't you simply take me to the other side of the river?"

"Vell, Durzey," said Zfevvy. "Now thet ve ere approachin ze location of yer family, I zpooze I'll move on. And good luck ta ya."

"Ya zvinzycroot," muttered the annoyed Durzey, looking up at Zak.

Zfevvy began to trot along the bank in the direction of the way the river ran. As he moved away, his feet made rhythmic clicking sounds as if he trod a path of grass heavily glazed over with ice.

When Durzey, irritable and wordless, began trotting across the tundra toward the east, Zak heard a similar clicking sound, which he could now tell came from the caribou's foot joints.

"The sound from your feet, sir," said Zak. "Is it like that with all members of your species?"

Zak's attempt at conversation was altogether ignored. The indignant caribou continued clicking his way across the tundra toward an outcropping of boulders. As they approached the rocks, Zak saw among them a female caribou grazing in the grass and small willows. Her calf was with her. The young caribou walked along next to her and stopped for a moment to gaze in the distance before he burst into an awkward lope across the grass. After having made a little circle, he then ran back to his mother who seemed completely oblivious to his actions. Durzey slowed and approached them with care.

"Ow ere ya, me leetle biffen?" said Durzey in a new tone of sweet affection. "And 'ow'z our youngun? I've mizzed ya two, ya noo? Ya cutie thinz!"

"Vell," she said. "Ya mizzed uz two cutie thinz. And now ya come ta pee yer rezpickz. And I'm zpoozin now ya be a'tellin me vyat ya mean ta leave me 'eer alone vid ze leetl'un. I'd zay vaz cuz ya been a'runnin ze femalz on ze ice lak a zeely ztoot. Thet'z vy. Yer a zarry'un, ya ere. N'good a'tal."

"I vaz not runnin femalz, Mum," Durzey said.

"I 'eered aboot yer beer," she said. "Vord gitz aroon, ya noo. Zo I noo yer on ze ice, ya noo. I zpooz ya be a'tellin me now ya vaz on ze ice fer ze grazen, eh? A new kinda ice grazz, eh? Good fer ze bools, yeah? Ya come ta git me an ze leetl'un zo'z ve can git a taste o' ze good frezh ice grazz. Eh?"

"I vaz not chazin no femalz, Mum. I vaz thar fer anoother rizen."

"Vell, I can zmell yer oozin' moozk. Ya can't fool me. Ya 'ad coortin on yer brin fer zhoor," she said.

"I vaz not oozin' till I come roond ya, Mum. Me thoots meeby ve could moogle. Ya an me behin ze rockz, eh? Poot ze leetl'un doon fer a zmal rezt, eh, Mum? Vell, come on. Ze rockz ere a'vaiten."

Durzey came closer to the female. Zak was beginning to get nervous.

"Mooove! Ya grizzl o' grizzly beer grub. I von't be a'pootin ze leetl'un doon. Not on yer life. Kridz! Vyat'z thet on yer 'ood? Now ya gone en got yerzef a parazyt in yer bracken! Ya broon bag o' villerleaf bloat. Zchnapoopz-o-coozhkin! Look vyat ya done to yerzef! A dizgriz iz vyat ya ere. An ya 'eer expoozin et ta me an ze leetl'un ez ve zpick."

"Et'z not a parazyt, Mum. Et'z a leetle proozent I brung ya. Et vaz vy I vaz on ze ice. Ta git yer proozent from Zark. Et come from Zark'z retrit. Et'z a leeazard thet come from ze joongle. Now ya zee, don't ya Mum—ow come I vaz on ze ice—now ya zee, don't ya?" said Durzey, feeling rather confident in his usage of the tactics of devious diplomacy.

"Vell, I zujoozt ya take et back ta ze joongle var et belongz, ya noockle-noozd unguloot zhoups! And ya better be a'oopin et ent catchin, cuz iffin I ever zee et a'growin on ze airs of ze leetl'un I'll unt ya doon, Durzey. Of thet ya can be zhoor."

Zak could contain himself no more.

"Good day, madam!" he said, following up the greeting with a hissing grin.

"Huzh yerzef, ya voormin," said Durzey in a low, teeth-clenched voice.

"Kridz!" she said. "Et zpickz! Ze parazyt zpickz! I don't lak et a'tal, Durzey! Go! Ya and thet thin vhatz come ta roozt in yer arb. Back to ze joongle! Ze two o' ya! Go! And leave uz alone. An ya callin me a voormin, too. Thet thin'z took a'hold o yer brin, Durzey. Go!"

Durzey trotted away from the female and the calf, continuing his way across the tundra at a steady, clicking pace. Zak had no idea where they could be going, and he wasn't even sure why he was staying with the obdurate caribou at all. But he was certain that his perch offered a better view of the horizon than did the ground, which might facilitate his ability to spot Sir Sark. Finally, Durzey stopped.

"Vell, I zpooz I could ezk ya 'ow long ya be a'viztin me 'ood. I zpooz I could; but I'll tell ya thiz. I'll tell ya thet ez long ez yer up thar ya git no varter. I'll zee ta thet."

Zak thought that water was about the last thing he wanted after what he had been through for the last few days, but food was a different matter. He was hungry, but just in case any negotiations might be biding in his future, he kept that thought to himself.

# 27

THE SUN SWUNG round in a circular path before the eyes of both bear and mastodon as they, too, rotated round and round on their backs in their ice-water rivulet. All they could do was wait it out as the sun, and they, made loops. But there was a certain peace in simply relaxing and watching the sun make its rounds as it cast its own bright eye down upon them, its magical glare signifying their existence and locking them forever in its brilliant history. Finally, the rivulet expelled the two bulky forms when it made a sharp angle on the ice. But before they came to a stop, they had bisected a medium-sized herd of caribou.

"So that is why you were here," said Sark, looking in the direction of the caribou who were hastily refashioning their ruptured herd. "You were after the caribou, were you not? And you almost got yourself killed. Where is the possum? And what slothish lowbrow of the grizzly bear clan would try to run down a caribou on the ice? Well, I suppose I am looking at that particular specimen presently, am I not? Where is the possum? O. Possum! You have caused me to lose the possum. Where is he? Have you seen him?"

As soon as he got to his feet, the bear happily loped away from the irascible mastodon without acknowledging a single question. *What is a possum?* he thought.

"Grizzlyboor!" said the mastodon as he got up and began to stroll in a southerly direction, searching the blue-gray horizon for any evidence of possum visitation. He soon adjusted to the brightness of the day, and, despite the absence of his little friend, the fresh, cool air brightened his spirit. It was not long before he could see in the distance the orange tundra and the river with its raft of brown, ant-like figures of swimming caribou. *Hundreds of them must have fallen through the ice,* he thought. *Down there is where I will find a wet and cold and irritable possum. He will have a word or two for me, I expect.*

Finally, Sark reached the southernmost edge of the ice, and it was from there that he saw his fifty female black mastodons in a line, all patiently waiting at the river's edge. *How do they always know when I am coming back?* He broke into a trot.

Before he approached them and before they saw him, or so he thought, he made a detour back into the river. But, of course, they did see him.

"Well, the lop-ear of the ice is returned."

"Lizards that look like birds."

"He looks as full of himself as ever."

"And as full of bad gas."

"I wonder if he saw his black cat."

"More cat tales."

"I would like to see the black lion."

"'Hello, my fifty dearests!' he will say."

"'Hello, my fifty fairests!' he will say."

"'Hello, my fifty fine friends!'"

"Lizards that strut."

"Why isn't he in the river?"

"It's dirty."

"Look! He's going into the river now."

"But why didn't ..."

"Birds that look like lizards."

"The old fool!"

"He always comes down the river."

"Look! He's floating on his back."

"And spinning in the water."

"He thinks he's an otter. Look at him smiling."

"Why did he go into the river if he was already on the bank?"

"An unfurled youthful frond of fern's thy nose."

"He told you that?"

"He told me that, too."

"He is going to spin past us!"

"Here. Take my trunk, dear."

That said, the last in the line of fifty female mastodons waded into the river with trunk outstretched to the big, smiling, muddy male black mastodon known as Sark.

"Yes, my dear!" he said. "Unfurl thy youthful frond of fern, my beauty, and levitate thy servant's serpent. O love! I thank you kindly."

With his trunk coiled around that of the fiftieth female, Sark arose from the river like a breaching whale, dripping a volume of the gray glacial muddy water copious enough to create yet another sizable rivulet that ran back down the beach to the river. He then released the female's trunk and ambled up the bank, where he made a half-hearted body shake.

"Ah, look at you all! My fifty dearest true loves. My fifty fairests. My fifty finest female friends! I can see you have missed me as I have missed you. Terribly!"

"We thought you were going to spin and grin your way right on past us," said the forty-ninth member of the female mastodon line. "Were you having trouble leaving the river behind, or had you forgotten what female mastodons look like?"

"I was entranced," he said, "mesmerized—paralyzed by the beauty of the shore's fifty finests. O raven warmth! O ebony rapture! I was a sure goner." Then, glancing back at Number Fifty, "But for you, my passion, I am saved from the ghastly Death by Drowning."

"But we saw you go into the river only a little way upstream," said Number Twenty-Two.

"Did you, now?" asked Sark. "Well, I must have fallen out of the water somewhere along the way. And, dazzled by your precious forms, I suppose I must have lost my wits and fallen back in."

"The chump is returned," said Number Three.

"Why don't you want us to know you came back on the ice?" asked Number Seventeen.

"Are you afraid we would follow you to your tropical valley retreat?" inquired Number Thirty-One.

"You know, my loves," said Sark, "as I have told you, the only way to reach my wintergreen oasis is by swimming up the river, and only I am a strong enough swimmer to accomplish the feat."

"But didn't you almost drown in front of us just moments ago?" asked Number Forty-Seven.

"All these questions!" said Sark. "Well, I have a question for you. Have you seen a possum today?"

# 28

THE NEXT MORNING found Sark sleeping late. As his great dark body absorbed the sun's rays, his consciousness began to stir to its presence among the sounds of buzzing flies and the faint chirps of a sparrow in a nearby willow bush. When, finally, he became fully awake, he got to his feet and took his bearings. Not far away he could see the river, now in its banks and flowing gently. And in the far distance, he saw his fifty females, scattered and grazing in the great rusty-red landscape that made up his surroundings. He had indeed caught up on, among other things, his sleep; and he was hungry. But he decided that the first thing that he wanted to do, even before grazing, was to take a bath.

For Sark, the muddy river was not an option, so he made his way through the grass and bushes in search of a pond. The tundra ponds, always deep blue and clear and inviting, were like precious gems to Sark; a collection of polished sapphires scattered upon the vast carpet of his grand tundra salon.

When he reached his destination, he plunged into the clean water, scattering the resident ducks who gained altitude to choose another, more peaceful, pond environment. He dove under the water and gracefully glided along the pond's bottom, twisting and corkscrewing his way until his large black body was free of the gray slag it had collected from his long journey down the glacial river.

Satisfied with his bath, the mastodon walked out of the water to the grassy bank, where he lay down upon a knoll in the sun. From his position, he was able to regard the water's surface, and when it calmed to its natural glassy peace, he could see his reflection. *Ah, you beautiful creature*, he thought to himself. With the end of his trunk, he took up small scoops of the water with which to clean and polish his tusks.

"What yew dew?" came a clear voice with a distinctive, somewhat metallic, musical tone.

"You are a little out of your range, aren't you?" said Sark to the dire wolf who was sitting, unmoving as a boulder, nearby at the pond's edge.

"That iss vanity. Alllll vanity."

"Of course," said Sark, "vanity is one of life's necessities. To be contented one must be adored, therefore it is one's first duty to see that the job gets done."

"That iss what yew dew, all right."

"Yes. Yes. That is what I do," said Sark, becoming a little annoyed by the wolf's verbal intrusion into his sapphire solitude but continuing to regard his reflection while polishing his ivories to the point that they gleamed in the sunlight.

The dire wolf remained silent awhile, staring out over the pond. Then he raised his head and gazed out over the landscape toward the distant grazing female mastodons.

"Yew dew vanity foh yew females. Foh yewself. That makes sense. That makes common sense."

"Common sense," said Sark. "Now there is a deep subject indeed. It should be further investigated. I am certain that its study could become the lifelong endeavor of the finest members of the scholarship."

"I tink I iss retired from da females. They iss lottoh trobbles foh me."

"They can be that. Sometimes I go into temporary retirement myself. But only temporary, mind you. I must always return to my dear ones."

"Now I devote my time to da art of trokkin."

"Were you tracking the ducks? I must have certainly disrupted that endeavor."

"Nobody can trok a duck."

"Then what exactly is it that you pursue?"

"Da black ponter."

"Black panther? You mean you want to track Moksoos? Is that whom you are speaking of?"

"Yoh. I want him to trok."

"Dear fellow, what would you do with him if you caught up to him?"

"Nottink. I iss only a trokker. Now that I iss retired."

"Perhaps I should ask you if you have given any thought to the matter of what Moksoos might do with you if you find him."

"Nottink. I haf him trokked foh very long time. Ant I tink he knows about me. He knows that iss what I dew."

"Is Moksoos in these parts presently?" asked Sark. "I would like to see him."

"That I cannot say. I haf him lost. I come to look foh him, but I dew not know. I dew not know where he iss. But that iss not a bad tink. Yew see? That iss da interestink part."

"The interesting part, eh?" Sark was brewing up his own interest in this peculiar wolf with the musical voice. "Dear sir, do you track anything else these days besides Moksoos?"

"Yoh. Yoh. Of course. I trok everytink. I trok alllll da animols. But I dew not eat them. I iss wogotarian like yew. I only eat da plonts. Grass, leafs, roots, berries. Tinks like that. Yew see?"

*Well, I have never seen anything of the sort before*, thought Sark. *A large, broad-headed, heavily canined dire wolf who is a vegetarian, who tracks only for the love of the sport.* Sark was becoming pleasantly consumed with affection for his new mild-mannered acquaintance.

"My name is Sark," he said.

"Ah?" said the wolf.

"My name is Sark, sir."

"Ah."

"And your name?"

"Ah?"

"And your name is?"

"Ah."

"Yes. Your name?"

"Name. Woll."

"Well, what?"

"Woll. I dew not rightly know," said the wolf. "I guess I lost trok of it."

"Well, then," said Sark, "I don't suppose Moksoos has much to worry about, does he?"

"Noh. He has no neet to worry. But a name iss not ant animol. Ant I am a trokker of da animols. Ant I am very good at what I dew."

"Yes. I am sure you are, my tracker friend who has gone and lost track of his name. Do you think you could track a possum?"

"Ah, yoh. Once I trok a possot from faaaaah to da south alllll da way to da ice. But that iss where I draw da line. Yew see? That possot, he was lost. I never see that before. But I dew not go ont da ice foh no possot."

"Sir, are you talking about a very long time ago?" asked Sark.

"Not that long. When da sun was long int da sky."

"Lost Track, sir, I know that possum. But pardon me, the name fits somehow. Do you mind me calling you that? Lost Track? You see, sir, I must find that possum. Will you help me?"

"That possot iss not ont da ice?"

"I am quite certain that he drifted out of the ice by way of the river only yesterday. Perhaps you can pick up the scent. As yet, I haven't been able to. But of course, I have been rather occupied by my females. And I confess to not being a bit handy at tracking things."

"Yoh. Woll. Moppy we should go to da reefer. Check foh da possot there."

Sark and Lost Track left the pond and walked toward the river, the mastodon hastily snatching along his way anything that remotely resembled a leafy meal.

When they reached the river, the big wolf quietly studied its gently moving surface, taking light whiffs of the cool, damp air into his flaring nostrils. They walked back up the river to where it flowed from the giant, partially collapsed cave in the ice; then they turned around and walked slowly back downstream, stopping from time to time for sniffs of the river air. Lost Track slowly and patiently led Sark farther and farther south along the rocky shore.

Sark watched the wolf go about his work, and though he himself knew little about the art of tracking, he was intrigued by the wolf's demeanor and style that seemed to him to be those of a master at his craft. As they continued downstream, Lost Track methodically moved up and down the bank, forward, then backtracking, then sniffing the water, the rocks, the sand.

Finally, the wolf stopped and stared out across the water. He waded in slowly, then began swimming. He swam far out in the water with his nose up, making a path of a large figure eight; then he swam back to the bank where Sark was waiting. The fifty female black mastodons were now gathered next to him. Lost Track trotted out of the river and, seemingly oblivious to the fifty curiously staring pachyderms, walked straight up to Sark's feet.

Sark and the females were silent and motionless. Then Number Twenty-Seven jerked her head up and down threateningly.

"This is Lost Track, my loves," said Sark. "He is going to help us find a possum."

"He is going to help us find a what?" said Number Twenty-Seven.

"Why do we need the wolf?" said Number Five.

"A possum?" said Number Twenty-Two.

"Did the wolf come from Sark's oasis?"

"He said he lost his possum."

"Lost Track will help us find it."

"Sark, what is 'possum'?"

"My poor things!" said Sark. "When Lost Track helps us to find O. Possum, I shall take all of you provincial madams on a lovely field trip to the South. There is so much for you to see and learn. You poor knowledge-starved creatures."

"O! possum," said Number Sixteen. "It is O! possum."

"O possum!"

"Lost Trok tink that possot has been int da reefer," said the wolf.

# 29

DEEP IN THE forest, and away from his army, Mungo sat before the flames of another raging bonfire and watched as a terrified newly appointed medicine male awkwardly danced and sang chants before the blaze to summon a spirit from its torrid orange-and-yellow undulations. The scene was eerie and heavy with the potential for violence. Above in the canopy, and invisible to the sans-pelage forms below, were Moksoos and the great horned owl perched on the hard, furrowed limb of a black hickory tree. They were there primarily on a spying mission.

*Might you have a theory as to why it doesn't rain, owl?* Moksoos was speaking only with his thoughts.

"You certainly seemed to have been playing your roles quite well, such as that goes," whispered the owl. "But now it looks as though you have completely reversed roles with me."

*Why, on this great blue sphere, would you say such a thing, owl?* Then Moksoos turned his gaze upward toward the sky.

"Because you are quizzing me on a subject about which I should think you would have an intimate knowledge. As if I should know the details instead of you. I am only an owl. Remember? Forest-folk. Might I suggest that this lovely, clean moonlight has effectively disarranged your thought processes—And why do you keep looking up at the sky?"

*We members of the Shadow World don't know everything, friend.* Moksoos then turned his full attention back to the owl. *Our vision can often be as restricted as is yours. I really don't know when the drought will end. That is why I asked you. But it will end at some point, I am certain.*

"Probably. But the rain may come too late. It is a sad thing how it is too late for so many already. And that nasty beast and his hunting party have certainly taken full advantage in the regions where the droughts have occurred. Seems to me to be a pattern to it. You recall I have mentioned this to you before. I think the problem originates from inside. Your world. And it is tearing the atmosphere apart.

*Don't be ridiculous. The wayward fool has an infirm mind. It is sick. It is deranged. And nobody is controlling the weather. Although—I must say—the sky at times does have a peculiar quality about it.* Moksoos briefly glanced upward once again.

"It is sick? It is deranged? What rubbish! Look at him sitting there. He is not deranged. He is not sick. Only he is never satisfied. Is he really going to kill that medicine male?"

*Of their familiarity they die.*

"Oh, stop it, Moksoos. Listen to me. What we need is *help*. Haven't you tinkered with the balance before?"

*Very rarely, owl. And that is long in the past.*

"Well, if it has been done in the past, it can be done again. And this time it could save more than some old philosopher-mastodon."

*What did you say?*

"Word gets around to the owls."

*I'm impressed that you would know about that. Would you like to elaborate?*

"Actually, Moksoos, you told me that story yourself. Are you getting forgetful? Oh my! I do believe that medicine male is done far. Why don't you give his chief what he is asking for from the flames? That would be a clean finish for the two of them. You wouldn't even have to touch them. They'd die of simple fear alone."

*I am only—*

"Yes. I know. Only a cat. Cat! Cat! Cat!"

*Thank you, owl.*

"Now, just look at that. Why doesn't *he* go into the flames to jabber with a spirit, such as it is? Or is not. How uncivilized."

"There is no such thing as civilized!" Moksoos snapped aloud, but in a low voice filled with passion. "There is no such thing as civilization! No species is in possession of anything remotely resembling the physical capabilities required to attain it. You will find it nowhere, foolish bird. No evolution of that intellectual magnitude has ever occurred on the Great Blue Sphere. Not on the land, not in the water, not in the air. Even the whales shun the weak and the dolphins head-butt one another to death."

"You don't have to be so touchy, Moksoos, I only … Oh! That is nauseating. Oh! Listen to it howl. How cruel! Now he will have to find himself another medicine male. I do not understand this species, Moksoos. Why do they destroy themselves? Why do they destroy the forest?"

"The power of stupidity is immense. Never underestimate its force and fury."

As Moksoos and the owl looked on from their shadowy perch in the canopy, Mungo stood alone, waiting with his arms folded on his broad chest. He stared into the crackling fire as if he were fearlessly braced for the appearance of some awakened force, some resident of the midst of the flames' glowing embers to come forth and meet him, face-to-face, and ask him what it was that he wished for.

As he continued to gaze, with the dancing red flicker of the firelight in his eyes, the owl and Moksoos disappeared from their hickory limb and the moonlight and even the shadows of the night to traverse another darkness; and in the instant, in that tiniest pinch of time, or perhaps even in the very absence of any passage of time, Moksoos was once again sitting in the moonlight of the bison range, in the brushy clearing next to the canebrake where he had met Swrogah and the old bison on that day so long ago. The owl was perched in the buckthorn bush nearby. They were now a very great distance away from the bonfire, the lifeless burning body of the medicine male, and Mungo.

"You mention a curious matter regarding the sky, Moksoos," said the owl. "What do you see? What do you make of it?"

*It is a curious matter indeed, bird. The sky has come off its hinges.*

"Now, Moksoos, if the sky has, as you say, come off its hinges, might that not tell you that something, or someone, is interfering with the balance? Something, or someone, from your world? I suppose I should inform you, Moksoos, I heard an odd rumor. It was said to have come from an old female upland sandpiper. I haven't really taken this seriously, of course. But it had to do with this sandpiper seeing a wormlike object moving about in the atmosphere."

Moksoos turned to look piercingly at the owl. *Let me know immediately if you hear anything else regarding such matters. And the sandpiper—might it have been Stella?*

"I've wondered myself if it might not be her," said the owl.

\* \* \* \* \*

Presently the sans-pelage chief, in a muted rage, turned away from the fire and the stench of his medicine male kindling in the hot center of the blaze, his ashes of hair and hide already floating and tumbling in the billowing smoke. Overtaken by a paroxysm of intense indignation and wrath, Mungo staggered through the moonlit forest toward the company of his army.

Then suddenly, and silently, behind him, a blurred, bright-golden luminescence appeared and transformed into a being in Mungo's exact image. Unseen, and like a burning shadow in a comedic, synchronous movement with his every step, it followed him closely for a few moments. Then, just as suddenly as it had appeared, it mutated into a gliding, amoeboid yellow glow that streamed skyward, where it danced and skipped among the crowns of the treetops before it ascended, writhing in snakelike motion, into the upper atmosphere.

There, it became a glowing yellow lance with scales and the head of an eel. It shot through the dark sky in a silent explosion of sparkling points of pure yellow light that vanished into some profound blackness somewhere beyond the blackness of the night, which now seemed itself momentarily unhinged, somehow out of balance.

Mungo was totally oblivious to that which had just occurred in his presence.

# 30

Zak, clinging to the mahogany branches of his perch, bounced southward through the smooth chill of the tundra air, happily homeward to the clicking rhythm of Durzey's foot joints. In this fashion, they had traveled for days. Zak had no need for negotiation—no need, at least, if Durzey continued south. And if the caribou were to stray in a direction that was significantly counter to the direction that the river flowed, all a possum would have to do would be to drop to the ground and follow the river on his own.

But Zak continued to enjoy the advantage of his setting that allowed him to scan the horizon for Sark, and he was not overly concerned by his continued separation from his large friend. He assumed that the old black mastodon certainly by this time had gathered his females and led them southward as he had said he would do. But to be swiftly carried so far to the south on board Durzey's antlers was an opportunity too fine for a homesick possum to deny. He saw no particular advancement of his lot by going on a solo search of Sark. Besides, Sir Sark and his females should be along at any moment.

Poor Durzey, terribly self-conscious of that most embarrassing affliction in his horns, directed all his attention to isolating himself from the herd, avoiding his own kind altogether. This he accomplished with fast travel. With the river sprawled, bent, and winding as a serpent in the valley off to his right, he trotted along in the clicking hoofbeat of the caribou.

Durzey's plan to relieve himself of his peculiar burden had been a complete failure, for every time he lowered his head to graze, Zak, hanging from an antler beam by his handy tail, gathered berries from the tundra's brush and tender roots and grubs from its black soil. And every time he lowered his head to drink from one of the ponds along the way, Zak, likewise, was able to take in his fill.

The caribou's scheme to starve or thirst out his guest, if carried forth, would require his own starvation, a notion less than auspicious, to be sure. So the crafty, ill-humored Durzey, discovering himself in a nonnegotiable position, found the need of a more serviceable approach in dealing with his problem. Thus, a new strategy was born: That of simply giving up altogether would be the current, and to his way of thinking, realistic, means to an end.

One day, as Durzey and Zak approached the summit of a rise of the tundra, Durzey stopped trotting and slowed to a meandering walk, looking out over the landscape to his right and his left, sniffing the air and the ground; Zak took notice. Finally, the caribou stopped in his tracks.

"Vhen a carib qvitz 'e qvitz, and I qvit," he said with frustrated finality, finally breaking his long and obdurate silence. "Zfevvy and Mum vaz right. A parazyt iz vyat ya ere. Vell, I can tell ya, ol' Durzey'z right ready to fez up ta et. A zvinzey zkoorg of a parazyt iz vyat I've got and I'm banizhin mezef from ze 'erd for ze rezt of me dayz. I von't be expoozin mezef to no other carib. But 'ere'z vyat I don't underztoond. Ya can zpick. 'Ow can a parazyt zpick? Itz zoomtin exotic I've took fer zhoor."

Zak, who had long ago given up hope of having any conversation with Durzey, now, after hearing the caribou's woeful characterization of his state of affairs, felt a little sorry for his transportation and decided to respond, though with a dash of admonitory flavoring.

"Dear sir, I must say, it seems to me that you either have a problem with your hearing or a problem with your comprehension or, perhaps, both. As I have already told you and your horny mate, Zfevvy, I am a possum. A possum."

"And ow iz me vazted life improved by nooin ze name of ze diziz I'm a'carryin? Can ya tell me thet, epozoom?"

"My name is Zak, Durzey. Zak. And I am a possum, not a disease. Why do you not understand that simple concept?"

Suddenly, for no apparent reason, Durzey appeared distraught, even frightened, and his face took on a most forlorn expression. Zak studied him with growing curiosity and concern.

"Dear fellow, what is the matter with you? Why have you suddenly become so lugubrious? Do all caribou behave in this manner, or is it that you represent a most unfortunate exception to your race? Come now. What is the problem? Speak up."

Durzey sat down and lifted his nose in the air. His eyes filled. And then he broke into long, moving, piteous sobs.

"Eh hoooo. Eh hoooo. Eh hoooooooo."

"Incomprehensible!" said Zak, taken aback by the sad sounds that poured forth from the unexpectedly pitiful and emotionally shattered caribou. "What on earth?"

"Eh hoooo. Iffin etz yer vizh ta be a'takin me life, then take it now, Zik ze epozoom. I'm no good lak thiz. Me 'ornz ere pootrifide. Verminooted, too. Eh hoooo. And I miz me 'erd. And I miz Mum and ze leetl'un, too. I mizum al, I do. Eh hoooo. Am I dizoorvin of thiz end? Mibby tiz zo. I don't noo. Eh hoooo."

Zak, disturbed by Durzey's avalanche of emotion, began to feel disheartened, guilty, even a little like giving up himself, at least as far as his taking any more advantage of the caribou who, it now seemed, was a rather soft and sensitive brute, after all. Indeed, Zak felt like he needed to come to his rescue.

"Please, sir. Durzey. You must pull yourself together. I did not realize that I had become such a distressing cargo. If you like, I will leave you presently and be on my way alone."

"No! Ztay! Ya muzt ztay. It'z meant ta be. Yoor me poonizhment. Me retriboozhin and me caztigizhin fer not bein a good hoozband, fer not bein a good fither. Mum vaz right. I'm no good a'tal. I'm von mizerable carib, and I muzt be poonizhed. Eh hoooo. Ya zee now, don't ya? Ya muzt ztay. Old Durzey'z done fer. And it muzt be done good and prooper. Et'z too late fer old Durzey who muzt stand up and pee fer ze vayz of vikkidniz. Or mibby I've oonly been mizonderztood, ya zee. But etz me own falt. Of thet I'm zhoor. Eh hooo."

Zak was beginning to feel the growing, and gnawing, burden of responsibility for Durzey's sadness. *What am I going to do now? How am I going to put Durzey back together again?* Panic was blossoming. "My dear sir, it is not nearly so bad as you think," said Zak. "You have not been at all wicked. I'm certain that you are quite right. You have only been misunderstood. I am sure you are quite a decent fellow. Yes. I'm certain of it. A bit of a rogue, perhaps, but quite a decent one, I'm confident to say. Really. Yes, a quite decent rogue you are indeed."

Durzey again arose to his big round feet and, resolutely, renewed his clicking pace toward the South.

"Eh hoooo."

On they went while Zak tried hard to figure out how to unravel that which was bound so firmly in Durzey's mind. But as time went by, Durzey seemed to lose his spirit even more, which likewise caused Zak to lose spirit. A few times along the way, Zak allowed himself to drop to the ground from Durzey's horns in hopes that the caribou might realize that he was free and could go back to his herd, but Durzey would stop and point his antlers down at Zak, saying: "Ya muzt be a'climbin aboord now. Zo it ztayz a good and prooper poonizhment. Me life, iffin etz worth innithin a'tal, etz worth ztayin ze poonantz. Thetz me duty now. Now be a'climbin aboord or I'll die right 'ere and now befoor yer leetle blik eyez."

Despite this peculiar tribulation, Zak was at least getting distance behind him. So much so that the landscape was beginning to change before his eyes again, as the great meadow of fire-colored tundra was slowly becoming populated by green conifers and aspens. The tundra was transforming itself into the great Northern forest.

Onward they went until, one evening, they reached a small grove of aspens overlooking the river's delta. The trees' leaves, now beginning to turn yellow, quivered in the chilly breeze as if nervous about their future.

"Durzey," said Zak, "this would be a lovely location for a few days' rest. I am sure you must be totally tuckered from your unremitting pace."

"Iffin et be yer vizh, fer I'm at yer bik an cal. I'm but an 'omble zoorvent to me joozt dizertz."

"Yes," said Zak. "A little time to rest up. To think about the situation. Perhaps you will come to realize the advantage of our parting. I do recall your readiness to be rid of me a few days ago. Remember?"

"But now I underztoon ze zignificoontz of it. Don't ya zee? Don't ya ZEE? Eh hoooo."

"Yes. Well."

So for two days they rested and grazed and drank together, Zak unable to leave Durzey's horns without triggering the caribou's grave disappointment in any interruption of his good and proper castigation. Zak was becoming distraught. Even if Sark found him now, he would not be able to leave the poor caribou behind in such a bleak condition of unhappiness. They had become sad prisoners to each other.

It had been days since they had seen any caribou, and those they had seen earlier in the journey, Durzey had been careful to avoid. But one morning, as Durzey lay on the ground still asleep, Zak heard a clicking sound. It was Zfevvy who came calling.

He carefully approached the still and sleeping Durzey, who could have just as well been dead for all Zfevvy knew.

"Eh, Durzey," he said. "Ere ye al right? I don't zee ya moovin a'tal."

"Eh, Zfevvy," said Durzey, awake now, but still lying in the grass with his head on the ground, his large vapid eyes blinking sadly. "Don't be aproochin' me. Etz doongeruz."

"Et'z a parazyt. Eh, Durzey?"

"Et'z me retriboozhin. I'm doon"

"Ez it catchin, do ya think?"

"Et'z Zik, me poonizhment."

"Iffin et'z zik, thet'z a good thin. Mibby it'll fal off of ya."

"No. Et'z name iz Zik. Et'z epozoom."

"I say, Zfevvy," said Zak. "You must speak to your friend. Convince him that he must go back with you."

"Ere ye a parazyt, Zik?" asked the suspicious caribou.

"Of course not. That is a ridiculous notion," said Zak.

"Vell, look et 'im. 'E'z done. E'z qvit. And vhen a carib qvitz, 'e qvitz, an 'e'z qvit. Vyat av ya done ta 'im? Vyat kind of vikkid voormin of a zkoorg ere ya iffin yer not a parazyt?"

"Eh hoooo."

"Oh! Yoozt lizzen ta ze poor thin!" said Zfevvy looking at Zak. "Yer a coorz mibby. A coorz of a leeazard epozoom, eh? Ya gone an poot a coorz on old Durzey. Thet'z it. A doongeruz pliz iz Zark'z retrit. An vyat ya done to Zark? Av not zeed 'im a'tal. Iz femalz ere proobly ztill a'vaitin 'im. But yer no leeazard neither, ere ya? Vell, then, vyat ere ya?"

"When was the last time you saw his females?" asked Zak.

"Vhen ve zvam ze river an ya peed a vizit ta old Durzey's vife and leetl'un, ya coorzed foonguz. Ya frittened 'er alf ta deeath, ya did. And ze river'z been a'hactin ztrange, too. Von day et'z a'floodin ze delta and ze nickzt et'z in etz binkz. Did ya coorz ze river, too? Eh, Durzey! Yer vife zendz 'er regardz. Mum zez zhe mizzuz ya. Vantz ya to come 'oom ta 'er and ze leetl'un."

"Eh hoooo."

"I am not a parasite or a curse, sir," said Zak, at wit's end. "I do not know what is wrong with Durzey, but I do think it is in his best interest for him to go back with you. And the sooner the better."

"Then ze 'ole 'erd'l be expoozed ta ya. Ze 'ole 'erd coorzed!"

"But I will stay here," said Zak. "You and Durzey will never have to see me again. Just take him home with you. Please."

"Eh hoooo."

"Did ya 'eer thet, Durzey? Ze voormin zayz ya can be rid of 'im. Ya can go 'oom to ze vife and leetl'un."

"I cannot," said Durzey.

"Vell, vy not?"

"I'm poonizhed. Zik'z me poonizhment fer me trinzgroozhinz. I'm done. Ya av ta faze it, Zfevvy."

"I don't underztoon. Et zayz ya can go," said Zfevvy.

"I don't think et az no controol neither. Ze thin and me iz doomed to be ztuck ta von anoother. Till me 'ornz and me boonz in their ivory deeath zhine back at ze zun and ze moon. Et'z coorzed, too. Eh hoooo."

"That is ridiculous, Durzey," said Zak, half beginning to believe him. From his tail-hanging position he looked up at his nail-less big toes as if he needed to remind himself of something.

"Vell, vyat ere ya iffin yoor not a coorz and a parazyt?" demanded Zfevvy, stomping the earth with his right foot. "Out viz it, voormin! Foonguz! Out viz it!" Zak and Zfevvy momentarily stared each other down as Zak began to track an altogether novel avenue of thought. Then he broke into a drooling, sadistic grin.

"Well, then," said Zak, "since you put it that way, I suppose I shall tell you. Now get this, you two ungulate piles of permafrost poop. What I am is in control. And I am indeed the worst case of curse-and-lizard parasite that ever crawled from the sulfuric vents of Sark's—rest his ruined, routed, and rotted remains—retreat! And yes, it is true. I have placed a curse on Durzey for his wicked ways, and presently I am placing one on you, Zfevvy, for your insolence."

"Vyat?" asked Zfevvy, looking up at his horn rack, thinking that he could already see a new blemish in the crotch of a distal fork.

"But," said Zak, "I just might consider lifting your curses if the pair of you take me to the other side of the river immediately, as I have repeatedly requested you to do in the past. Do you not recall? And if you do not do as I say, then I can assure you that every individual in your herd of thorn-headed reindeer reversions will be very well parasitically 'epozoomed' from now on and forever and for eternity, too. Now let's get moving!"

Durzey jumped up in a panic. Zak had to hold on tight as the two caribou galloped to the river. Zak was thankful for the ride. The river was now filling the delta as Zfevvy had described; but the caribou carried out their swimming mission efficiently and without saying another word.

When they reached the other shore, Zak dropped to the sand. But he maintained his sardonic didelphid expression, drooling rabidly.

"One more thing, you pair of snot-snoozled tundra deer."

The caribou stood trembling as they waited in dread of what might be forthcoming from this nightmarish, serpent-tailed, fungal-lizard-sorcerer, Zik, the wicked "epozoom."

"Before I lift the curse, you must chant for me."

Durzey and Zfevvy looked at each other, wide-eyed and confused.

"Zhoont?" asked Zfevvy with a befuddled look.

"Yes, fellows," said Zak. "It is most definitely required."

"Choont," said Durzey.

"Zhoont," said Zfevvy.

"Czhoont," they said in unison. "Choont. Zhoont. Choont-Zhoont," they said back and forth to each other and to Zak. "Zhoont. Choont."

"No! No!" said Zak. "You blue-northern idiots of the ice! Be quiet!"

The caribou pair went into a gloomy silence, staring down at their big feet.

"Now, in unison, I want you to repeat after me. And you had better get this right: O where art thou Didelphis hagge."

"OO veer eert thou Deedeelphiz agg."

"Whose rotund belly boasteth bagge."

"Ooz rotoon billy booztith big."

"Wherein a suckling son once clung."

"Veerin a zucklin zon vonz cloong."

"Thou spreadeth milk upon its tongue."

"Thou zpreedith mook upon etz toong."

"And foible-tailed the naked rat."

"An fibble-teeled ze nekkid rit."

"Grew to the bignesse of a cat."

"Grew to ze bigniz of a kit."

"With sable ear and snout of swine."

"Viz zibble air and snoot of svine."

"Oh mother dear marsupid fine."

"Oo moother dear merzoopid fin."

"Well," said Zak, "your rhymes stink, but I do believe that, perhaps, the curse is lifted. Very well. Now you are advised to move quickly. Out of my sight, you click-clacking, club-footed cads! And do not look back or ... or ... well, I will not tell you. But it would surely be a very nasty surprise."

Durzey and Zfevvy galloped, clicking away to the north, not saying a word or looking back. Zak watched their bouncing buffy rumps become smaller and smaller as they moved along the distant shore of the river. "Goodbye, fellows," he said to himself. He then looked around and took stock of his surroundings and the fact that he was once again all by himself. *I've made it back to the forest*, he thought. *But where oh where is Sir Sark?*

# 31

"THAT POSSOT ISS like a duck. Ant a duck cannot be trokked."

"But I do not understand," said Sark. "You said you tracked him here from very far to the south, did you not?"

"Lost Trok dew not unterstant neeter," said the dire wolf. "It iss da same possot, but it iss not da same possot. He lifs no trail behind. That possot iss like a bord."

"What do you mean?"

"It iss like he flies like a bord—only every now ant then Lost Trok can catch a little possot int da air. Lost Trok tink tiss possot iss like a duck. Yew see?"

"Perhaps the river washed away all his scent," said Sark. "We were in the river for a very long time."

"No good. That iss not it. Sok, yew tink yew haf lost yew smell int da reefer? Noh. It iss stronker after da water. That iss wy yew vanity works foh yew ant yew females. Da water takes da clothes off yew. Yew see? But tiss possot—tiss possot iss different. Tiss Lost Trok dew not unterstant. How can tiss possot fly like a bord? Always da same tink. Int da reefer. Out of da reefer. On da otter side. Always da same tink. Always lose trok. Yew see?"

"The river is high again," said Sark. "Perhaps it is well we don't travel the other side. It would be dangerous to take the females and their little ones across."

"No good ont da otter side. Always da same tink. Always lose trok."

"What are we going to do to find O. Possum, Lost Track?"

"Lost Trok tink iss pig proplum. Tiss possot iss like a duck."

"Yes, yes—like a duck."

"Yew haf been to da South, no?" Lost Track asked.

"Yes. I have been to the South," said Sark, now distracted by his growing concern over Zak's mysterious disappearance.

"Yoh. Yew know what a possot iss. That iss how Lost Trok know."

"But we must do something to find him," said Sark. "I promised him. And my females have never traveled, and I, I'm afraid, have been a bit remiss in my attempts to further enhance the poor things' worldliness. I fear they would be disappointed if I do not take them on an adventure. O fastidious creatures are they. I fear they will soon press me to take them to my retreat in the north."

"Ant why not take them?"

"It is my only hiding place."

"Yoh. Woll."

"So you see, Lost Track, we must find O. Possum. It is most imperative."

"Why yew call that possot Opossot?"

"What do you mean?"

"Lost Trok tink moppy yew haf fohgot. Lost Trok know tiss possot. Ant hiss name iss Zak."

"That so? And how do you know this?"

"Because Lost Trok know tiss possot. Sok do not lissin."

"I heard you," said the mastodon.

"Sok, Lost Trok want yew to tell where yew tink tiss possot iss."

"But I have no idea where he is, Lost Track. Haven't we been looking for him for a while now?"

"Ah. That iss one lost possot, no?"

"I am afraid that is true."

"Sok," said Lost Track, looking intently at the mastodon's face, "Lost Trok want to know where tiss possot want to go."

"All I know is that he wants to go home," said Sark.

"That he want to go home."

"Yes. That is all I know."

"That possot want to go home?"

"Yes."

"Yew know tiss? That that possot want to go home?"

"Yes, yes, that I do know."

"Sok, yew ask Lost Trok to trok tiss possot, no?"

"Well, yes. Of course."

"Ant yew know where tiss possot want to go, but yew dew not tell Lost Trok. Tiss Lost Trok dew not unterstant."

"But you, I thought, are the great tracker, are you not?"

"Ant that iss why Lost Trok ask these questions. To discofer da cleeyews. Da cleeyews are very impottont. Yew see?"

"Yes. I suppose you do have a point, my friend. The clues are very important."

"Lost Trok tink moppy yew haf fohgot. Lost Trok know tiss possot."

"I haven't forgotten, Lost Track. I do recall your saying that."

"Woll, there iss only one tink to dew."

"And what is that?"

"Backtrok."

Next morning's daylight peered down upon a single-file marching wolf-and-pachyderm procession, Lost Track in the lead, followed by Sark with his fifty females obediently traipsing behind, each trunk clasping the tail of a forward mastodon. The females, in turn, were followed by a similar miniature tail-in-trunk procession of sixteen baby mastodons.

The happy lineage, questing the landscape for adventure, worldliness, and a lost possum, was pointed due west so Lost Track could seek out the ancient trail of Zak, laid months ago when a possum from far to the South was about to discover and explore the great ice sheet of the North. Finally, after a few days travel, they reached the old north-south-running path that Zak had himself traveled.

"Lost Trok tink tiss iss it," said the wolf, sniffing and studying the tundra turf for his ever-important clues. "Yoh, tiss iss it. All da cleeyews fit perfocly."

"Now we go south?" asked Sark.

"Yoh. We go south. But to go north da trail iss warmer. Even ont da ice, da trail iss warmer. Bot Lost Trok dew not trok no possot ont da ice. So we go south. Yew see?"

So Lost Track and his mastodon entourage that had traveled so far westward from the river, now right-angled to the left, and to the South the grand procession went.

"Let's go find that possot," said Lost Track.

"Come, my loves, to the South we go!"

"Possum hunting," said Number Seven.

"Sark says the possum is a poet," said Number Eight.

"How nice to go to the South," said Number Sixteen.

"He said possums have to be in the South for winter."

"To not freeze."

"What does one look like?"

"Maybe a bird that looks like a lizard."

"A tail like a snake."

"Sark said little black ears."

"Sable, he said."

"And a little pig nose."

"Snout of a pig."

"How big?"

"The size of a cat."

"The bigness of one."

"And the females have a what?"

"Where they keep their babies."

"I never!"

"How do they get in?"

"They find their own way."

"How do possums—"

"It's forked."

"The males have a forked tongue?"

"It's not the tongue that is forked."

"My word!"

"And we want to find this thing?"

"Be careful. The young ones are listening. Come along now. Hold on tight to the tail in front."

"Sok," said the wolf, "Lost Trok tink tiss iss go to be very interestink expedition."

"That so?" said Sark, trotting behind the dire wolf. "Well, then. Perhaps now you are willing to give up your search for Moksoos."

"When da turkey gopler lays ant egg."

\* \* \* \* \*

One late afternoon, far to the east of the wolf and mastodon caravan, the orange, setting sun peered down upon a pair of caribou males tracking northward along the river's bank to where the river was about to disappear underneath the southern edge of the great ice sheet.

"Et'z ez I feared, Durzey. Zark'z gone. Poor ol' Zark. Rezt 'iz rooted an rooned reminz."

"And 'iz femalz," said Durzey. "Veer ere they?"

"Oh! 'Iz femalz ere gone, too!" said Zfevvy. "Et'z a doongeruz pliz, Zark's retrit. A doongeruz pliz."

# 32

"REALLY, OPAL," SAID Old Ok, "do you think it is such a good idea to try to teach it something that is perhaps outside the scope of its evolution?"

"Well, Ok, the species evolved a nose like the rest of us did," said Opal. "Surely it is not going to cause problems for him to merely see the thing. Come, Pishiu. Look at Sena. Do it, Pishiu," she said. "Do like Sena."

Pishiu was watching Sena, who was sitting in front of him on the sandy bank of the stream. The bobcat was holding his right forepaw over his own right eye.

Pishiu reached out to tug at Sena's paw. Sena had placed it over his eye, hoping the little sans-pelage male would do likewise.

"Pishiu, put your paw over your eye, like Sena," said Opal.

"I believe it thinks that Sena has something in his eye," said the jag, who was sitting at Sena's left side, facing Pishiu in the same fashion that Sena was. She held this position in readiness to make a hiss to draw Pishiu's attention in her direction, and in the direction of his nose, if only he would do what Sena was doing, which he was not. Pishiu continued to pull Sena's paw from his face so he could see both of Sena's yellow eyes.

"I don't think you have anything to worry about, Old Ok," said the jag. "The species is far too dense for us to be able to teach one of its members tricks."

"Come, Pishiu, do like Sena," said Opal, ignoring the jag's comment.

"Pishiu," said Pishiu.

Sena allowed Pishiu to pull his paw away from his eye. Then Sena gently pulled back his paw and placed it back into the same position. The little sans-pelage pulled it away again. Sena pulled his paw free from Pishiu once more and put it back on his closed right eye. Again, Pishiu pulled it down. Again, Sena put it back. Then, suddenly, Pishiu did it. He put his hand over his own eye. But it was the wrong eye. The jag was out of position. But Old Ok, who was on the opposite side of Pishiu, Sena and Opal, was now in the perfect position to aid in the demonstration.

"Old Ok!" said Sena. "Say something! You're in the proper place to get the attention of its seeing eye so it can finally see its nose."

Old Ok, who up until this moment was only a spectator, was caught completely by surprise. Without thinking, he roared loudly.

"Old Ok, what are you doing?" said Opal. "That is too loud!"

"Look! Look at it! It is looking straight at me!" Old Ok again roared in excitement, delighted over his achievement.

"Be quiet, Ok!" said Sena. "You are going to frighten it and wake up its whole pack at the same time."

Indeed, Pishiu, with one wild right eye, was now staring to his left at Old Ok, while holding his left hand over his left eye.

"There you go, Pishiu!" said Opal. "That's a good boy. That's a good, good boy!"

Then the little sans-pelage male took his hand down from his face and looked at Opal with a quizzical expression.

"That is very good, Pishiu," she said. "Now let's try the other eye. Show him, Sena."

"How do you know it saw its nose, Opal?" asked the jag.

"He must have seen his nose," she said. "How could he have missed it?"

"Would you please tell me again, Opal," said the jag. "What exactly is it going to do with its new information?"

"Think," said Old Ok. "It is going to use its new information to think."

"He is going to use it to help himself understand what he is," said Sena.

"Thank you very much, Sena and Ok," said Opal. "I believe you two do get the picture now."

"Do you suppose his species has the same problem that our possum-poet has?" asked the jag.

"What are you talking about?" asked Opal. "Zak doesn't have a problem seeing his nose."

"He did before he left the mastodon trail," said the jag.

"I believe you might be right," said Sena, looking at the spotted she-cat with an expression of great interest in his face. "If Opal's theory is correct, I believe that Zak and the sans-pelages just might have a common deficit."

"What exactly do you mean?" said Opal.

"I believe it is time for us to go," said Old Ok, looking back up the bank at a staring adult sans-pelage form standing next to the furrowed trunk of a willow tree.

"His mother!" said Opal. "Yes, I do believe we should go now."

"And quickly," said the jag.

The three cats and the bear bounded, splashing their way across the stream, and disappeared into the forest. Pishiu's mother walked quietly down to near the water's edge and squatted next to her young. They smiled at each other, making gentle vocalizations. Pishiu raised his hand and held it to his eye for a moment. Then they both looked toward the silent forest on the other side of the stream.

# 33

*T*HE RIVER GOES *south. Follow that river. The river goes home. Follow* ... Those words became a mantra to Zak as his southerly riverside pace penetrated deeper and deeper into the northern forest whose trees were now larger and much more varied in ancestral stock. And so, too, were the other plants and animals he saw along his way.

The river, larger now, snaked along with its valley through the green landscape, maneuvering an audience of hills and foggy, blue mountains.

*The river goes home. Follow.*

On Zak trotted in earnest, slowing only for food and sleep in the evenings, but unremittingly onward, always keeping the river's glistening sheen in his sight, and losing its sight only at night when he slept. And onward he went in parallel with the dire wolf and mastodon formation coursing its southerly way, as a great, lumbering millipede, somewhere in the distance to the north and to the west.

Zak's homeward-bound determinedness had spiraled to full blossom since he had parted with the caribou Durzey. Being relieved of that burdensome vehicle seemed to allow him to remain more focused on his travel ambition.

But one morning Zak awoke with a chill and a headache. He lay on his back with his nose pointed at a large pine limb above his head where pine siskins were busily working over its cones. He felt a bit disoriented and scolded himself for not seeking any kind of shelter the night before. He arose and began to forage the forest floor for his breakfast, and after a little while, he continued in his trotting gait. He felt feverish and not at all himself. But despite his condition, he was able to continue, stopping only for sleep and food.

But now, it seemed to him that something was different. *Perhaps,* he thought, *there is something a little different about the river.* Or perhaps he could simply see it better now. *Or perhaps it has turned or twisted upon itself. Must follow that river. Curious, though,* he thought. *My nose. I see my nose differently. My left eye sees it better now for some reason. Something has shifted.*

Zak continued, though he felt a weariness overtaking him. He was getting sick. Then, one afternoon, with perplexity fading into throbbing confusion, he decided to stop and walk down to the river's edge to try to think. *What is going on here?* he wondered. He then waded into the river a little way and studied the water for a moment. *Yes. Something strange.* He walked out of the river and up the shore back to the forest's edge. Then he stopped and turned around to look again at the river. *Have I been here before?*

He felt dizzy and tired and decided to sit down for a moment. Then he heard a noise. A haunting, frozen chill surged down his spine as he looked along the shore and saw, bearing straight toward him, a pack of seven angry-looking gray wolves that seemed to have come out of nowhere. In a panic, he turned to run back into the forest. But it was too late. The wolves quickly caught up to him and surrounded him, panting and snarling.

Crouching in the middle of their circle, he looked up into their faces and saw the youthful clarity of their yellow eyes. They looked hungry and greedy, and he imagined that soon they would be fighting each other over his carcass and its bloody pieces. *Please let this be a terrible dream,* he thought. *Please let them understand that I am not ready for this. This is way too sudden. Surely it cannot be that important to them that I should have to die. Please, brothers, no!*

He decided to turn again to run toward the river, for what real purpose he did not know except that he simply could no longer bear seeing the vicious circle of fangs that gleamed so menacingly down upon him. He made a lunge at one of wolves who, upon seeing Zak's hissing mouthful of pointed teeth, jumped aside, allowing him to pass and scurry down to the water's edge. But just before he reached the water, he was stopped cold in his tracks, for there arose before him from the river's shallows, like a puff of rising steam, a ghastly figure— the most terrifying-looking predator he could ever have dreamed or imagined, who he immediately recognized as Moksoos, the famous emerald-eyed black lion.

But he was many times larger than Zak had remembered him— for now, he was four times the size of a mammoth. The frightened wolves bounded away at the sight of this bizarre feline apparition who sat calmly in the water staring, with cold, green-glowing eyes, down upon their possum. Then Zak noticed that the great cat's fur was curiously dry. *How can this be?* he wondered. He remained for a few moments in stunned motionless silence; then he turned and began to creep, as if perhaps unnoticed, away from the monstrous creature. *This is all a dream*, he thought to himself. *I am overcome with fatigue and sickness. What is the matter with me?*

"Zak, stop," said Moksoos in a curiously gentle tone of voice.

Zak froze in his tracks again, not daring to look back at the menacing-looking cat figure.

"Zak, we need to have a talk. Would you be agreeable to that?"

He was completely speechless.

"Cat has your tongue?"

"Sssss," Zak hissed.

"What was that?" said Moksoos. "Did you wish to say something?"

"Sssss."

"Go ahead. You may speak."

"Sssss," was all Zak could utter.

"Yes? What is it that you want to say?"

"Ssssir."

"Is that what you wanted to say? 'Sir'?"

"Yyyess, ssssir."

"Zak. Do not be afraid. I merely wish to ask you something."

"Yyyess, ssssir."

"What do you think about the river lately?" Moksoos asked.

"Ssssir?"

"Do you think there is something strange about how the river lies?"

"Yyesss, sssir," said Zak, still looking away.

"I want you to think about that."

"Yyesss, sssir."

"Take a moment and think about it."

"Yyesss, sssir," said Zak, before enduring a short and somewhat painful period of silence.

"And your nose, Zak. How the river lies in relation to your nose."

"Yyesss, sssir."

"I want you to think about that, too, Zak."

"Yyess, sssir."

"Zak. It is quite doubtful that a possum could survive the winter here. Have you considered that?"

"Yyess, sssir."

"Zak. Look at the water for a moment. Look how it flows."

"Yyesss, sssir."

A great horned owl flew down, from out of nowhere it seemed to Zak, and lit on the sand a short distance down the beach. The owl then moved his head from side to side, drew closer to Zak, and began to curiously stare at him.

"I did not bring you here to interfere," said Moksoos. He now turned his gaze from the owl and back to the possum. The owl moved away and stood motionless.

"Look around you, Zak," said Moksoos. "Look at the river. Look at the bank and the trees. Don't you see that you have been here before, Zak?"

"Yyesss, sssir."

"What do you think about it all, Zak? About the river. The way the water moves. Its position according to your nose and left and right eyes. What do you make of it, Zak?"

"I-I was going north again?"

"Ever since you woke up on your back under that big pine limb a few days ago, north has been your fixed target."

"Yyess, sir."

"Yes, sir, Zak. It certainly has. Do not make this mistake again, Zak. Do you understand?"

"Yes, ssir."

"Zak, I want you to come down to the water where I am. Yes. Now, please."

Zak turned and walked slowly past the owl toward Moksoos. He dared not look him in the face but fixed his eyes on the cat's massive, chest. He stopped and stood before the great black feline with its peculiar green eyes staring down upon him.

"Very good. Now look past me at the river, Zak, and close your eyes."

Zak looked at the river, then he closed his eyes.

"That is good. Now open them, Zak."

When he opened his eyes, it was morning, and he was again lying under the same large pine limb busy with foraging pine siskins. His fever was gone as were the owl and Moksoos. A black jay, dripping wet, as if it had just stepped from its bath, hopped from the ground upon his belly. The bird puffed his feathers to dry them and walked up Zak's chest and looked into his face. Zak was startled to see that its eyes emitted an emerald glow.

"It's time for you to hit the trail, Zak," said the black jay.

"How do you know my name?" asked Zak. "How long have I been asleep? And it is morning, is it not?"

Without another word, the jay flew into the forest and disappeared.

Zak arose from the ground, shook himself, and took his bearings in accordance with the river. He felt fit and ready for southerly travel.

*He did not say my name*, Zak thought to himself, smiling. *It was merely the squawk of a jay. What a very strange dream. Rather disconcerting, too. I must surely from this moment on remain at post for wolves and black lions.* He shook his head again and continued south along the riverbank. As he trotted along he began to construct a new rhyme that he thought coincided with his purpose.

Homeward, home the river flows
As the sliding adder goes
What gossip waiting at your mouth
Keeps this possum pointed south
So he can learn what the adder knows
Homeward, home the river flows
Southward, mouthward, homeward goes
The river.

*But why,* Zak thought, *wasn't Sir Sark in my strange dream?* He felt a sting of disappointment in the fact. *Where is he? If I went back upstream, North, why did I not find him; even in a dream, why didn't I? Where is Sir Sark? Where is he now? If he followed the river as I am presently, then he should have overcome me by now. I should be traveling toward my home in the South, perched upon his hairy head at this moment—he and I and his fifty females. A most pleasant caravan. What happened? Could he be injured? Dead? Could he possibly have taken leave of the ice before I did and bypassed his females to search for me in the South? Why didn't he come out of the ice when I did? And what happened to that ferocious bear?*

*Is Sir Sark presently somewhere ahead of me wondering where I am and why he cannot find me? Too many possibilities. He is somewhere ahead looking for me at this moment. I believe it is the only way to explain it. He is presently somewhere along this river to the South.*

*But if he is traveling south as I am, how will I ever keep up with his pace? And even if, by chance, we did find each other, we would surely have to go back for his females—another delay, and summer coming to an end. And Moksoos reminding me in my dream that the far-northern forest is no place for a possum in the winter.*

*How ever did I become separated from Sir Sark? I do not wish to go home without him. I will be of no help to my friends. I will have nothing to show for my long absence.*

*Why is it that when events begin to unfold in a proper fashion something like this has to happen? Why is it that one must expect the unexpected? Who ever invented the word anyway? Unexpected. It is a misnomer.*

*Perhaps the pious raccoons should consult their Hierarchy about that one. How do the Hierarchy and his followers deal with misnomers? Discard them in the tailings of their excavation sites? Put them back in the ground somehow?*

*As for me, I would recommend that unexpected be reburied. A granite stone marked Do Not Disturb should be placed on top of the grave. And a very heavy stone it should be. How disruptive unexpected is. How depraved. How uncivilized! The raccoon who discovered it should be banished from the forest. Or from the religion. Or whatever. What was it thinking? The Hierarchy himself should be forced to explain the purpose of such an oddity. His toes should be held to the hot coals of accountability. The very idea.*

"Certainly no squirrel would behave in such a fashion," he said aloud to himself in Rodent tounge. "Incomprehensible! That's what it is. How could a clan of pious raccoons possibly know what they are if all they can do with their time is to go about disturbing the peace by uncovering regrettable units of discourse? Yes. And their silly views make them think that they are somehow set apart from the rest of us. I do believe that is indeed treading upon the territory of not knowing what one is."

But just before Zak's mental, and then vocal, diatribe was about to escalate to a declaration of war against Lavratonianism and its ring-tailed practitioners, he heard from a bough high above his head the tongue in which he had just spoken:

"Ler szay ootreh! Ma darsupee! Ick! Ick!"

Zak was stunned to hear the old language of rodents, but the sound made him feel at home, for that single phrase ("I have found it! The marsupid! Ick! Ick!") uttered by a fox squirrel, was, he knew, his notice that he, finally, was about to reestablish contact with the Canopy Connection.

# 34

"So that iss why da possot got hisself lost. He was out on a sarch foh da knowledge, no?"

"That is right," said Sark as he and the rest of the tail-in-trunk procession traipsed obediently behind their vegetarian dire wolf tracking agent presently touring under the mastodon-given appellation of Lost Track.

"Ant dew yew tink he find it, Sok?"

"I believe he did. At least in part. He said that he found out what he is, although, I don't believe that is what he was looking for originally. Actually, he was not entirely clear on what exactly it was that he was seeking in the beginning. I believe he forgot his original plan, as his conversation wandered onto something else—some wish on his part to seek contact with rodents in another region. As if it would somehow help his friends at home. I really couldn't make sense of it. I suppose I should have pressed him on the matter more thoroughly."

"Ah, that iss good."

"What is good, Lost Track?"

"To know what one iss. No?"

"Yes, of course it is."

"Moppy someday Lost Trok find out what he iss."

"Are you telling me you don't know that you are a dire wolf and a member of the forest-folk?"

"Lost Trok know that he iss dar wolf, but there iss otter lefels. Yew see?"

"Other levels, perhaps, but I think it is quite enough to know one's niche in the animal world. I strongly suspect that there exists an entire species that is roaming about without the knowledge of what it is, even on that most basic level."

"They iss like yew possot friend was. That iss pig proplum."

"A big problem indeed."

"But da otter lefels, Sok, are impottant tew. If one dew not know what one iss on any one lefel, then one dew not know what one iss. Woll, for that matter, one dew not know what anytink iss."

"Tell me, Lost Track, just why is it that you wish to track Moksoos?"

"Because Lost Trok iss on da sarch foh da knowledge, tew. Yew see?"

"No, I don't see."

"That ponter iss different from allllll da otter animols. Very different. Lost Trok has trokked da trail of da ponter when da trail was warm. Many times. But when Lost Trok iss about to find that ponter. About to see that ponter. About to look that ponter int da eye. When Lost Trok get so close to that ponter da trail ends. Da trail vanishes. Gone. To trok da ponter iss to trok da knowledge. Ant if Lost Trok can trok da ponter Lost Trok can trok anytink. Except a duck. Ant a duck cannot be trokked. Woll, foh that matter, anytink that flies like a bord cannot be trokked. Ant now that possot iss like a bord. Tiss Lost Trok dew not unterstant. Yew see?"

"I see," said Sark.

"Sok, iss yew certain yew nefer see that possot fly like a bord?"

"Of course I am certain. O. Possum, or *Zak*, as you say his name is, cannot fly. I can assure you of that."

"Lost Trok iss not so certain that yew know tiss. Tiss possot iss very different. Like da black ponter."

"No."

"Woll. Yew must tink about that, Sok. Possots dew not swim very woll."

"I believe that is a true statement."

"But tiss possot, Sok, can swim like a fish, no?"

"No. Of course not. He is a hopelessly feeble swimmer. Why would you think any differently?"

"Why yew say tiss, Sok? That possot can swim like a fish. That possot swim downt that reefer with yew, no?"

"Of course not. He rode the whole journey on top of my head or in my ear. That is always the way we travel together."

Lost Track stopped dead in his tracks. To keep from running over him, Sark and the first five females had to come to an abrupt check, creating many mastodon collisions in the rank.

The dire wolf slowly turned around and sat down on his stout haunches. He stared determinedly at Sark's eyes, all the while remaining silent.

"What? What is it now, Lost Track?" asked Sark.

"Ahh!" he said.

"What is it, my friend?" Sark asked again.

"When yew ant that possot trafel together, that possot iss on yew head?"

"Why yes. Almost always."

"On yew head."

"Yes."

"When yew ant that possot trafel together int da water, that possot iss on yew head?"

"Yes."

"When yew ant that possot trafel together on da ground, that possot iss on yew head?"

"Well, yes."

Lost Track continued to stare; then he raised up a paw and pointed it straight at Sark's face.

"Yew see? Tiss Lost Trok dew not unterstant."

A discomforting notion was gaining popularity in Sark's mind that something in the form of one of his obturations in the path to conversational pleasantry might be headed his way. And he was beginning to feel a little embarrassed.

"I ... I—" he said.

"Sok, how come you not say tiss?"

"Well, I—"

"Sok, yew ask Lost Trok to trok tiss possot, no?"

"Yes, but—"

"Ant yew know how tiss possot trafels."

"Yes—"

"But yew dew not tell Lost Trok."

"But I—"

"Yew see? Tiss Lost Trok dew not unterstant."

"Well—"

"Yew know all tiss intformation ant yew dew not tell Lost Trok."

"But I thought you ... I thought he would be afoot now ... I—"

"Da cleeyews, Sok. Da cleeyews are very impottont. But Sok has fohgot alllll about da cleeyews. Tiss Lost Trok dew not unterstant. Yew see?"

"Yes, I see," said Sark. His eyes were tightly shut.

"Why don't you help him if you know the clues, dear?" asked Number Five.

"The clues are very important, Sark," said Number Seven.

"Sark, don't you want to find Zak?" asked Number Four.

"He already told you to tell him the clues, Sark."

"Yes, dear, we all heard him."

"Don't you want to find the poet?"

"Unfurl thy frond, Sark."

"Can you think of anything else to tell Lost Track?"

"Think."

"Think."

"Stay right where you are, little ones. Hold tight to the tail in front."

"Please accept my apology, one and all," said Sark. "I have indeed misbehaved. I have committed the most mammoth of mastodon sins. I have made myself into an example of the veritable essence of dull, dumb, dimwitted, and moronical obtuseness." He moved his big head from side to side and trumpeted loudly; then he smiled. He knew when he was beaten, and he enjoyed it immensely.

"Sok, iss yew got any cleeyews that yew haf not say to Lost Trok?" said the wolf, smiling slyly at the females as they were smiling at him.

"No, Lost Track, I don't believe I have. You may now grant me absolution. I can assure you that I am leached of all sin. At least for the moment."

"Yew iss certain of tiss?"

"I am quite certain," said Sark.

"Sok say to Lost Trok that he iss certain," said the wolf, again smiling at the females.

Muffled chortles and giggles rolled like a wave down the line of females to the baby mastodons, who remained obediently silent in their standing tail-in-trunk positions.

"Lost Trok has to go back to da reefer now."

"What on earth for?" asked Sark.

"Because Lost Trok know how that possot can fly like a bord."

The dire wolf turned and loped away through the forest to the east, leaving the bewildered Sark to his females and the babies.

Sark and the herd spent the next few days grazing and exploring the great northern forest that they had, by now, so deeply penetrated. Sark, an old veteran of many previous travel expeditions, happily tutored his females on the vegetation of the region and the abundant forest cuisine that surrounded them. But he wished that Lost Track had given him some idea as to when he might return, and, though he knew it was his place to stay with the herd, he wondered why he had not been invited to go with the wolf. He was curious about Lost Track's intention to return to the river. *Why go back to the river now?* Sark wondered. Until now, he had thoroughly enjoyed the concept of backtracking Zak to his homeland and surprising his possum friend when he found him. Yet Sark did not really mind a change of events should that arrive. It rather fit his personality.

One evening, as the old mastodon lay on the ground resting between Number Thirty-Two and Number Forty-Seven, who were both fast asleep and snoring loudly, an idea came to him. *So!* he thought. *O. Possum, Zak, must have climbed onto the horns of a caribou when I lost him in the river. Of course. It only makes sense. There were hundreds of caribou in the water. That's it. That is the most reasonable way to explain why Lost Track could never pick up O. Possum's trail originally.*

*And now that he knows what happened, that is why Lost Track has gone back to the river. But how did he figure out that O. Possum climbed aboard a caribou? And how far south would a caribou go? I suppose Lost Track will find out. Perhaps he will have O. Possum with him when he returns. Who knows? But isn't it all a grand adventure? A magnificently mysterious adventure? All my eight hundred years have been a mysterious adventure. I hope I have another eight hundred years of adventure ahead of me. And if I attain that goal, I shall apply for an extension. Everything is mysterious, nothing is truly familiar. O how, familiarity, you lie.*

* * * * *

When Lost Track reached the river, in no time at all he found Zak's scent and trailed it north for a while, and, after determining with certainty that it only grew colder in that direction, he turned back and followed it south. *Lost Trok haf da possot now*, he thought to himself. *That possot iss on tiss reefer to da South.*

He continued, trotting and loping along the river's shore, tracking the faint but ever-so-lightly strengthening scent of possum. In this way he traveled for days, making only brief stops for food and rest. Then, one day just before noon, he felt his heart sink, and the hair on his neck and his back bristled.

*Tiss iss no good. Tiss iss no good. Wolfs! Lost Trok dew not like tiss. There iss seven wolfs on da trail.* He stopped to think, and, circling with his nose to the ground, he rechecked his count of the wolves whose ominous scent was now comingled on the river's bank with Zak's. *Tiss iss no good. Now Lost Trok haf somtink to worry about.* He continued at a slow, methodical walk, cautiously making certain to gather all the details of the scent scene that lay spread on the beach like an invisible scroll of hieroglyphics for him to decipher.

As he worked his way south, he noticed that the wolves' scent was much warmer than that of the possum, and he took it as a good sign. Perhaps the wolves were not interested in Zak's cold trail. Perhaps they were not even hungry for possum. Perhaps they had not noticed it, for he knew that even the combined sense of smell of seven gray wolves was inferior to his own powerful sense.

From his long experience and his acumen for the detection of details, he was able to determine that the wolves' trails intermingled with one another through wasteful ramblings. From this he gleaned that they were all young males, and he took it as a bad sign. Youthful wolves might not contemplate the significance of the taking of life as would older individuals who might, if they were not hungry, let a possum go free until perhaps another day when the need for meat presented itself more acutely. And he did not look with fervor on the thought of meeting up with the wolves himself. As a slower and heavier species, he would almost certainly find himself an outsider under attack. Perhaps he would even become their prey.

But on he went south, moving and sniffing slowly and meticulously along the beach until he reached a point where the wolves' scent turned away from the river and toward the west. He was able to determine that they had been in a hurry, too, as if something had spooked them. He also determined that Zak was not with them. *Good*, he thought. He then decided to follow the trail back to the river, and there, to his amazement, he found Zak's scent to be as fresh as that of the wolves. There had been a wolf-possum encounter. What had happened? He followed Zak's trail down to the river's edge, and to his utter amazement again, he found the scent of Moksoos. Lost Track was dumbfounded by his peculiar accumulation of evidence. What did it mean?

For the next two days, he remained at the site, studying, checking the water, casting to both the north and the south and, again, to the west. He even swam to the other side of the river and meticulously worked over its east bank. Nothing. He swam back to the west bank and spent hours in contemplation of this most perplexing puzzle. And he thought that one of the most peculiar aspects of it was that, as he went south along the river, Zak's scent trail, which seemed to have doubled on itself, grew weaker and weaker.

So the two trails of Zak converged—from the south and from the north—and they ended at a site near the shallows of the river's west bank where Moksoos had been. But where did they go from there? There was no fresh scent trail of panther or possum that led away from the site. *Tiss Lost Trok dew not unterstant. That possot ant that ponter, they iss like a duck. Ant a duck cannot be trokked.* He decided that there was nothing more for him to do but go back to the mastodon herd.

# 35

D USK DESCENDED WITH stodgy lackluster upon the creatures
of the day while it arose with shining contingency for those
of the night. And as a day possum, Zak naturally saw it
as the time for him to look for a safe place to lie down to sleep
for the night; but the great horned owl perched on a dead limb of
the black gum whose hollow base a possum was about to enter had
other ideas.

"I say, possum, you've had an interesting voyage, haven't you?"

*Who is there?*

"I am the owl perched on the dead limb above your head, such as
it is."

"Who is there?"

"You wish to repeat the question aloud? I am the owl perched on
the dead limb above your head. But please. As I know you are aware,
it is not necessary for you to repeat your thoughts out loud."

*I do believe it is you, sir, who has a question.*

"Yes. I did ask you something. You have had a fascinating journey
so far, have you not?"

*Indeed, sir. Practically every incomprehensible step of the way.*

"And you seem to have learned some important facts along the
way."

*I would hope so, sir.*

"Yes, indeed you did. A genuine possum specimen you are. And
now you know it. That is no small treasure, possum. So, on behalf of

all forest-folk, I would like to express my heartiest thanks to you, for it is positively in the best interest of us all that each and every one of us knows what we are. But that's not all. You have been chosen."

*Chosen?*

"Yes."

*What in the name of the laughing leopard frog, sir, are you talking about?*

"But of course, he has revealed himself to you. That's what I mean by *chosen*. Indeed—he saved your life! He's done that sort of thing before—only, very rarely."

*I don't understand you. Why don't you clarify that which you seem to wish to express?*

"Why, I speak of our green-eyed feline friend, of course."

*Moksoos? Yes. I had a dream about him recently. And you were also in my dream. But I also remember you from some time ago. You had spoken with the old sans-pelage with stripes on its skin and the thorny moss structure on its head. And you told Sena and me about the evil sans-pelage.*

"So you think Moksoos was just a dream? Well. Then I have said too much already. I'm afraid I cannot discuss this matter or any other such matters in further detail. But the jay—the jay spoke to you, did he not?"

*There was a black jay with green eyes. In my dream.*

"You heard it speak to you. The jay, that is. The black jay with green eyes. And you think it was a dream? Well, then, that remains a secret, too, I suppose. It is all for the balance, Zak."

*But how on earth do you know—*

"I know a lot about a lot of things," interrupted the owl.

*Well, then, do you know of a mastodon—*

"I will not tell you where your Sir Sark is. One must not interfere."

*Interfere with what, sir?*

"Nor can I tell you about your friends at home. For the same reason. Indeed for the same reason that I do not act as an interpreter. For the same reason I am not permitted to say many things to the forest-folk. They trust me with their secrets. And, as our mutual friend says, it could disturb the balance—the symphony. Such as it is."

*And just who are* they, *sir? Whatever do you—*

"Never mind about who they are. That is a secret business. I'm afraid I cannot answer your questions. I have said too much already. Good night, possum."

When the owl lifted off from the dead limb, its brittle shaft snapped and fell to the ground, barely missing Zak's nose. In the next moment, a flying squirrel glided down from a nearby white oak and lit on the trunk of Zak's tree, near his head. The little flying squirrel's name was Pitsee, and over the last few days of Zak's river-journey to the South, she had followed him, making known her presence around this time of the evening. As the spoken language of great horned owls was a universal one for all members of the forest-folk, including the rodents (and even the sans-pelages), she had, during her eavesdropping, understood every word that the owl had said to Zak.

Zak was now alone no more. For not only was he in the company of Pitsee, but the rodents of both the canopy and the ground followed his movements with great curiosity ever since he had been discovered by the excited fox squirrel some days earlier. Zak had become a Canopy Connection curiosity and gossip source when, many months ago, the famous architect and dam builder known to the nonrodent forest-folk as Quarral had announced his presence.

A possum from the South who understood the language of rodents was indeed grand gossip, but only, of course, after it had been declared so by someone of such high standing within the rodent clan as was the genius little beaver Quarral. And the fox squirrel who had made the talking-possum rediscovery a few days earlier, months after Zak's departure from the northern forest, became famous himself, so much so that in the future he would be known as "the wise fox squirrel who had found the architect's lost talking possum."

And over the course of those evening visitations, Zak had some revelations for curious little Pitsee, who presently acted as a historian for the Canopy Connection. Indeed, little Pitsee had begun documenting the story to string the interviewee's pearls of truth upon a flimsy, almost beadless, filament stranded for all those months in the spongy mire of rodent conjecture.

Zak had happily handed over shiny pearls like: "I tried early on in my travels outside of my region to communicate with the squirrels in order to gain information regarding the poisonous sans-pelage Mungo, but I was met with displeasure only; eventually, with the help of a friend, I was able to make contact with the illustrious dam-building beaver Quarral, who was very accommodating indeed, but, in the end, really had no useful information for me." Of course, Pitsee, as well as the rest of the members of the Canopy Connection, knew that sad fact. That lonely pearl was strung a long time ago.

"And," she asked in Rodent, "what was your impression of the architect?"

"Good," Zak said, sensing his own preeminence in the delicate hands of the skillful interviewer. "Very good. Incomprehensibly so, in fact. All the deportment of gentlemale genius I should suspect, considering that I, not being one—a genius, that is—can only divine such a thing. And comportment, too. I could sense that, you see, being, though not a genius in the strict fashion, a highly sensitive possum. Oh. And his voice and accent. How elegantly spoken was the immaculate beaver Quarral. Just incomprehensibly so."

"And who was your friend?" she asked.

"So bright and full of kindness and good manners. Very accommodating; walking and talking with all the grace of a swallow in flight; always with his arms folded on his chest, then raising his right hand to his cheek; and so admired by his workers."

"And where," she asked, "did the name *Quarral* come from?"

"I'm glad you asked that," he said. "He, the architect Quarral, is apparently so famous that the nonrodent members of the forest-folk population named him so."

"And where did the name come from?" she again asked.

"Oh, I see. That I cannot say."

"You mean it is a secret?"

"No, I simply don't know where the name came from, except, of course, from the nonrodent forest-folk. But isn't it interesting?"

"Yes, it certainly is. Now let's get back to the topic of your friend—"

"Well, anyway, I was lost and I wanted to go home, but I kept going in the wrong direction, north, secondary, I suppose, to some defect of my physical being, possibly along the lines of an intracranial metallic foreign body; that is to say, a magnet in my head—"

"Oh?"

"Yes, until I found myself in Sir Sark's beautiful wintergreen oasis far onto the great ice sheet."

"Ice sheet?"

"The far north is frozen in, you see."

"You mean like winter?"

"Yes, but more so; all is ice, madam. It's where Sir Sark goes to get away for a while and where we, Sir Sark and I, became good friends."

"And who is this Sir Sark? He's not the friend you brought up earlier—"

"Sir Sark is a northern black mastodon who has fifty lovers whom he leaves on the tundra when he vacations at his oasis—"

"Rather boorish, don't you think? But this oasis; could you elaborate, please?"

"Oh yes; a beautiful tropical paradise—"

"But you said the far north is frozen."

"It is—with steaming brooks and ponds full of iridescent catfish and shadowshine more spectacular than any I had seen before or have seen since. And Sir Sark swimming in the river like a giant seal—now, *there* is a splendid swimmer for you. And he had, early on, told me to be on the lookout for the lights in the evenings, but I always went to sleep too early. But one night he woke me up and I got to see them. Oh! So gorgeous."

"The stars?"

"No, the beautiful night lights; first pink and then emerald, spreading, then folding themselves into shimmering beings of various contortions as we watched them; but for the most part, they were as emerald as was the valley itself where there live lizards that look like birds and birds that look like lizards—"

"What did you say? Would you repeat that?"

"—and a beautiful, beautiful jungle it is! Or was. Who knows if it even still exists after the thunder."

"Slow down, please!"

"We finally left his oasis by way of an under-the-ice river that flooded, but we became separated by the bear, and I had to travel all the way down the river, in and out of it, to the northern range of the great Northern forest on the horns of a caribou who goes by the name of Durzey."

"A bear, you said?"

"An obstreperously obstinate race the caribou are. Have you ever met one?"

"Well, no, not personally."

"But from the beginning—" he said.

"What do you mean?" she said.

"I merely, as I said, wanted to seek information about this Mungo fellow—perhaps wisdom, too—from the rodent folk of other regions."

"And why would you think that sort of information, if you were able to obtain it, would be of any benefit to you?"

He didn't know the answer to that question, but those pearls had rolled like raindrops off a *Colocasia* leaf, and she had strung enough of them to become more famous as a reporter for the Connection than was the wise fox squirrel who had rediscovered the architect's lost talking possum.

Pitsee also had some revelations for Zak. For in the midst of these twilight interviews, she had informed him that the trail he had left behind months ago had since become a rather busy one; that not long after he had left the region, a peculiar plant-eating dire wolf, sniffing and studying and following the trail of possum, had climbed along the great dam of the architect to its very end; then swam underwater to the beavers' cave entrance that led to their den, entered their den, sniffed and peered wordlessly into the eyes of each beaver (including the architect's!), and then left them there, huddled in fright, to explore the rest of the mountain cave.

Then, upon exiting the mountain, he had followed the trail of possum away far, far to the north, until, finally, that last lonely Canopy

Connection observer at the northernmost Canopy Connection out-post had made note and relayed the news back south that the dire wolf, just as the possum had done weeks earlier, disappeared on the horizon of the great tundra where the Canopy Connection no longer connected—because the tundra rodents have neither a canopy nor the time and energy to spend on gossip.

But. The Canopy Connection of the great Northern forest, she told Zak, became abuzz in gossipy wonderment over the mystery of the fate of possum and wolf, especially that of the possum, whose actions and whereabouts were deemed of such great importance because of the notice given by the architect. During those days *before* the architect's lost talking possum had departed from the forest and made his way onto the tundra, every individual member of the Canopy Connection and even the body as a whole had indeed long waited in breathless anticipation, then, in respiring consternation, for any further sign of query from that "friendly talking possum, roving the countryside, seeking information." But no further query had been made by said possum.

"And," Pitsee told Zak, "after possum and dire wolf were long gone into Northern oblivion, and just as the buzz was about to wane—only slightly, of course—along came up that very same trail a ruby-throated hummingbird, two nuthatches, a redstart, and a spotted skunk who walked on his hands, making peculiar sounds like *oooo frremmit.* Yes. He and those birds walked, and flew, right up to the edge of the tun-dra and stopped, then turned around and went all the way back home along the same trail. But as far as your interest in Mungo—"

*Elbon!* Zak thought.

"I myself, Zak, have heard gossip that filtered through the Connection in very small trickles from the South, where it is very dry. And it is not passed around much at all by us rodents, because it is not good gossip—but simply awful, Zak. That kind of sad business we just do not talk about, you know. You should know that. You, Zak, and your story, are the sorts of gossip business we like to engage in—after notification by the architect, of course."

"So I was of no interest," he said, "until I was agendafied by the dam builder."

"You are correct. Now, do you really want to know?"

"Yes," he said.

"It is just awful, Zak. That terrible thing and its army just seem to skip from one dry region to another. Such misfortune. Many, many rodents have perished in the fires. Many, many squirrels have lost their homes and their young as well as their own lives. Birds' nests and the birds themselves, Zak, exploding into angry yellow flames. Fawns separated from their mothers. Poor spotted fawns with perished mothers, who were instructed by their mothers to lie still in their absence, lay still and were consumed by the hungry fires and turned to clumps of soot. Think of the terrible circumstances in which the reptiles found themselves. The turtles, Zak. Nowhere to go.

"So much displacement. Refugees everywhere. Families of cat, moose, weasel, raccoon—yes, possum, too—coyote, rabbit, wolf, skunk. Sundered. Even sans-pelages who like fire. Murdered. Some were eaten, which is understandable, of course, even to a flying squirrel; but not the wastage. So much waste. So much forest, vegetation of all kinds, fish, too. Murdered.

"Is there anyone who can save them? Anyone who can rid us of this beast? Anyone that powerful? Even the clouds and the rain are afraid to go near it, and the sky itself becomes confused and unfriendly."

*I cannot believe he and his birds followed me all the way to the tundra*, he thought.

"But, you know, Zak, in our region of the Connection, we just don't gossip about a thing so awful as this is. Indeed, for a certain period, we squirrels were successful in sparing our ground rodent kin of this terrible news. And I fully expect that's been the case in other regions, too. I do not consider myself at all lucky to have heard about these kinds of goings-on. I can assure you of that, sir."

*And why would a dire wolf follow my trail so far?* he wondered.

"What," she continued in her language, "did that owl mean? 'He has revealed himself to you.' 'He has done this sort of thing before.'

'The black jay spoke to you.' 'They trust me with their secrets.' What is that all about, Zak?"

"Dy contoe. Nah payshu," he said.

"Oh, well," she said in Rodent. "But in the meantime, congratulations, Genuine Possum Specimen."

# 36

"YEW SEE?"

"Actually, I don't see, Lost Track," said Sark. "Really. Just how do you expect me to see how O. Possum and Moksoos are like a duck? How do you expect me to see how they just vanished, as you say? Just flew up and away. Come now, you were fooled by a complicated scent trail. Perhaps the wolves' scent got you confused.

"How could O. Possum's trail have come from the north and from the south only to vanish with the scent of Moksoos, which itself came on the scene with no trail attached to it at all? And now you tell me you also smelled an owl!

"I do not see anything yet, Lost Track. But I am quite certain it all can be easily explained. Think about it. We will both think about it. The two of us will sort it out, my friend. There were simply too many scents for you to unravel at one time. Now. You see?"

"Noh. Lost Trok dew not see. Lost Trok know what Lost Trok know. Da ponter ant da possot iss like a duck. Ant a duck cannot be trokked."

"Well, then, that is all there is to it," said Sark. "There is only one thing left for us to do, Lost Track."

"Ant what iss that?"

"Keep on backtracking. We will surely do ourselves no disservice if we continue to the South. It must be the right direction, at least, in a general sense. Don't you think? Anyway, there really is no other direction for us to go. Now, is there? I am correct, and you know it."

"Moppy."

"Then let us carry on."

Without another word, Lost Track turned and proceeded once again in his southerly dire wolf trot; the great black pachyderm caravan followed behind.

"Lost Track," said Sark.

"What?"

"It occurs to me that there is something else I haven't told you. But I am certain it is of no great importance. I report it as merely interesting coincidence."

"Oh no," said Number Six.

"What?" asked the wolf without stopping.

"Well, once, a very long time ago, while residing at my wintergreen retreat to the North, I accidentally—and rather clumsily, I must say—stumbled and fell into a pool of very hot water. I thought I had surely come to my trail's end, for I was, I thought, in a helpless and hopeless circumstance. From the intense heat, my ears melted into their present size and shape, which, of course, is quite an advantageous condition after all—but never mind that. Anyway, I was certain that I was about to croak as I began to lose consciousness. Then, the next thing I knew, I was lying on the bank of the pool, in a perfectly healthy state of body and mind and staring into the green eyes of your black lion, or panther, as you say. He introduced himself and, in a blink, disappeared. It all sounds a bit mysterious, but if all the facts were known, I am certain rational sense could be made of it."

"Sok. Yew haf already fohgot. Lost Trok know tiss ponter. Lost Trok say that ponter iss different. But now yew haf fohgot."

# 37

YOU KNOW WHAT *their problem is. Don't you, Moksoos?*
*Why don't you tell me anyway?*
*They don't know what they are.*
Thank you.

*Your conversational skills, such as they are, seem truly ebb-tidal this evening—and you're looking at the sky again, Moksoos.*

Be careful what you say to the possum.

I am careful.

*I think you are, owl, but the other members of the Shadow World don't know you as I do. There are certain members who possess a keen sense for any disturbance in the balance, and words as well as actions may create a detectable anomaly. Whether they take an interest or not, those particular members will be aware of it. I can assure you they took notice when I saved that black mastodon from boiling and, perhaps as well, when I saved that possum from being eaten by wolves.*

You won't let the other members get the wrong impression, will you?

I would never break the trust, you know.

*Yes, of course, but you know that as long as I walk with the forest-folk, they look upon me with a certain scorn and—*

So they might not believe what you tell them.

I might not be very convincing. Besides, I have very little communication with the inside.

*The Shadow World is no more civilized than ours is.*

Perhaps you are right, owl.

*Surely, Moksoos, you can interfere just a wee bit without overly disturbing the balance.*

*I will think on it, but I will do nothing to disrupt the balance.*

*I would suggest that if that varmint keeps on converting his drones into medicine males and subjecting them to spirit-hunting bonfire deaths, his army, and his very power, will surely wither.*

*That would be nice.*

*But he has a great deal of power doesn't he, Moksoos?*

*Yes, it does.*

*Why don't you ever use Mungo's name in our discussions?*

*I find it distasteful.*

*Why doesn't it rain, Moksoos?*

*I do not know, owl.*

*But how could you not know? Moksoos! Do something!*

# 38

"So, how do *we* know, I mean, for sure know, what we are?"

"We are bobcats, are we not?"

"Well, yes, but the sans-pelages, by the mere exercise of their own logic, must call themselves something, just as we do by the practice of our bobcat contemplation."

"I believe that if they cannot see their own noses, Sena, then their logic cannot take them very far. It seems to me that they must take their first bearings from that point of reference, so they can see themselves from that unique perspective before proceeding. I thought you and Old Ok finally understood that. The prolongation of a wink can be quite educational if, in the process, one gazes upon one's snout."

"Yes. Yes. I like that theory, Opal, I think. But what if we somehow have it wrong and we really don't know what we are? Then we would be no smarter than the sans-pelages. Maybe they are even better off for not knowing. How do we know that they don't know more than we do by not knowing?"

"They don't know more by not knowing, Sena, because they don't know that they don't know. If they knew that they don't know what they are, then that might be another thing altogether. But if they don't know that they don't know, then it leaves them quite in the dark, dear. *We* know what we are. You and I are bobcats, Sena. Shinboo is a wolf. The jag is a jaguar. Old Ok is a bear. And we all know it. We are, *all* of us, forest-folk; sibling-offspring of the great symphony of the evolution of life.

"If you're alive, Sena, then you should know what you are, even if you haven't yet invented a designated vocalization for it. Normally, you should know what you are because you can tell *that* you are, that you exist. And you can tell where you are coming from because you use your nose as a point of reference. And from there, you can see how you fit into the scheme of things. You know, Sena, the balance, the symphony. That you fit into it as a wolf or a bobcat or a frog or whatever. I should think that that is the what of it. There, I've fed you knowledge on the hollow of a pelvic bone. Surely you get it now, dear."

"But, Opal, if the sans-pelages don't know *what* they are, then they must surely know *that* they are, don't you think?"

"Why, yes, Sena. I should think that. But without that basic point of reference, I'm afraid it is not good enough for them. They can gain all the knowledge about their existence that they want to, but it will not help them in the end if they miss the step that shows them how they fit into the scheme, the sphere of the living. I really don't believe they know that. Perhaps they knew it at some time in the past, but somehow, over the course of time and wayward evolution, they simply forgot it. Who knows?

"It may surprise you, but aside from this particular defect of their nature, I believe they are otherwise of a rather sound intellect. But their dreadful shortcoming alters their perception so much so that, with any new knowledge acquisition, they become more and more disconnected from what they are, which causes them to rely more and more on their familiarity of their surroundings. But their familiarity lies to them. They are not truly familiar with anything. So it's round and round—the more they try to learn about the complexities of the world, the more their identity eludes them. All because they missed one single basic step. Or they just forgot it."

"They forgot that they are sans-pelages, that they are forest-folk like we are," said Sena. "That's what you're saying."

"Yes. I believe it has totally slipped their minds."

"Maybe it is good to avoid the complexities and keep it simple," said Sena. "At least it does no harm. I wonder if Zak knows what he is by now. If he does, I'm sure he will keep it simple. And Pishiu—do you think he knows what he is?"

"I don't know. But I believe, perhaps, for the moment he does."

"And will he keep it simple?"

"I don't think so."

"Opal, do you think it is ever again going to rain?"

"I don't know anymore. It is becoming frightening. And what has happened to the Canopy Connection? There's not the slightest buzz. I haven't seen a single rodent, not even a chipmunk, for quite a while."

The pair sat alone in the meadow near the edge of the forest. A big, bright orange moon was rising over the treetops.

"There is the full moon, Sena. Look at it, and pay very close attention. I believe it is trying to tell us what we are."

"That we are bobcats?"

"Yes."

"One more question, Opal. What if the sans-palages finally learned to see their own noses, and the theory didn't work—that is, they didn't learn what they are?"

"Well. If that were the case, then their problem would be much deeper than I think."

# 39

"WHY DO YOU wander the tundra, Moksoos?"

"Stella," said Moksoos, slightly startled. He then walked out from behind the dwarf willows that he had thought provided some concealment. "I did not realize you had noticed me. But of course I should have known, shouldn't I? You with those eyes of yours. Dear, you are as lovely and elegant as ever. And for that, I cannot take my own eyes off you."

Stella glanced around at the flame colors of the tundra foliage, both near and far into the flat, distant horizon, and then she glanced at her four brown-and-white spotted offspring who were, in their own elegant fashion, curiously watching Moksoos. They were presently almost exactly the same height as their beautiful slim-billed upland sandpiper mother, who stood upon long, delicate yellow legs. Her slender neck was perfectly vertical in its typically perfect upland sandpiper posture.

"You're the sweet-talker, Moksoos. As always," she said admiringly. "But these eyes of mine are here primarily to see that my young are properly cared for, so they can have their own time to experience the beauty of the mystery of all this that surrounds us. I'm afraid the existence of my big dark eyes is not at all for the seeing pleasure of tall dark cats. But surely, Moksoos, you were not stalking me, were you? Whatever brings you here to the tundra?"

"In a manner, Stella, I *was* stalking you. I came here to ask for some information that I believe you might be privy to."

"You are quite the traveler, Moksoos, for you must have come a very long way to find me. But if you had waited only a few days longer, you would have had to stalk me in another prairieland in another hemisphere, and on another continent, for it is almost time for me to move my family to our southern region. But what is it that you seek, tall cat?"

"Stella, I have heard a rumor from an owl that perhaps at some point in the past, you saw a peculiar celestial event."

"Yes. That is true. I did not find pleasure in the experience."

"Please describe for me this event, Stella," Moksoos asked in a serious tone.

"Why are you interested in such matters, Moksoos? Why did you come so far to ask me about this?"

"Stella, I—"

"Never mind, Moksoos," she said. "You well know I trust your intentions."

"And I hope you well know that you have always had my admiration, Stella. That is why I have come."

"Moksoos, what I saw was an unbalanced sky. I am very old. Some say I am wise. If that is true, then it has nothing to do with my old age. I am not wise because I am old. And I am old only because I have had the good fortune to know when and how to avoid danger. I seem to sense its presence in a way that does not utilize touching or hearing or smelling or tasting or even seeing. I can trust this sense purely, and that is why I have no fear of your presence at this moment.

"When I saw the sky that day become unbalanced, this sense fiercely came over me in a way more powerful than I had ever felt it. The blue sky shimmered and flickered and danced about in the form of flames of cobalt and cerulean and azure. I suppose it should have been beautiful, Moksoos. But it wasn't. All that I could sense from it was foreboding and horror.

"But I saw more that was disturbing—much more disturbing. It was the golden eel against the blue fires of the sky. Its awful stare. It stared into me, Moksoos. It stared inside of me! Into the very core of my life. And I know that I will never be the same again.

"But the eel was not simply golden, Moksoos. It was of an unimaginably intense yellowness. It shot across the sky like a sans-pelage killing device. And then it was gone. Actually, it exploded in silence." Stella gazed out over the prairie. Then she glanced back at her chicks, then again at Moksoos. "I cannot put this scene behind me, Moksoos. I cannot put it behind me. I simply cannot."

Moksoos had been watching the distant tundra as the upland had recounted this story. He felt sadness for Stella, who did not deserve this burden, and a greater sadness by this news that he had come to dread. When he turned to look back at her, he could see the fear in Stella, the same fear that he had just heard in her speech, and he noticed that she was shivering.

The upland looked at Moksoos with her large eyes that now glistened with fear and melancholy. "I have had a good life, Moksoos. And I have few regrets. I am lucky. But I will always grieve the knowledge that my beautiful blue home above the prairie can turn into a monster."

# 40

THE RIVER'S DELTA had become wide, so the river, as if it were a giant flatworm afraid to leave the lap of the land, maneuvered the earth in great, gliding back-and-forth turns and twists, stretching the distance to its destination to many times that of the length of the delta itself. But recently, Zak had begun to follow the edge of the delta rather than the bank of the roving and reluctant river. He had made good time and had come very far. By now, many weeks had passed since he had left the great Northern tundra behind. His voyage had been efficient, direct, and swift; much more so than his months-ago journey to the North had been.

Now fall, with its cool, dry clarity of breath and sunny demeanor, was sweeping, as to a waltz, over and through the Southern forest; as always, it was a gala affair. But it was very dry. And in the breeze, the leaves crackled, many falling to the earth long before they would have in a normal, wetter season.

*I never in my life saw a sorrier cynic than is Sir Sark*, thought Zak as he trotted along on the dry earth. *And to think he said that cynicism is a virtue.* "A virtue of utmost charm."

*Sir Sark, you are not a cynic! Not a cynic at all.* "I regard facts as sinister creatures to be avoided at all costs." *Yes, Sir Sark, I believe you do.* "What one says is of no matter so long as one confounds—I assure you that wisdom is no virtue, but mystery certainly is."

*I understand that now, Sir Sark. Quite clearly, you old, blubbering, log-nosed philosopher. You were right. But it is not at all confounding. Perhaps Mystery is the chief virtue, Sir Sark. Or at least a very important one. And I believe it is as slippery as your Truth is. And it's quite shy, isn't it? Always hiding from one's familiarity. But blossoming everywhere—everywhere!—when one is attentive. O ubiquitous Mystery. No, Sir Sark. You are not a cynic. A disciple, perhaps. A connoisseur. A maestro! Yes. That is what you are. And I, Sir Sark, am a possum. O possum I am!*

> "As the sliding adder goes
> Homeward, home the river flows
> Southward, mouthward, homeward goes the river."

This he recited out loud as he kicked up dust from beneath the leaves along his way. He was in pleasant spirits today and looked forward to his twilight chat with little Pitsee, the flying squirrel historian, whom he had asked to entreat the Canopy Connection on his behalf for information regarding the whereabouts of Elbon, as well as those of Sir Sark and his fifty females. Who needs the services of a riddlesome owl when the great Canopy Connection is at your disposal?

Onward he went without slowing his pace, as he had done the day before and the many days before that, stopping only for sleep and conversations with Pitsee, relentless in his southerly migration. But as this day drew to its end and its shadows elongated, Zak came to realize that the river was no more. It had become a very large body of water, for now a great lake lay to the port side of his nose. And he came to the realization, also, that he was approaching his own Southern region.

The hairs on his neck prickled. *Is it really true?* he thought. *I have almost made it? I am in my home territory? Yes, it is the lake, alongside of which Sena and I traveled. Where Sena caught rabbits. Where Sika and Shypop told me about the fires started by that awful sans-pelage, Mungo. And somewhere ahead we met the grumpy tern who preferred to fish in privacy. And now the persimmon trees have a few ripe persimmons in them. How did it all happen? I am almost home. I have almost come full circle. I must find Sena and Old Ok and tell them what Pitsee said. Now, finally, I have important news to share. But where is Sir Sark?*

# 41

*N*ow, what is the matter?

*I had a conversation with Stella. I know why it doesn't rain. I now have all the answers to the riddle.*

Whatever do you mean, Moksoos? No doubt she is on the tundra with a batch of chicks. How could you have had a conversation with her?

*She and I were both on the tundra when we spoke.*

You went all the way to the tundra? But how? You have been with me all this time.

*Is that what you think, owl?*

Perhaps I should know better. I wish you had taken me with you. But I'm glad the rumor I passed to you bore fruit. Dear old Stella. She must have raised hundreds of lovely upland sandpiper offspring throughout the course of her many seasons.

*She is a wise bird, owl. But now she carries a burden because she saw something that she was not supposed to. Her equanimity is permanently damaged. But she is strong, and she will carry her burden well. You should have taken the rumor regarding her seeing a worm in the sky more seriously.*

So, why doesn't it rain, Moksoos? And what about this worm?

*There has been a lack of poise, a lack of stability, of the atmosphere, owl. It only happens infrequently, but I have noticed it enough to be satisfied that it represents a real disturbance of the balance, and I think it has had a profound effect on the weather in certain regions. And I think—in fact, I am certain—it is the Little One.*

*Who? What on earth and in the Shadow World do you mean, Moksoos?*

*The Little One wishes to play with the sans-pelage, to tease it, because it keeps demanding that one of us grant it spirit status. By stopping the rain, the Little One is helping it to destroy and conquer and thereby grow more powerful among its kin, which further aggravates its perceived notion that it must become a spirit. It is just the sort of activity that would bring great pleasure and entertainment to the Little One. Owl, I once spoke to you of certain members of the Shadow World who are keenly sensitive to any perturbation of the balance, especially if such an anomaly is the result of an action by one of the other members. Even a minor action, such as my rescuing the black mastodon, is considered by most members as truly meddling. And I agree. But of all the members, the Little One is, I believe, the most sensitive. Indeed, the Little One is known in the past to exit the Shadow World and investigate, even going on spying missions, tracking the member who did the meddling, so to speak. Tracking, spying, employing its rude and injurious stare in places it shouldn't, which, in turn, is in itself disruptive to the balance— hence the permanent injury to Stella. It is ironic that a member of the Shadow World who is so on guard to changes in the balance would yield to its own whimsy and create such havoc. I am all but certain that the Little One is well aware that it was I who saved the black mastodon and it was I who saved that possum from a wolf attack.*

*So, in the same way that we are spying on Mungo, your Little One is spying on you. Tell me, Moksoos, would the Little One give Mungo spirit status?*

*No one can bestow spirit status. We are what we are. The Little One is teasing it as a kitten teases its captured prey; however, in so doing, it is disrupting the balance and throwing the atmosphere into a conundrum. If this condition persists, I fear there is risk of damage to the equanimity of life on the great blue sphere.*

*This Little One, it is a sort of demi-spirit?*

*Oh no, it is a fully ripened one, only it is called the Little One; it is a Yellow—and when it exits the Shadow World, it usually prefers to take the form of a javelin with an eel's head. Or perhaps it is an eel in the shape of a javelin. I've never quite figured out the Little One's intent in this matter.*

*An eel? A javelin? A Yellow? So what are you?*

*An Emerald—and, as I seem to so often need to remind you—a cat.*

*I don't know what all this means, Moksoos.*

*Understandable, owl.*

*But I knew it was coming from inside, Moksoos. That someone is meddling with the sky. And I told you that!*

*I did not permit myself to believe that one of us would interfere so overtly. I have been proven mistaken, as it seems that the Little One is perfectly capable of the mischief. It seems I owe you an apology, owl.*

*Where is the Little One now?*

*Inside, I suspect.*

*What happens now?*

*I must have a word with it.*

*And you are sure it is this Little One who does not permit it to rain?*

*Yes. The other members know better. At least I hope so.*

*Why don't the other members stop the Little One? They must surely be aware of such a breech.*

*Because I don't think they really care anymore. As they rarely go outside, they seem to have lost interest.*

*In the balance, such as it is?*

*Yes, bird, what happens to the balance. I'm afraid it is sad testament to the state of affairs inside. It breaks my heart. It breaks my heart in the same way that Stella's heart is broken by the rude enlightenment that her blue-sky home can never again be trusted.*

*Are the other members bored with our world, Moksoos?*

*Familiar, I think.*

*So you are the only one who cares about the balance?*

*So it seems.*

*If you stayed inside, you could keep up with what the other members are up to.*

*If I stayed inside, owl, I'm afraid I would become like them.*

*Are you going to have to go back inside now?*

*That will not be necessary, owl.*

*Then all will be well when you have a word with the Little One?*

*No, not entirely.*

*Why not?*

*Because now the sans-pelage will have to be dealt with.*

*Well, deal with it, Moksoos!*

*The only way to deal with it is to take its life, and for a spirit to kill a mortal is too much interference. I will not do it, bird. How many times do I have to tell you that?*

*But you kill other mortal forest-folk.*

*When I do, I do it as a member of the symphony, and that is quite a different matter. It is for food or to win a mate or just plain jealousy or anger, but it is all part of the balance. But to kill as a spirit—as an outsider, so to speak—is disruptive, highly so, to the balance.*

*But won't Mungo lose his power if it rains?*

*Only for a time, but his thirst for spirit status will continue to be a temptation for the Little One.*

*But if you have a word with the Little One, he—it—will not be convinced for long?*

*Not as long as the sans-pelage craves spirit status, owl. I know the Little One will figure out some other way to give it power and continue to tease it. I believe that the Little One has now developed a taste for interference.*

*So Mungo must be dispatched.*

*It must be done, for that will be the last thing needed to put the Little One back into the proper frame of respect-reference.*

*Well, then, who will do it? I mean, who will dispatch Mungo?*

*That, owl, I do not know.*

*We have a dilemma, then, don't we, Moksoos?*

*Apparently so, I'm afraid.*

*Why so many loose ends?*

*Loose ends are part of the symphony, bird.*

*Why are you giving me so much information?*

*You said you were curious.*

*Then how will you do it? I mean, how are you going to "have a word" with the Little One, such as it is?*

*You will see.*

*Will it be dangerous?*

*It is the only way to restore the balance.*

*I am glad you are finally acting like a cat spirit; it is what we have been needing.*

*I am happy that you are glad.*

*As you said, we are what we are.*

*I wish only to be a cat, as I think you well know.*

*What are you going to do about Swrogah?*

*Restore the balance for her so it can rain.*

*That is not what I mean, Moksoos.*

*I know.*

*Why are you different from the other members, Moksoos?*

*Because I like what you are.*

# 42

"THEY CALL IT the what?" said Sark. "The Hoky Tree? What on earth is that, Lost Track? I thought you said the Hoky was a raccoon. Hoky Tree—where do you get this stuff?"

"Noh. Noh, Sok. Da Hoky Tree. Da Monostorry Tree of da Hoky. Yew see?"

"But how do you know this? How do you know what it is called? And how in the world do you know that there are exactly one hundred raccoons who live in it? I mean, they all wear masks and seem to look alike. How does one keep that many raccoons straight so one can be certain as to the accuracy of the count? With that many raccoons, how do you know that it's not one hundred and one? Or ninety-nine?"

"Lost Trok dew not tell a lie offer one raccoon, Sok. But why yew worry? Because yew haf fohgot. That iss why. Lost Trok know tiss possot. But now yew haf fohgot."

"No. No. I haven't forgotten that you know that possum. But I still do not understand how it is that you know the name of this big tree we are about to see. And that you know that there are exactly one hundred raccoons living in it. How do you know that it is called a 'mono starry tree of the hoky.' I don't understand. Are you sure this thing, this particular raccoon, is called a hoky?"

"Yoh. Yoh, Sok. They iss relogost raccoons, ant they haf a hoky."

"They are religious, you say? Then you must be trying to say hierarchy. Is that it, Lost Track? Hierarchy? They have one raccoon whom they call their Hierarchy?"

"Yoh! That iss exoctly what Lost Trok say, but Sok dew not lissin. They haf their Hoky ant da Hoky live int da Monostorry Tree."

"Yes. Yes. But how do you know this? I mean, it seems to me that you must have been speaking to someone along the way to find out about all of this, to know what O. Possum's real name is. And how did you figure out that the raccoons are religious without someone telling you? Do you understand what I am saying? I am certain that you would be very frightening to a raccoon, even if it knew that you are a vegetarian, which, of course, it wouldn't. So who was giving you this information?"

"Ah! Yew haf already fohgot."

"I know. I know. You know this possum. But that does not answer my question."

"Da cleeyews, Sok. Da cleeyews. Yew see?"

"Yes. My word! I see, all right! I see one big white oak. Look, my beauties! You don't see anything like that growing on the tundra, now do you?"

The mastodon formation folded into a noisy, chattering, rotating mill of pachyderms, circling the tree, inspecting, closely studying the scaly plates of bark of the grand old Quercus beast standing as the anointed potentate of all woody beings of the forest. The acorned sod crunched beneath their feet. One of the baby mastodons tried to enter the grand portal to its cavernous interior but was jerked back by its tail by a female elder.

Sark walked up to inspect the entrance, gingerly peeking into the darkness. He probed the wooden blackness with his trunk; after a moment, he pulled back, squint-eyed.

"Sticking your snout where it is not invited, are you?" said Number Thirty.

"Whew," said Sark, "it's a bit ripe in there. Come, my love, have a smell."

"I shall pass, thank you," said the female.

"That iss da Hoky," said Lost Track.

"What is the matter with him?" asked Sark. "Doesn't he ever take a bath? Do you think he is inside there, presently?"

"Yoh. Da Hoky iss int there."

"Are all the raccoons presently inside?"

"Why yew ask that, Sok?"

"Just curious, Lost Track."

"But Lost Trok dew not unterstant."

"What do you mean?"

"Yew want to know if alllll da raccoons iss int da monostorry tree?"

"Well, I suppose that is what I asked," said Sark. "Yes."

"Woll."

"Well, what?"

"Woll, why yew ask that when yew tink Lost Trok go to lie offer one raccoon?"

"I did not say that you would lie about, or over, as you say, one raccoon. I merely wanted to know how you know about these things. That is all."

"Sok. Yew haf already fohgot."

"I know. I know. The cleee-YOOOS."

Lost Track and his mastodon procession spent a little while breakfast-foraging the leafy greenery near the monastery tree before they all, once again, gathered and proceeded on their southerly way. And as they marched along, they all lapped up the gift of the scenery of forest life, its breathing botanical and zoological inhabitants of snail and moss and squirrel and shrub and snake and tree and turtle and fern and beetle and the many, many others; and they took the great pleasure of greeting these fellow passengers who lived at the same time that they lived, and rode in the same bubbly froth on the crest of Sark's great wave of life.

The woodland spectacle that passed by as they made their way did not go unappreciated. They took it all in. And in so doing, each felt thankful to be a part of it all. The notion of familiarity did not exist in a single member of the caravan.

When Sark became aware that the day was coming to its end, he felt a little stunned. He had been so engrossed in his expedition that time had slipped past without his noticing.

"Where do days like this go, Lost Track?"

"Days like tiss?"

"Yes. Where do they go? What happens to them? Can they ever again be found?"

"Lost Trok dew not know where they go, Sok. They iss like a duck."

After a time, they had crossed the hardwood bottom with its stream that, so many months ago, had almost taken the life of the possum they were seeking. They hiked on into the hills, where they passed the log where Grumley, the grumpy possum butler, had showed Zak that he was truly a possum and he could always remember it by inspecting his nail-less big toes. And it was only a little later when they arrived at a mountainous cul-de-sac, wherein lay a small lake created by a mighty dam crafted by the famous beaver architect whom the nonrodent forest-folk of the region knew as Quarral.

"Look, loves!" said Sark. "What a gorgeous dam. Magnificent detail! Where is the lodge? I don't see it yet."

"There iss not one, Sok. Da lotch iss part of da mountain. Yew see? Offer there."

Sark looked across the lake to where the winding dam joined the steep bank at the base of the mountain. "So they live inside the mountain. That is interesting indeed."

"Da beefer's name iss Quol. Lost Trok tink that beefer iss like Lost Trok. That beefer iss very good at what he dew. Ant his name iss like Lost Trok, tew. Not really his name."

"But how do you know all this, Lost Track?"

"Sok."

"Never mind," interrupted Sark. "My fifty dearests! You should go in for a swim. Take the little ones for a bath. And don't let them walk on the dam. We don't want to leave behind damages. Will you join us, Lost Track?"

"Sok. That dam iss very strong."

The big black tour group scattered and rumbled down the hillside to the little lake that soon became a roiling and rollicking vessel of fifty-one adult mastodons, sixteen babies, and a dire wolf. A maintenance crew of beavers looked on from their positions on the dam as the waves rolled and sloshed against its wooden infrastructure. They decided that the distraction of the raucous crowd and the presence of a dire wolf was good reason to leave their jobs to the next shift and call it a day, so they all quietly slipped into the water and swam into the underwater mountainside shaft that led to Quarral's den.

Sark and Lost Track walked out on the bank and shook themselves.

"Did you go inside, Lost Track?" asked Sark. "I mean, did you see this talented beaver?"

"Yoh, Sok. But da beefers dew not like da dar wolfs. So Lost Trok dew not botter with them."

"How did you get to the den? Where is this entrance to the inside of the mountain?"

"Da mountain iss full of da caves. Ant there iss a pig chomper, tew. That mountain iss very interestink."

"Caves and a what?" said Sark. "A pig chomper?"

"Noh, Sok. Pig chomper. Chomper!"

"Chamber? A big chamber?"

"Yoh, Sok. Chomper. But Sok dew not lissin."

"That so," said Sark. "Full of caves and a big chamber, eh? I would like to see it, Lost Track."

"Lost Trok tink iss dancherous foh da mastodonts. Da caves iss too narrow. Woll."

"Well, what?"

"Woll, there iss one cave that iss pigger. On da otter side of da mountain. But Lost Trok dew not know. Moppy iss dancherous. Yew see?"

"No. But I would like to. Let's all go. My females would like to see a cave. We don't need to stay long. I will watch them."

After Sark gathered up his crew, the formation filed tail-in-trunk along the side of the mountain above the lake and crossed over the ridge to the mountain's opposite side. Before long, they were all standing in front of the entrance to the shaft where Zak and Elbon had once been instructed to leave the premises by a most inhospitable bear.

"My dearests," said Sark, "Lost Track says that the mountain is full of caves, and there's a large room. But this cave here is the only entrance big enough to accommodate anyone our size. We must proceed with caution and take it slow. Does everyone understand?"

The hillside roared with the trumpeting sounds of agreement from the fifty females. Sark moved near the door of the cave and extended his trunk a little way inside to sniff and inspect; but just as he did, the same young mastodon who had earlier tried to enter the hollow of the Great Monastery Tree, ran past him, entered the cave, and disappeared. His mother stepped forward in a panic.

"It is all right, dear," said Sark. "I will retrieve the little beast myself. Everyone wait here."

With Lost Track following closely at his side, Sark slowly and carefully made his way into the cave.

"That one iss trobble, no?"

"Yes, he is," said Sark. "Reminds me of me a few hundred years ago."

They continued along on the dark and winding uphill grade of the shaft until, only by feeling their way, they found a steep wall on which was a shelf they would have to reach to continue their forward progress. It seemed to Sark that perhaps a long time ago the floor of the shaft on which they stood had somehow dropped to a level lower than the rest of the cave that lay ahead of them.

"There iss a bar that live here. Lost Trok tink that Zak ant Olbont meet tiss bar."

"Zak and who met the bear?"

"Olbont."

Lost Track attempted to jump to the next level of the cave, but the try was not a total success. His paws gripped the side of the ledge as his hind limbs dangled free, scratching the dusty wall beneath him. Just as he was about to lose his grip and fall backward, Sark lifted the wolf's rump upward to the floor of the shelf using his trunk. Then Sark reared up and began scrambling his way up to the next level where Lost Track was waiting. How did that little rascal make it up here? he thought, thinking of the young mastodon somewhere ahead in the darkness.

As Sark made his last push and stretch to attain his destination, he inadvertently jerked his head upward, forcefully raking the roof with his great tusks. From the insult, the roof shuddered, and rocks and boulders began to fall; then they rained down.

The mastodon and dire wolf bolted forward and quickly ran up the winding path to get away from the dangerous melee. On they went into the darkness, bumping into the walls of the twisting tunnel, just barely ahead of the cave-in that eventually filled almost the entire cave with rocky debris.

As they finally burst into the colossal chamber with its gray columns and burly stalagmite figures, they were followed by a blast of dust from the tunnel that was no more. It had made its last stand against gravity and now was transformed from a maneuverable cylinder of space into that which was the very substance of the mountain itself.

For a while, they rested, panting, in the gray, dusty dim light, waiting for the cloud to settle. When Sark caught his breath, he began walking around the great, dimly lit room, inspecting, to his amazement, its grand bestial formations.

"Would you look at these ghostly behemoths, Lost Track? How long it must have taken them to grow to their present size! Simply lovely. How I wish the females could see this."

Then they heard a thumping sound. It was the little mastodon trotting up to greet them.

"There you are," said Sark. "Well, little fellow, I hope you have found another route to the outside world, for we certainly won't be going back the way we came."

"Sok, Lost Trok tink tiss iss pig proplum. There iss no way foh yew to go out. Not event da baby. Tiss iss pig proplum, Sok."

"Well, then," said Sark, "go tell the females that we're at least still alive and in good health. I'm certain they must be in a dither by now."

"Tiss iss pig proplum," muttered the wolf as he trotted through the narrow corridor that coursed around to the other side of the lake, leading, eventually, to the cave entrance on the hillside above the beaver dam. It was where Zak and Elbon had, themselves, once exited and soon parted company.

When Lost Track reached the opening and its welcoming, waning sunlight, the wolf loped back around the lake and over the mountain ridge to where he found the female mastodons all frantically pulling and pushing rocks and boulders in a futile effort to reestablish the cave's existence. Already their dusty trunks were scratched and sore.

"There iss no way," Lost Track told them. "Da cave iss now part of da mountain. It iss a cave no more. But Sok ant da baby iss not hurt."

Without yet having a firm course of action in his mind, Lost Track decided that it would be prudent to make one small maneuver: Move the herd back to the other side of the lake and in the vicinity of the cave entrance that he had last exited and would, he figured, continue to use in order to stay in contact with the stranded Sark. It was, he thought, a maneuver that would save him from wasting so many of his tracks.

By the time he and the female mastodon herd got to the other side of the lake, it was night; but along the way, he had fashioned a stopgap strategy. Sark and the baby mastodon had been fortunate to be the victims of such circumstance in the company of someone who was an expert in the trade of tracking, someone who so thoroughly probed, so meticulously gathered, and so well remembered, the details of the scene.

The tracker wolf informed the anxious and attentive females that tomorrow he would take them to a place high on the mountain. Here would be an opening in the rocky ceiling of the great chamber where Sark and his young companion and offspring now whiled their time. And it would be through that rocky rent in the mountain that they would have to supply them with food and water.

Water? they asked. How would they get water up there? Lost Track further assured them that he was certain they would find a way to accomplish this feat, before adding that he was already considering that they might, as they carried food supplies, also carry mouthfuls of water that they could blow into the opening so it could run down the room's great columns for as long as the trapped pair needed it. Of course, he said, that was only a suggestion on his part—and that he was quite certain they would figure out something more "reasonopple" on their own.

After submitting these instructions and humble suggestions, he entered the nearby shaft and followed its long and dark way back to the great chamber that was likewise lost in complete blackness when he entered it.

"Lost Track. Is that you?" asked Sark.

"Sok, Lost Trok tink tiss iss pig proplum. Yew see?"

"Yes," said Sark. "I believe that I have caught up to your train of thought on the matter. A big problem indeed."

"Sok."

"Yes, Lost Track?"

"Lost Trok tink moppy yew need da hop."

"Need the hop?"

"Noh. Da beefers. Moppy da beefers hop yew. That Quol iss very smot beefer."

"Lost Track. How are you going to get this beaver and his crew to help us? They won't have anything to do with a wolf. And we don't even know their language. Besides, how could they possibly rescue a pair of mastodons from this place?"

"Zak know da langotch."

"Yes. That is a fine thing indeed, Lost Track. And where is Zak the interpreter when you need him?"

"Moppy Olbont can hop."

"Who is this Olbont, anyway?"

"Olbont iss a friend of Zak. Ant he has visited Quol ant hiss beefers. With Zak."

"This Olbont. He is a rodent, I take it."

"Lost Trok tink tiss iss da only way."


When the first dim light hit the chamber the next morning, Lost Track left the cave, gathered the females, and familiarized them with the mountaintop and its dangerous roof entrance. He informed them that they must approach the opening only one mastodon at a time, since the roof of the cavernous room was thin and might not take on the weight of any more than one adult pachyderm. But before they all went up the mountain, they each took a trunkload of greenery and a mastodon cheek-bulging mouthful of water so Sark and the young mastodon could survive the grind of life in the dark prison in which they now resided.

With these tasks accomplished, Lost Track set out for the South to find the neurotic little stargazing spotted skunk Elbon, whose scent trail the wolf had noticed ever since he and the mastodons had left the tundra and entered the northern forest. He made his way by rapid, efficient wolf travel, stopping only for water, vegetable matter, and short rests. And as he went the distance, he hoped as much as any dire wolf had ever hoped, that the little skunk had not, for one reason or other, disappeared from his old home ground.

Indeed, he had not. For when Lost Track arrived, late one night, to the patch of forest Elbon knew as his home, he heard a thumping and ooing sound coming from the top of his old polished sycamore observatory log.

"Oooo. Cridit. Cridit."

Of course, now, there was another problem. Elbon did not know Lost Track from any other dangerous, meat-hungry wolf. So Lost Track knew that he had to utilize the very best of diplomatic means at his disposal to coax the little skunk into going back north with him for the sake of forest-folk he had never even met. And the only way Lost Track could think of accomplishing such a feat was by slowly sneaking up to the log and pouncing on Elbon as if he were indeed prey to a dangerous, meat-hungry wolf.

# 43

ZAK HAD NOT followed the shore of the lake for very long at all. He had not even reached the location where, last spring, he and Sena were asked by the tern to leave his fishing territory. In his excitement to be nearing his home and his family of friends, Zak had lost patience with southerly travel altogether. He had decided to take himself a shortcut, and he found himself heading deeper and deeper into the vast forest that sprawled to the west of the lake, and as he traveled onward, he began arcing increasingly northward. A recalcitrant old habit was beginning to reestablish its authority. The magnet was summoned again.

Now, once again, nothing was familiar to him; but he thought that surely, somehow, he would stumble upon the old forest-field interface where weddings occurred and meetings were called. Or, better, he might happen upon one of his companions—Old Ok, perhaps, or Opal or Tal. Yes, he thought. Now that it was fall, maybe the red mastodons had returned from their summer grounds that lay somewhere far away to the west. Or the jag. Or Sena. By now, he had about given up on Sir Sark. He seemed to be indefinitely detained.

Late one afternoon, as Zak mistakenly continued northwestward and nightfall descended, so did his vigilant optimism begin to wane. And while it did, the old ponderous, forlorn sense of being lost again crept into his thoughts. He did not even know in what direction the lake was anymore.

He came to a small clearing that supported a grove of dead, dry salt brush, next to which stood a massive red oak elder. He sat down and leaned against its old, hard, and furrowed trunk and waited for Pitsee. The little flying squirrel, he thought, would surely give him a proper travel plan to follow the next morning; so he sat for a good while, waiting. And as he waited, he realized that he had not seen a single rodent for quite some time. Where were they? *And where is Pitsee? She is late.* He felt a little annoyed. Had he somehow temporarily disconnected himself from the great rodent communication system?

Then he heard a noise on the other side of the little salt brush meadow. It was a pair of coyotes. Zak thought it prudent to climb, so, without further hesitation, he began working his way up the vertical tough ridges of bark that the old tree seemed to provide for climbers such as he. The coyotes spotted him and ran over to his tree, leaping up, snapping and snarling for what they hoped would be their evening meal of possum. Well out of reach of the deadly coyotes, Zak looked down upon the ominous intruders and thought how this day had earlier been so bright and full of hope, but now turned so sour and mean. *And where is Pitsee? She is not coming*, he thought. *Not tonight.*

Since it was becoming quite late, he figured that the tree was his safest, and, with coyotes on the ground below, his only option for his place of rest tonight. So he continued climbing higher and higher, well into its immense crown, where he picked himself a broad limb and walked upon its surface distally, until, in the darkness, he found a branch on which to curl and anchor his tail. But it was not a branch of the red oak. It was a branch of mistletoe of a very large size—its span, one and a half times the width of the spread of a condor's wings; its shape was somewhat like that of a huge butterfly with its wings outspread, but three dimensional.

Zak did not realize this. Nor did he realize that, either because of drought or disease or age or the combination, the mistletoe was dead and had been so for a long time.

# 44

B Y THE TIME he reached the big chamber where Sark and the young mastodon waited, Lost Track was completely "oooed" out. The frightened Elbon had moaned the whole journey, and the wolf figured he would hear those pitifully anxious little sounds in his sleep for the rest of his life.

"Lost Track," said Sark, "will you please go back outside and tell whomever is constantly bombarding us from the roof with tree limbs to cease at once. And where on earth is all this water coming from? There must be a downpour outside."

"Sok. That iss yew females."

"I thought as much," said Sark. "But we have enough food supplies and water in here to sustain a whole herd of mastodons. Tell them to take a rest."

"That keeps them busy, Sok. So they do not worry so. Yew see?" he said, grinning. "Sok. Lost Trok want yew to meet Olbont."

Sark looked down at the timid little upside-down skunk.

"I thought you were a rodent, Olbont. Wait. Ah! But you are Elbon, are you not? The stargazer who doesn't know where he is?"

"Oooo."

"Yes," said the mastodon. "O. Possum. Zak. Zak told me all about you, Elbon."

"You don't know where you are either," said Elbon, in his little insecure voice.

"Well, now, isn't that interesting," said Sark. "I should have known that being stuck in the middle of a mountain would not meet your standard."

The little hand-standing spotted skunk gazed up at Sark's face for a moment. A nuthatch was perched on the bottom of each foot.

"Let's see, now," said Sark. "There were two other birds, weren't there? A hummingbird and a redstart they were, according to our possum friend. Are they missing?"

"They don't know where they are," said Elbon. "But they are not really missing. They have gone to their jungle hideaway far to the south. And they will not rejoin the nuthatches and me until the winter's snow is gone and the little white blossoms appear on the huckleberry bushes and I can see my handprints in the dust of pollen on my sycamore log, and there are new green leaves growing in the cottonwood trees and the wood thrushes call for their mates because they don't know where they are either. None of us do. And it's all verrry disturbing. Have you looked at the stars lately, Mr. Mastodon?"

"The name is Sark, Elbon. In fact, our mutual friend, Zak, calls me *Sir Sark*. But, as you can see, the inside of this cave is not a very fine perspective from which to gather astronomical inferences."

"Well, we must go outside tonight and have a look, Sir Sark," said Elbon. "Is Zak with you presently?"

"Olbont," interrupted Lost Track. "Sok ant da baby iss stuck int da cave. They cannot go outside. Yew see?"

"You are Zak's friend?" Elbon asked Sark.

"Yes. Of course."

"I don't see him. Why isn't he here with us?"

"We don't know exactly where he is presently, Elbon."

"No, you don't know. Nor where anybody else is, for that matter."

"Elbon," said Sark, "do you know the rodents' language? I understand that you and Zak paid a visit to the architect beaver."

"Yes."

"Excellent. Then you can help us, Elbon. Please go and explain to this fellow that there are two mastodons stuck in the mountain. If he's as scandalously clever as they say, then perhaps he can come up with a plan to get us out of here."

"But I don't know the language," said Elbon. "How can I ask him to help you if I don't know the language?"

"But you just said you did."

"No. I merely agreed that Zak and I and my hummingbird paid him a visit. But Zak did all the talking. I cannot speak to rodents."

"Olbont, Lost Trok tink moppy yew try anyway."

The wolf trotted over to the tunnel from which he and Sark had entered the great chamber and sat down beside its obstructed entrance. Elbon looked on with interest, recalling the time that he and Zak had fallen from a ledge somewhere in its dark interior and had landed onto the back of a bear. He wondered where the bear called home now that his cave was ruined.

"Yes," said Sark. "Do anything. Make hand motions. Whatever it takes to get this beaver to come and see our condition. If you can get him to come, then surely he will figure it out from there."

"But I use my hands for walking," said Elbon.

"Elbon," said Sark. "How do you think Zak would feel if you didn't help his mastodon friends out of such a mess as this is?"

"You can send the wolf."

"So you think that beaver is going to follow a wolf into a dark cave?"

"But I might lose my way."

"Lost Track can lead you part of the way to keep you from getting lost. And he can stay out of sight so the beavers will not be intimidated."

"I don't want to follow a wolf into a dark cave either."

"Elbon, are you going to help us or not?"

"But the bats don't like my birds."

"You can leave your birds with me. I will watch them until you return with the architect."

"But I don't want to go without my birds."

"Elbon, son. Go!"

"Oooo," said Elbon as he and his birds scampered and flew to the shaft that led to the lake side of the mountain where the beavers resided.

Inside the blackness of the tunnel, the two nuthatches perched, huddled together, on the bottom of Elbon's right foot which caused his upthrust rear end to sway from side to side, with an exaggerated tilt to the right side, as he traveled. Elbon continued until the tunnel led him downward and into the shaft that, with a turn to the right, brought him to the beavers' den.

After a little pause to build his courage, he quietly entered the beavers' room, and in the dim light, he could see several of them huddled around their master artisan. They were the shift supervisors attending a regularly scheduled meeting for their continuing instruction and education, for dam maintenance under Quarral's watch was a fluid pursuit, requiring an avaricious open-mindedness to the many new concepts so well provided by their chief officer. Presently they listened with great interest as Quarral discussed a visionary idea that had come to him the previous evening while exploring the forest neighborhood around his great dam.

For Quarral, the forest was a great source of inspiration, a boundless stockyard of data and materials from which, if in the right hands, even wisdom itself could be constructed; and both practical and theoretical applications could spring forth in multitudes like crickets on a damp summer's night.

But the new idea that he presently shared with the supervisors came not only from his last eve's forest excursion, it also came from a months-ago visitation to his den by a peculiar possum who knew how to speak Rodent.

Quarral had never gotten over his profound fascination with Zak's tail. He had seen possums before from afar, but the encounter with Zak was the first time he had ever seen a possum tail up close so he could really examine it, appreciate its strength and pliability, its weaving, serpentine properties, its nakedness, so much like his own tail's nakedness, but, otherwise, so different.

He was amazed by it. It had to be revolutionary. But how? And how could such a revolution be ignited? He wished he could borrow the tail of some friendly, obliging possum so he could take it for a short stroll around his dam and see how it might fit into the scheme. Then, when he had the answers he sought, he could, with an abundance of gestures of appreciation, hand it back over to its owner. But when he thought about how he would feel loaning his own paddle-appendage to even his brightest and most trustworthy supervisor, he saw the impracticality of such a notion. He had to shudder at the thought.

But ever since the previous afternoon he had no more need of such a gruesome impulse. For now, he had vines. Specifically, muscadine. Once again, the forest had shared a secret with the bright little beaver. But why had it been a secret up until now? *Why hasn't it come to me before?* he thought. He had seen the great muscadine vines clinging to the tree trunks and dangling from the limbs a thousand times. *Why, oh why, have I not seen their application? Too busy thinking about cutting trees to think of how to utilize the vines that lived in them.* He chastised himself. *Foolish! How like a possum's tail they are! But stronger and longer. Much, much longer. Perhaps not as pliable, but I can work around that.*

"Ay, ay yay voov," he said to his infatuated supervisors as he stood up and leaned back on his beloved paddle in awe of what the future of vine usage in dam construction might bring. But just as Quarral brought his hand to his cheek to strike his well-known contemplative pose, he noticed Elbon and the nuthatches timidly hiding near the chamber's entrance across the room.

"Per paa qazhoor!" he said in disbelief that, at that very moment, he was staring at the friend of the very possum of his inspiration. "And after all these months!" he said out loud in Rodent. How could it be? How mysterious. Surely the vine revolution was about to commence in grand fashion, for it seemed that fate herself was attending his supervisors' meeting and taking an active and most interesting role at that. Having the sense that destiny summoned, he peremptorily sauntered past his group of supervisors toward Elbon and the birds to greet them, at the same time inquiring as to the whereabouts of the possum and the hummingbird.

But just as Quarral approached his guests, Elbon began to lose his balance, his rear end tilting more and more to the right, and as it did, it rolled slightly so that when his hind feet hit the ground, his rump, with tail straight up, was pointed directly at Quarral's face. By now, having abandoned Elbon's right foot, the nuthatches had flown to a new perch near the room's entrance.

At first, Quarral froze, speechless. Then he panicked. "Nah! Nah! Veevooaylp! Veevooaylp!" shouted the beaver as he dove backward to land outstretched on the floor, his own flat tail raised in defense of whatever ominous attack was about to befall. "Veevooaylp!" he cried for mercy into the dirt floor of the cave. The supervisors flushed in different directions before they, too, hit the dirt to lie still with their eyes closed to give themselves the sense of being invisible.

Elbon lifted his hind end back to its upright position, this time without the weight of the birds on his right foot to cause him to tilt. He didn't know what to do or say now that his diplomacy had taken such an ungainly turn. He hand-walked over to Quarral, whose earth-ward-facing head was on the same level as his own and tried to get the petrified architect's attention.

"Mr. Beaver. Mr. Quarral."

There was no response.

"Mr. Quarral," said Elbon, "do you like to look at the stars at night?"

Quarral and the rest of the beavers remained silent and unmoved.

"I do. But it can be verrry disturbing," said Elbon.

Quarral turned his head slightly and opened one eye so it could see Elbon's little face just inches away.

"They tell us we don't know where we are, Mr. Quarral," Elbon whispered.

Quarral, of course, had no idea what the skunk was saying, but at least his voice did not seem to carry a threatening tone, so he slowly pulled himself up into a squatting position, eyeing, as unobtrusively as he could, the little spotted creature as he spoke in his own foreign tongue.

"I like to use my sycamore log," said Elbon.

The beaver blinked in silence.

"Have you ever looked at the stars from a sycamore log, Mr. Quarral?"

Quarral made a slight, neutral nod to try to appease the chattering weapon holder. To whatever politics belonged to the skunk, Quarral, at this moment, extended welcome with open heart and mind, practical diplomacy having, most courageously, taken full command of his senses.

The thrill of having a captive audience at his disposal had almost caused Elbon to forget the very purpose of his visitation to the beavers' den. But then he remembered.

"Mr. Quarral, Sir Sark and a baby mastodon whose name I don't know are stuck in the mountain. They need you to help them."

Of course, Elbon knew he wasn't getting his point across, so he leaned his weight onto his left hand and used his right to give a small tug at one of Quarral's ears. Then he walked toward the den's entrance and waited. Quarral sat watching for a moment until Elbon came back and repeated the effort. Curiosity was too much for the bright beaver, so this time he followed Elbon to the door. The nuthatches flew down from their rocky perch to light on Elbon's feet as he continued into the dark tunnel; Quarral now followed him with great inquisitiveness.

When the pair reached the great chamber, Quarral was startled to see its floor so strewn with the wet, leafy tree branches. *Is this the work of beavers?* he wondered. *How peculiar.* Then he saw Lost Track munching on the leaves at the end of an ash limb. In an instant, his tail reactively slapped the floor of the cave, and in that same instant, he recognized Lost Track as the dire wolf who had visited his den months ago. Elbon gave Quarral another gentle ear tug to calm his nerves, but by now, Quarral was more curious than afraid.

"Sir Sark and Mr. Wolf—" Elbon began.

"Da name iss Lost Trok," interrupted the wolf.

"I want you to meet Mr. Quarral. He is a very bright fellow, and I do believe he has his own sycamore log."

"I should imagine he has many sycamore logs, Elbon," said Sark. "Good day, Mr. Quarral. Thank you for coming."

Quarral recognized the greeting without the need of comprehending the words. He nodded pleasantly with raised eyebrows.

"Zhoorbau," he said, looking around curiously at the wet, limb-cluttered room.

"Elbon," said Sark. "Good work. Just look what you have done. You have brought back the famous architect beaver. But now what are we going to do with him?" he said, glancing over at Lost Track, who seemed suddenly distracted by a leafy hickory twig.

Elbon gave Quarral another ear tug and waddled over to the sight of the cave-in; then he turned around and started back over to where the beaver stood, but before he could reach him, the astonished architect was already on his way to the obliterated cave entrance to inspect the damages. The picture was clear—the mastodons were trapped. Quarral knew very well that that old entrance was where they had entered the great chamber.

"Teemaynaw vwoijer," he said as he placed his hand upon his cheek. Then, as the rest of the cave's company followed his movements, he began strolling around the room, looking at the walls and ceiling of the chamber and at the two mastodons; taking inventory, measurements, and seemingly plucking from the atmosphere whatever abstractions only the very bright are permitted to pluck.

Quarral looked up at the chamber's cracked ceiling as yet another tree limb came crashing to the floor. Water rained down upon the calcareous columns and burly figures to form vast puddles at their bases. He walked back over to Elbon who was also staring up in wonderment at the dome. Then Quarral lifted his hands and pointed them outward with palms up in a questioning gesture.

"I don't know what that's about either, Mr. Quarral," said Elbon.

"Elbon," said Sark, "it's my herd of female mastodons. They are dropping down food supplies for the baby and me, as well as for Lost Track."

"You mean that wolf really eats those things?" said Elbon.

"Yes, Elbon, Lost Track is—"

"Lost Trok iss wogotarian, Olbont," interrupted the wolf.

Quarral stood by, politely enduring the mysterious conversation's progress.

"What?" asked Elbon.

"He is vegetarian, Elbon," said Sark.

"Vayjur tooret," said the beaver as he turned to leave the damp and noisy room. But before he reached his exit, he stopped and turned, as if upon reflection, and stared at Lost Track for a moment. Then he walked straight to the dire wolf and gave him a tug to one of his ears.

"He wants you to follow him, Lost Trok," said Elbon.

When Lost Track and Quarral left the great chamber, Elbon followed them all the way back to the beavers' den. The little skunk was intoxicated by his success in giving notification of the plight of the mastodons to the famous architect. For the moment, even the stars were of secondary importance; and he took particular relish that upon Lost Track's and his entrance into Quarral's den, the supervisors once again hit the dirt in fright. Quarral quickly admonished their outstretched paddle-tailed bodies, informing them that there was no time for such antics when a vine revolution was about to commence.

# 45

"ODD," SAID SHINBOO, the red wolf female, "how it is that this time it's the absence of the hum in the trees rather than its presence that precipitates a council meeting. Rather boring, actually. But what do you make of it, Opal? Or might the jag have any declarations on the matter?"

"Nobody knows what it means, Shinboo," said Opal, gazing at the empty canopy above her head. "But remember, dear Shin, boredom generally implies the absence of calamity."

As the sun was already beneath the horizon, the fall air at the forest-field interface was chilled and so dry that it was unlikely that dew would visit the big grass clearing on that eve.

"My declaration on the matter, wolf, is that it is not a good sign," said the jag. "I fear that something has frightened the rodents into mass migration."

"That is what I think about it, too," said Sena. "It's very peculiar. And disturbing."

"They found out about something. Something that we don't know," said Old Ok. "Something that caused them to leave the premises in short order. For only a couple of days ago, the Connection sounded like a cicada convention—it was difficult for an old bear to get in his nap."

"Maybe the rodents went to live by the big lake," said a gray fox. "And my guess is we will all join them if it doesn't rain soon. I believe there is something very wrong with our weather. This is no mere drought. Something is the matter with the sky itself."

"Nothing is ever going to be settled when there is only unsettling conversation about," said a young raccoon.

The meeting had been small to begin with and soon disintegrated. Of late, many inhabitants of the community had begun to avoid such gatherings, electing to stay at home instead. There were no more weddings, and the meetings were becoming depressing, for the long and oppressive drought of the region seemed to be the only surviving topic of discussion; and no one had any ideas for a solution for the drought except, perhaps, abandoning the region. And no one thought they would ever again lay eyes upon their poet-possum, so no one would ever get married in the future.

The very reason for council meetings in the first place was beginning to diminish, especially now that there was no more Canopy Connection to ignite a sense of urgency to call one. The excitement over the evil sans-pelage chief, Mungo, had also seemed to dissipate. There had been no news of him for a long time; not really since the time that the jag had left the region to seek out the famous black lion, Moksoos, and Zak had left the region to seek out information from other regions (nobody ever knew exactly why) and had never returned.

When the herd of red mastodons had returned a few weeks earlier, Big Tal, the young bull, said that there was no such dry weather in the region of their summer feeding grounds—that this horrendous drought, it seemed to him, was presently restricted to this region only. In fact, seeing that survival might be challenging if they stayed near the forest-prairie interface, the mastodons had, after a short reacquaintance with the community, continued on to the big lake at the eastern edge of the region. At least there they would not go thirsty.

Long before the coming dawn, Opal, unable to sleep at all that evening, quietly went to pay a visit to the jag, who also couldn't sleep and even seemed to be expecting the call.

"I know what you are thinking," said the jag. "And I'm afraid it would be more dangerous than ever."

"I should go alone," said Opal. "But I do need to go. Besides checking on my Pishiu, I might gain some information that we all need. Maybe find out some reason for the disappearance of the rodents."

"I don't like it, Opal. Its mother knows about us. The whole camp might be waiting this time."

"I don't think Pishiu's mother would want us harmed," said Opal. "I saw into her eyes that day by the stream. I trust her."

"Opal dear, the species is far too distracted for any of its individuals to be trusted. I do believe you know that."

"I will go alone," she said.

"No," said the jag. "You will not go alone. Sena and Ok and I will go with you, as always."

"I wish Moksoos were here," said Opal.

"What could Moksoos possibly do? He is just an old cat."

"Still, I do wish it. Don't you?"

"He would be completely worthless," said the jag.

"Why didn't he come back with you?" asked Opal.

"He said he doesn't like to interfere."

"Interfere with what?" asked Opal.

"I don't know, and I don't want to talk about it," said the jag.

"You really do wish he were here, don't you?" asked Opal.

"Opal! Madam!" called Old Ok from somewhere in the darkness. "We should be going now. Tomorrow will be here before we know it."

Opal and Swrogah were startled by the words. It seemed that the foursome had all been insomniacs that evening and thinking the same thing; so there stood Sena and Old Ok, ready to gather the two female cats and go to the little sans-pelage village to pay a visit to Pishiu.

Without another word, the three cats and the bear loped across the prairie and into the dark woods to the north. By the time the sun was in the sky, they were very near Pishiu's home. But as they drew nearer to it, each silently felt a growing, and very peculiar, urge to turn around and run as fast as possible in the opposite direction. And they noticed the woods were filled with smoke.

# 46

MUNGO HAD COME to believe that those whom he had previously called to medicine male duty were not made of the clay it takes to go into the bonfire and drag back a kicking and hassled spirit to meet his demands. So this night, he decided to use one of his generals for the job.

A most grim and frightened general, shaved completely bald and painted completely white, half-crazed from being held and force-fed a peculiar herb, was summoned away by the cold-blooded chief himself, who pushed, with his long, jagged stone dagger, the trembling pale sans-pelage deep into the night forest.

Mungo had shaved—scraped, actually—the big sans-pelage, himself, by clutching the poor maniacal beast by the throat with one powerful hand and squeezing off his air when he tried to fight. Laughing as he worked, the burly chief had used his flat, serrated-edged flint dagger for the job, which left long abrasions that oozed orange through the white dye that covered the terrified male's naked body.

But, except for the replacement of medicine male by the general, this night seemed no different from a whole procession of previous nighttime events. For it was exactly in this fashion that the powerful and invidious chief had, with whimpering medicine males in tow, disappeared from his generals late at night only to return the next morning alone and infuriated and still completely mortal, his scarred and wrinkled face bearing glazed, bloodshot eyes blazing hatred for the neglectful spirits, especially the one who resided in the flame.

That one, in particular, was becoming the focus of his fury. And it was exactly this pattern of boiling jealousy and rage in Mungo that so intrigued one mischievous member of the Shadow World, so much so, that it incandesced pure yellow light—which was, of course, the Little One's way of expressing great pleasure.

All totaled, there were twelve medicine males who had mysteriously disappeared and were never heard from again. Of course, the generals knew the routine with the medicine males, at least regarding their disappearance (for they could not guess what happened to them); and they were, tonight in particular, growing nervous and discomposed with such a suspicious state of affairs. But none questioned, or even dared discuss with one another, the actions of their leader who, on this particular eve, had his biggest ever plans of marching the next day, alone, behind his army's plunder and into the next conquered, burned-out sans-pelage holdings, this time glorified by spirit status. His army would be waiting for him: Mungo, the war spirit.

Tomorrow would bring the perfect conditions for burning and slaying and the taking of slaves and feasting, as an earthly war spirit chief, on that grand youth-and-power-giving flesh of the young ones. For, as a spirit, he thought, the power of the youthful brains, bones, and flesh he would chew would be many times richer than ever before; and, perhaps someday, it would enable him to gain enough strength to conquer all the spirits of the Shadow World that the old, and dead, medicine males used to talk about.

He salivated as he poked and bloodied the back of the naked and hysterical general staggering before him, reeling from the herbal chemical that flushed through his brain as might some evil suffusion of noxious fumes from some other, forlorn world. On they went into the night, winding in the darkness through the vines and trees and shrubs, along the darkened floor of the forest until they reached a little clearing thickly infested by dead, dry salt brush. It was the perfect location with the perfect fuel for an intense bonfire.

Mungo set the psychotic general to work gathering the brush and packing it tightly into an explosive mass of brittle wood. With the general busy at his work, Mungo sheathed his dagger into a fold of rawhide that hung from the back of his cougar-skin loincloth as some fearsome appendage of death. But from time to time, out of impatience and the unquenchable demand for his own show of authority, he would remove the great knife and whack the sans-pelage on the back of the head, causing him to fall to the ground but daring not to question or even look back at his frighteningly volatile chief.

Crazed by the herbal drug that pounded his senses and by fear as well, the general could only hope that his work, whatever it would be this night, would indeed help to convoke a spirit of the flame; for he trusted his fate more to that unknown Shadow World commodity than to the hand of Mungo. He reached to the ground to pick up what he thought was a large limb. He pulled hard to lift it, but it would not move, for it was an above-ground root that ran across the brushy clearing. It was one of several, in fact, that originated from a massive red oak that stood at the clearing's edge; many of the limbs of its great canopy extended far out from its trunk to cross the airspace of the clearing.

Mungo, agitated by the stupidity of his general tugging at a large, living, and well-lodged red oak root, whacked him three more times on his bald scalp, leaving behind gaping, bleeding lacerations. The dazed and bloodied sans-pelage staggered back to blindly continue his task of pulling and piling salt brush until, finally, a large portion of the clearing had been denuded of the shrub and the immense brush pile was in place.

As the general plucked more bushes from the clearing's perimeter, Mungo squatted and, with his great dagger and a stone, flint-started a little fire of twigs and papery bark and crisp leaves; then he carried it to the pile. Cupped in his leathery hands, he carefully inserted the little flame deeply into the base of the pile, adding still more splinters and dry bark. Soon there was a roaring blaze, and the general was ordered to commence dancing and chanting to the spirit in the flames. The chief then sat down on the ground behind him and watched with great anticipation on his large and wicked face.

The orange-and-yellow flames licked high into the darkness above the two sans-pelage beasts. And as time went by, the general became more and more engrossed in his dancing and singing as the drug seized his consciousness and carried it to some peculiar land between his world and that of the supernatural. Mungo had seen its effect on the medicine males, how fervent it made them in their supplications to the spirits, but he did not partake of the medicine himself. It was the medicine males' task, and tonight the general's, to engage in invocation. Mungo would be treated as nothing less than an equal by whatever being came out from behind the flame to visit him, for he was genuinely fearless in the quest.

A stiff breeze stirred the red oak's limbs high above the fire as Mungo sat and watched while the noises and movements of the general's dance reached their febrile latitudes. But it did not take long for him to reason that, as well as the fervent general went about his tasks, it was not enough. The spirit wanted another sacrifice. It wanted his general. Now.

So Mungo, once again furious with the fire spirit's insult, arose and walked up behind his general and slapped his large right hand on his back, and in one powerful grip of bloody skin, he raised the general completely off his feet and tossed him into the flames that so brightly licked back and forth in the wind. And just as the wounded and screaming sans-pelage crashed into the main body of the blaze, a dark, bird-shaped phantom with wings outspread wider than the width of a condor's entered the fire from above to land on the back of the burning sans-pelage. Then, instantly, in one wobbly jump, it exited the fire as a great butterfly-shaped lump of exploding mistletoe sparks moving directly at Mungo.

The chief was startled into taking a step back from the fire and withdrawing his flint dagger from behind him, but just as he did, he tripped over one of the great red oak roots and fell backward upon his dagger. The trajectory of the dagger's flat, flint body carried it, slicing and tearing, through the bone of his spine, completely transecting his great abdominal artery and penetrating several other vital structures, before its tip ended as a ruby belly edifice that Zak had to sidestep before he could continue to blindly scurry across the chest and over the face of the quivering and exsanguinating sans-pelage chief. And it was at just this instant that Zak decided that the great parasitic branch of dead and burning mistletoe was no longer of any use to him, so he deposited it on Mungo's head before continuing his way on into the dark forest.

Maintaining their usual surveillance of Mungo's peculiar late-night activities, Moksoos and the great horned owl had observed the scene from a limb in the distance. For a few moments, the owl and Moksoos were surrendered to speechless disbelief. Finally, the owl spoke out loud, "Well, sir, it looks as though our possum has taken care of half of your duties."

"I cannot believe it," said Moksoos. "I cannot believe it! And I didn't even know he was in that tree. Why did he wander away from the lake? Do you suppose he is lost again?"

"Moksoos," said the owl, "tell me: Will this most unexpected event anger the Little One?"

"Oh yes," he said. "It already has. And I now predict that the Little One wishes to have a word with me for saving that possum from wolves."

Somewhere deep in the dark interstices of the world of the spirits, the yellow glow of the Little One flickered and failed.

# 47

WHEN THE RED disk of the sun arose on the little sans-pelage encampment that was home to Pishiu and his mother, smoke was in the air, drifting and curling around the tree trunks and through their great crowns. The blue-gray shafts of the smoky light leaned toward the east, acutely, as if drawn by some invisible force. The forest-folk, including the birds, began leaving the eerie village vicinity, immediately, almost in unison, as if they, too, had been sternly instructed to do so by some mysterious coercion.

The little pool, alongside the stream, that had supported the many tadpoles and frogs and the mushy bottom that Pishiu had tried not to disturb because of the wealth of tiny living things it harbored no longer existed. All that was left in its place was an elongate depression of cracked, dried earth in which stood the yellow-brown skeleton stalks that had once supported so many graceful blossoms and vital-green leaf blades of iris and cattail. The cracked depression sprawled in parallel with a likewise elongate sandbar and the paltry trickling remains of what once was a vigorously flowing creek that, according to the sans-pelage elders of the camp, had never been so small.

The smoke that suffused the air of the forest and encampment this particular morning was not that of the little village fire; it was attack smoke. The members of the encampment had known this event was coming for many months. There had been many consultations among the chief and the elders and the zebra-striped medicine male with headdress of moss and sinew and turkey feather shafts.

Of course, they had done all that they could do. They had organized as well as their species was able. They had prepared for battle as well as such a little group as theirs could. Everybody had been warned; everybody expected that this time would come; everybody knew the plan, which was to stand up and defend their small territory of the forest that they thought they had sovereignty over.

They believed it was their only choice. They had long ago excluded, without even much discussion, the consideration of marching themselves far, far away, as refugees, to another location in which to live out their days, but, in so doing, begin for themselves the precedent of living as prey, running away in fear from predators—predators of their own species at that. They would not stand for such a thing. They would stand up for themselves and face whatever fate the hideously corrosive aspect of their own species had to offer. This small part of the great forest was their home, and there they wished to stay, no matter what.

Whether it could be said that they were caught by surprise or not on this dry and hazy morning was not particularly germane to anything. The smoke was simply there, and with it, Mungo's army. The warriors were everywhere in great numbers, snatching the young and the females, skewering the males, old and young, the would-be defenders, with their spear devices; smashing the heads of the old females with oak clubs or the stony protuberances of their daggers.

Pandemonium overtook the members of the little village almost at the commencement of the attack. When it came to birth, as a hellish brood parasite, it quickly murdered its less developed, feeble sibling-nestling, war. So there was almost no fighting that day, and no war. Only pandemonium was to survive. And it all went according to Mungo's strategy. He did not need to be there to oversee the fruition of his design; his army, by now automatic and efficient, was moving at its own hideous momentum. He, according to plan, would presently be undergoing a metamorphosis into a war spirit by the aid of a haggard, and surely frightened, fire spirit. His next great leap of power would be at hand.

But, of course, by this time, a small flock of vultures was what was at hand, visiting Mungo's carcass, each member puzzling over the way this foolish sans-pelage had met his demise. They discussed several theories as they commenced to dine.

Pishiu's mother had taken her little offspring by the hand and run to the stream where they could move quickly along its sandy bed, to where they did not know, only some faraway place to hide. But they had not slipped away undetected, for several of the males of Mungo's army had spotted them, as did one of the generals who regarded the two as particularly valuable specimens for capture. For he already envisioned soon pleasuring himself with the pretty young female; and her male young, of course, would surely be the finest of fleshy prize of youth and power for his leader, who, perhaps, would share with him the precious victuals.

So a chase was on that soon caught the attention of more warriors and generals. Some of them ran along after the frightened pair, while others, seeing that the mother and her young seemed to have chosen to remain in the streambed, made a detour through the woods to shortcut the winding stream and to cut off the frightened pair.

As Pishiu and his mother desperately fled, they were surprised to be joined by the three cats and the bear, who appeared at the streamside, as phantoms, to lope along by their side. And they, too, soon realized that a dangerous chase was on, that Pishiu and his mother were close to becoming prey to the many males now closing in. The warriors and generals were perhaps a bit surprised themselves that they had, during their pursuit, flushed a bear, two bobcats, and a jaguar. This was a fine hunt indeed.

Sena pulled ahead of his little group, looking from side to side for a place for them to make a break into the forest, for he knew that the open streambed was not an option for safe retreat much longer. Soon they came to a sharp bend in the stream with a steep bank that arose as a high, dirt bluff. Jutting out from the dirt face of the vertical bank were many exposed roots provided by the tall trees on its top. As they were about to go around the bend, they were met by an army of warriors and generals who had taken the shortcut through the woods to meet them. In desperation, they ran back to the tall bank that became the backdrop of their entrapment.

The powerful cats could have climbed the roots of the bank and escaped, but Pishiu, his mother, and Old Ok could not carry out the maneuver. Of course, Opal would not leave Old Ok and Pishiu behind to die alone, so she decided to make her stand. Sena, likewise, would never contemplate leaving Opal, or Old Ok; and the jag would never consider abandoning a fight and her pride, so she, too, held fast to their territory.

So the two bobcats, the jaguar, and the elderly bear crouched, ears back, snarling, and faced the oncoming sans-pelage attack, as Pishiu and his mother crouched in the dry streambed and leaned in fear against the dirt wall of the tall bank. Presently the line of angry and hungry-looking sans-pelage males began to move upon them in a semicircle of terror. Their number had by this time become so large that they had no fear; not even of a bear or a jaguar.

"This is it," said Swrogah.

"With friends like you," said Old Ok, "my life is fulfilled. But I sure would like to grab the throat of one of them. Just one. That would give me peace at the end."

Suddenly, there was a loud roar that came from the top of the bluff. The sans-pelage predators looked up above their prey to the crest of the bank. And there stood Moksoos, calmly looking over his audience below him. Then, in long strides, he leaped down the face of the bluff to the sandy streambed and stood motionless. The sans-pelages stood wide-eyed, in fearful amazement.

"What are you doing here?" asked a surprised and flustered Swrogah. "Why did you decide to come now? You old fool. You are going to be killed with the rest of us!"

Moksoos turned to the jag, smiling. "My dear Swrogah, what is this? I remember very well your telling me once that I would never grow old. And now you greet me in this way."

"Well, you are not going to grow any older now," she said.

He looked out over the motionless, wild-eyed sans-pelages, and then looked back at the cats and the bear. "Look. Do you see that? I have their complete attention now. But it won't last for long. So I am going to have to ask you to kindly leave the premises at once."

"I am not leaving you," said Swrogah. "And Old Ok can't climb this embankment."

"I will see to his safety," he said. "You must trust me now. That is all, Swrogah."

"I will not leave them, Moksoos," said Opal. She looked at Sena who nodded to her his approval and allegiance.

Moksoos again turned from the stone-faced sans-pelage crowd, this time, to stare piercingly into Opal's eyes. His green-eyed stare was powerful and unexpected, and influential.

"Now, you will do as I say," said a very serious Moksoos. "I will attend to the safety of your friends. You and Sena will follow Swrogah. She will lead the way."

The three cats began climbing the dirt bluff with the jag in the lead. When they reached the top of the embankment, they trotted into the forest as directed, without saying a word, without looking back, and without comprehending why. They just went, in much the same manner as the forest-folk of the vicinity had left the premises at sunrise.

"What are you going to do, Moksoos?" asked Old Ok, his curiosity outweighing his fright.

"Well, Ok, what I am going to do is nothing. Nothing but wait here until they become familiar with me and kill me. You should know by now it is their way."

"I don't think I like the sound of that," said the old bear.

Moksoos moved his hindquarters downward to sit rigidly on the sand. He sat silently, waiting. Old Ok was now speechless. The ominous crowd, presently practically all of Mungo's army, began to stir and come to life, making sounds of confusion that were soon followed by the sounds of aggression.

They began to slowly and cautiously move in to inspect this famous cat spirit of legend. *What will it do?* they wondered. *It doesn't move; it just sits there. Is it going to lash out or not move at all? It is not so fearful as we were told. Not really much bigger than a jaguar. Looks to be elderly, gray-faced. So this is really the cat spirit—just sitting here. Captured, perhaps? Somebody should do something. Are we all going to just stand around? Who here is afraid of this thing with the cracks in its tusks? It needs to be tested. Somebody should kill the bear. See what it does then. No. Take the woman or the boy. Take the woman. The boy will follow her. A good idea.*

Somebody tried. One of the warriors began to slowly approach the female who was nestled hard against the dirt bank with Pishiu. Moksoos trotted toward the warrior, snarling, and it moved back into the crowd. There was a small commotion as some of the warriors began to back up, while watching closely the movements of the tall green-eyed cat, who again sat down to remain motionless.

But the warriors quickly returned to their former position. *Is that all it will do? It is acting like any other old cat guarding its meal or its young or its mate. There is nothing special about it. Doesn't look like much of a fighter at that. Now, does it? It let one of us almost approach the female and return to the crowd unharmed. It hasn't killed. It doesn't have a taste for battle. It is old. It is captured. Somebody should approach it. See what it does. Stick a spear in it. See what it does then.*

Somebody did. Somebody who saw and seized that last opportunity to be the one who slew the great cat spirit while it still had some, though apparently not much, life left in it. Somebody who would become forever locked in legend, forever respected, forever the name named whenever the question would arise from the young ones as to who among us killed the mighty cat-member of the spirit world.

But, no. They would not need to ask such a thing, because that name would have been driven into their thought processes in their infancy. It would be the first lesson in the life of every sans-pelage in the future. The most magnificent benchmark of all of sans-pelage history—the slaying of an evil spirit. For it wouldn't take long for today's events to become so embellished and twisted so as to delete the small detail of the cat spirit being nothing more than a gray-faced, old black cat with funny-looking eyes and a peculiar dental problem.

So the warrior charged forward, courageously, and in one fluid athletic motion hurled his spear into the side of Moksoos's chest.

But then something strange happened. The atmosphere seemed to shudder. For, as the sharp, ragged stone point entered Moksoos, fracturing feline scapula and ribs, time slowed, profoundly, so all could see the spear slowly move with grinding momentum, driving through the chest, tearing, perforating, extending completely through to break contralateral bone, and, tenting contralateral hide, to exit, red-headed and become again a complete and viewable bloody spear.

Old Ok's silent and confused amazement had now become a gloomy, ponderous heartbrokenness. Pishiu sat in wide-eyed horror; his mother's face was turned and pressed into the dirt wall.

Moksoos never moved. He sat with red rents on both sides of his chest from which now appeared scarlet beads, then teardrops, of blood that glistened in the light; then red rivulets began pouring to the earth. But the sand did not soak up the blood, for each drop, as it hit the ground, turned into a hard, red marble-like sphere. The spheres began to stir in the sand and roll along the ground and around Moksoos's rigid body.

The spear, as it floated slowly in the air, now was no longer covered with blood; it had become a shining, bright yellow lance with scales and, curiously, the head of an eel. No one had ever seen such unearthly clarity of yellowness before, for it seemed as if it was of the purity of exact wavelength from the exact center of the spectrum of yellow light. The glowing shaft, as if now a pliable structure, began to bend upward toward the sky, curving above Moksoos's head until it became straight again, with the perfect yellow pointed nose of the eel head directed straight between his eyes. And the eel's eyes, black and foreboding, stared deeply into the eyes of Moksoos, penetrating his being; searching, violating. But Moksoos never blinked.

As the blood poured forth from Moksoos's chest, more and more red marbles formed in the sand, rotating en masse. And as they accumulated in greater and greater abundance, they swirled faster and faster around Moksoos. They began to rise and form a spinning cloud that became an opaque rotating blur, blocking out completely any evidence of cat form inside of it. The audience stood in fearful shock at the spectral yellow spear and red funnel cloud form before it.

The twisting funnel began to grow, and as it sucked in the smoke and ash in the air from the burning forest, it became a loudly cracking, then roaring, tornadic mass that turned from red to the blue gray of the smoke, and then it began to emit a glow that was green.

Then the spinning opaque object mutated into an enlarged, emerald cloud apparition of Moksoos. It arose skyward, with the yellow light-emitting javelin moving in tandem so that in one synchronous motion, the two forms, cat and spear, faced one another as they rose. Then, the Moksoos cloud again mutated. It became enlarged to massive proportions, blossoming explosively into a monstrous cloud mass, expanding, billowing, gaining in darkness and body, spreading over forest and prairie, blotting out the sun and the yellow spear as well, until all was darkness.

Then the lightning came. It came as no one had ever before seen it; as great blinding arborous bolts and fireballs of yellow followed by those of emerald, dominating the sky and the earth below; the great forest reflecting the yellow and emerald flashes of that heavenly ferocity lingering so violently above it. The thunderous shock waves it produced were so powerful that they knocked Old Ok and Mungo's army off their feet. The ground shuddered, and clods of dirt fell from the bluff's wall down onto Pishiu and his mother. It became difficult to breathe, for the air was thick with the odor of sulfur.

Once again, pandemonium dominated the now yellow-green strobe scene of the world of the sans-pelage. Mungo's army was broken into visionless fleeing animals having no taste remaining for their old allurements.

In their blind fear, they tripped over objects on the ground, ran into trees and into each other. They became starved for air and for their own sanity, sometimes spearing one another or stabbing one another with their daggers. The army was driven into a complete mad disarray by the punishing, thunderous concussions and the yellow and emerald bolts of unearthly luminescence.

The storm raged on. Yellow then emerald went the tormented sky that seemed as if it might itself crack and explode outward and into the great black space that resided outside of the sphere of life. Hours went by before, finally, the powerful thunderclaps began to subside. But the eerie yellow and green flashes continued with ferocity.

One of the Mungo's panicked generals, who had tripped on a root and fallen hard to the ground, lay for a long spell in a semiconscious state. When finally he tried to rise, he was pushed back to the earth by the bare foot of the old zebra-striped medicine male with the headdress of moss and sinew and turkey feather shafts. The general looked up and saw in the flashing spectral light a great horned owl perched on the medicine male's shoulder. The old medicine male bent over the frightened general and, with one hand, pulled him upward by his throat so that their faces almost touched.

By the crude, raspy vocalizations of the old medicine male, these actualities, as had been reported to him by the owl, were administered to the general: First, that his ill-advised chief, Mungo, was dead, killed by the Great Fire Spirit.

Second, the Great Fire Spirit was becoming weary of being treated with disrespect and that, in truth, it was a distinguished hero of the Shadow World, a hero spirit who deserved from the sans-pelages their profoundest adoration and doxology.

Third, that it would surely be in the best interest of all sans-pelages to never provoke the Great Fire Spirit, that it fulfilled its duties, such as they are, quite well and never needed to be given instruction by mortals, and if anyone doubted this fact, then they should visit the corpse of their chief in the nearby salt brush thicket.

Finally, the old medicine male squeezed the throat of the terrified general tighter and asked him if he understood what he had just been told, and the gasping general indicated that he did indeed. So the medicine male let him go his way to inform the others of his ilk of those actualities.

In the flashing light of the war above, the medicine male, with the owl giving directions, began to gather what was left of his clan, for he was told by the owl that if they survived the raging storm above them, then it would surely be a long, long time before they would again have any such sans-pelage threat as Mungo and his wayward army.

The atmosphere, what was left of it after having been sucked into the melee above, was dank and foul. The fires in the forest seemed to lack the air they needed to thrive, so they remained in a state of quietude as stalled, flickering embers, waiting.

When, by the flashing light, Old Ok saw that Pishiu and his mother were taken under the care of the old medicine male with the owl perched on his shoulder, he took it as a sign for him to try to make his way back home. He was confused by what he had seen, and he knew that, besides the owl and the sans-pelages, only he had been witness to what had happened and continued to happen to Moksoos; that the storm above his head was some kind of raging war involving a yellow sans-pelage spear device for killing and an emerald Moksoos cloud. As he lumbered along in a near-fugue state, he heard a voice. It was the owl.

"Old Ok?"

"Yes. It is I," droned the old bear.

"Old Ok. Well. I wonder—must ask you, that is—if you can keep a secret. You know. Keep mum, such as that goes?"

"What do you mean?" asked Old Ok, in a spiritless voice.

"I mean, sir, that business with Moksoos. Uh, I don't know what is going to happen, of course. Or if things don't work out … well … in that case, it probably wouldn't make any difference. But I am quite certain that Moksoos would request it of you, you understand."

"What are you talking about?"

"You see, sir," said the owl, "I must tell you that you are privy to something that, uh, you are not supposed to be privy to. You do understand."

"I don't understand," said Old Ok. "I don't understand anything anymore. I understand only that the more I understand, the more I don't understand. Do you understand?"

"I do understand. I understand completely," said the owl. "It is a sign of wisdom, such as it is, to understand that you don't understand. But, of course, that is a little beside the point here."

"And exactly what is the point?" asked Old Ok.

"That you keep it a secret. What you saw happen to Moksoos today. You keep it a secret forever. Wise old bear, I know you can do that."

"But I still don't understand," said Old Ok. "I mean, why should I keep it a secret? I don't understand at all."

"Moksoos is an Emerald," said the owl. "The Little One is a Yellow. They are presently, I think, having a dispute. Yes. Well, I can see that I must better explain it."

"Indeed!" said Old Ok.

"You see, Ok, Moksoos is a, well, of course he is a cat, but he is also a spirit of the Shadow World, as is the Little One. And you see, the forest-folk—except for me, of course—are not supposed to know about any of this business. It can have a dire effect on the balance. Now, do you understand?"

Old Ok stood silently for a few moments to gather his thoughts and assimilate them. "Well, I don't want to do anything that would disturb the balance."

"It is extraordinarily important for you to keep it a secret," said the owl. "I thank you for speaking out loud. I do believe that—at such a time as this is—it is better than reading. But I would simply love to hear the words, with my ears, that you know I want you to say."

"I will keep it a secret," he said. "But the sans-pelages clearly have seen it all. What of them?"

"It doesn't matter so much, I think. You see, Ok, they are generally too distracted for it to have much of a long-term effect."

Old Ok stood a few more moments in silent contemplation.

"Well, Old Ok," said the owl, "I have spoken frankly with you so far; so, not to break the trend, I shall tell you some gossip I believe you will find most interesting, and pleasantly so."

The owl paused momentarily. Old Ok remained silent.

"It seems that your possum friend, Zak, has stumbled onto the fields of the famous—famous to not only the forest-folk but to the sans-pelages as well, who will have him firmly locked in their legends as their Great Spirit of the Flame and killer of Mungo the Monster.

Indeed, he will be an object of worship for them whenever they are around fire. Of course they, perhaps, will not envision a possum, but they will love him from now on just the same."

"Zak? Killed Mungo? Zak is alive?" said Old Ok.

"Oh yes. Quite. Such as it is."

"Where is he, owl? We must find him! This is cause for celebration!"

"I will not tell you. The balance, Ok. Remember? But I will give you this advice: Have your jaguar friend Swrogah lead the search. But you are getting ahead of yourself, old bear. Look at the sky. It might have toned down a bit, but the war continues. We don't know what is going to happen. We don't know what our future, if there is one at all, will be. So goodbye, Ok. And good luck."

When the owl flew, Old Ok continued his pace toward the region of the forest he called home, the interface between forest and field where sometimes weddings occurred, or used to anyway. He felt guardedly optimistic, guardedly elated, from the news of Zak's existence and the possibility that he might, after all, see his old friend again. And he didn't mind at all keeping a couple of secrets to himself, for the rest of his life if need be, especially if it was for the sake of the balance.

As he ambled on his way, he felt something hit his nose, then his back, then his face and his nose again. It was raining. He looked up at the sky. Now it was glowing, faintly, emerald. The yellow flashing had ceased. He broke into a trot. *This must be good news*, he thought.

# 48

"THEY'RE TRYING TO kill us, Lost Track!" shouted Sark as a sixty-foot-long ash log tumbled from above to bounce with a loud wooden echo.

The thud vibrated the ground underneath the feet of Sark and the baby mastodon, who were huddled against the wall of the great chamber. Then more logs followed to pound the earth in galloping succession.

"That iss yew females, Sok. Da beefers cut da trees foh yew females to carry."

"First they try to drown us and cover our bodies with limbs; now they wish to pummel the remains."

"That iss yew starway, Sok."

"Stairway?" he asked, looking at the large and growing log pile, then back at Lost Track and the famous beaver architect, who was standing at his side.

Ever since Quarral, Lost Track, and Elbon and his birds had left the two mastodons behind, trapped inside their calcareous prison, Quarral's mind had transmogrified itself into a rapidly evolving blueprint, exponentially gaining the full raiment of complexity of detail required to build a giant spiral stairway, one that would give the great gift of freedom to two deserving mastodons.

By his special intuition for such things, Quarral had recognized a lustrous intellect residing behind the eyes of the dire wolf. This wolf, he thought, will be a key component to the successful completion of my greatest masterpiece.

Quarral was fully aware that in this pursuit he had at his disposal the brute power of at least fifty-one mastodons; and all that was needed was a way to coordinate the efforts of beaver and mastodon with a language barrier that stood in between them. So, in no time at all, as if the two bright objects attracted each other, which they indeed did, Quarral and Lost Track had worked out a crude but effective system of body language for communication between the two of them.

So they always worked as a unit of two, never separating, and by early the next morning, a large team of beavers, under instruction by Quarral, was cutting timber, and the mastodon females, by dictum of Lost Track, were hauling the logs up the mountain to deposit them into the crack in the ceiling of the great chamber.

The logging operation was highly selective not only for the proper size and species of the trees to be felled but selective for the presence of the large and healthy muscadine vines growing up their trunks. Before each tree was given over to a mastodon for hauling to the mountaintop, it was first stripped of its great vines. The vines were then gathered and beaver-hauled into the mountain and on into the great chamber where Sark and the baby awaited in puzzled wonderment.

"Yoh, Sok. A sprol starway that go alllll da way to da top. So yew ant da baby can be free. Yew see?"

At that moment, the first of many troops of beaver vine-haulers entered the chamber, dragging their long, frayed and twisted vine load, with Elbon and his birds riding on the top of the freight near its end. As it went rattling by, the little skunk and his birds gave up their perch to join their new group of friends. Quarral, who was standing next to Lost Track, scrutinized the tangled freight for specifications of length and diameter as well as other innumerable quality features as it passed. He leaned back on his paddle with satisfaction, folding his arms on his chest before raising his right hand to his cheek.

"Baysau," he mumbled, smiling to himself.

Phase one of the operation, the gathering of materials, had, by necessity, been far-ranging; for good trees with muscadine vines, though certainly not a rarity, were neither ubiquitous. So, when phase one, with its voracious appetite for vines, was completed, the possums, foxes, and raccoons who lived in the vicinity were left with dim prospects for a generous muscadine grape harvest next summer, and they were sure to look upon Quarral and his castorine engineering outfit with novel suspicions.

At the end of a few long days, a monstrous pile of timber, partially filling the great chamber, betokened the end of phase one. Next to the pile were rows and rows of muscadine vines. It was now getting difficult for a body to maneuver the room.

Lost Track gave the female mastodons a break from their labors as Quarral brought his beaver logging and vining crews inside the mountain to begin construction. Of course, a small dam-maintenance crew remained necessarily stationed on its sunrise-to-sunset duty, but Quarral made certain that its members were substituted from time to time so nobody would miss out on participating in the great historical event that was occurring inside the mountain—the construction of a great spiral chef d'oeuvre by application of revolutionary material—a classic of wooden architecture.

A spiral staircase had never been contemplated, and the application of vines in construction had never before been dreamed. So each arm of the project, as well as their combination, was a coup on the old standards. Quarral and his dam-building crew were in their glory.

Sark and the little mastodon, who had, prior to this time, been only spectators, were put to work, the baby sorting the timber by length and diameter, and Sark setting up the foundation of balusters. The beavers, now weavers, wove and cut and twisted and tied their precious vines and at the same time utilized many of the limbs about the room by the old standards of construction to supply the interstitial framework of the great stairway. The structure, now well tied to the cave's columns and burly beasts, was filling the room. Quarral was constantly in motion, running about the structure, inspecting, crawling in and out of its crannies, giving orders rapid-fire. The great chamber was quickly becoming a great stairwell.

As vertical progress was made, Sark had to carry his heavy logs higher and higher up the previously completed stairs. Quarral watched closely his every move and its effect on the structure, and any sign of weakness that presented itself in this test of strength was met by an overcompensation of weaving and bracing and casing so that the more weight testing that was done, the more the structure grew in robust solidity. Often, he would get Lost Track to send the baby mastodon up the structure behind Sark so he could determine the effect of the weight and motion of both heavy objects.

Finally, when the great vine-woven spiral balustrade was finished, Sark simply stepped outside onto the mountaintop. It was to where he had been log-hauling most of this last day anyway, ending up with his head far above the level of the ceiling's exit. Of course, Quarral and Lost Track were right there with him, and they climbed out, too. They took a whiff of the fresh air and sunshine, then turned around and descended the stairs so they could inspect the finished monument from below and tidy up the scene, which, of course, the cleanup crew had already done by the time they reached the floor.

"And I was just beginning to get a good feel for the place, Lost Track," said Sark. "But I suppose we can't stay here forever. Now, look at that! Isn't it a lovely sight?" he said, looking up at the magnificent wooden edifice.

"Verrry elegant," said Elbon.

"Lost Trok tink iss time to go. Yew want to find that possot, no?" asked the dire wolf, not wishing to remain in the cave long enough to bait the patience of mercurial destiny any further.

"I want to go with you to find Zak," said Elbon.

"Please," said Sark, "let us catch our breath, give ourselves a moment to admire our accomplishment."

As they stood silently looking on, Quarral walked around and around the structure, and from time to time, and surely for the ten thousandth time, he leaned against it, looking up. No matter where he did, the vertical casing, he noticed, was in perfect plumb. He leaned back with his arms in typical chest-folded position and his right hand on his cheek. His eyes were teary.

"Malpa," he said. Not bad.

Sark indicated to Lost Track that he wished to be the last to climb to the top; so, the long procession of beavers, followed by the baby mastodon, Quarral, and Lost Track began their ascension.

"Elbon, you want to ride with me?" Sark asked. "It's a long climb for a hand-walker."

"Oooo," he said as he waddled onto the mastodon's outstretched trunk.

The mastodon females and the beavers were all waiting together on the mountaintop, and when Sark and Elbon, and his birds, finally made their exit from the cave there was a celebration of trumpeting by the females and their babies and tail-slapping by the beavers.

Sark looked upon the rows of beavers and female pachyderms who stood before him. Quarral was standing a little to the side. The old mastodon studied them for a while, and as he did, a wealth of gratitude filled his eyes that they all could surely see. He turned to Lost Track. "How can I ever thank them, Lost Track?"

"Sok, Lost Trok tink moppy yew already haf."

"Lost Track," said the mastodon flatly. "Sark think maybe he has not."

"Come, my fifty dearests!" said Sark. "And bring the babies! I brought you to this mountain to explore a cave, did I not?"

"Come!" he said as he led the great thundering mastodon procession down the new stairway. It was a fortress that never budged, never quivered. And when the mastodons were finished with their cave experience and they exited one by one onto the thin layer of mountaintop, Quarral and his team stood proudly, amazed at that most impressive token of gratitude, the gift of complete confidence in their work. They would never forget the big flop-eared black mastodon whom the dire wolf called Sok.

# 49

"I TELL YOU, ELBON, I have never even been turned around," said Sark, "let alone not known where I was. This is most ridiculous."

The great wolf-and-pachyderm procession was back on the trail, headed south. It had been several days since they'd said goodbye to Quarral and his crew. In fact, they had only recently entered Elbon's home territory, where they had taken a short break so the little skunk could show everyone his beloved sycamore observatory log. And as they continued southward, naturally the subject of *where* homed to the conversation as a buzzard returns to his favorite roost.

"Fremmit! Cridit! Frrremmit, I say! The top of your pachydermal noggin is the densest log I have ever thumped!" said Elbon, bouncing on the top of Sark's head with persevering zeal, the nuthatches having long abandoned their skunk-foot perches for new and more sedate locations on each of Sark's bushy eyebrows.

"Perhaps it's the first one you have thumped that is not hollow!" said Sark. "Have you thought of that with that hollow little sycamore head of yours?"

"No! No! No, Sir Sark! You don't get it! Listen to me. You might never have been lost and not known where you were, both at the same time; but you have never known where you were anytime. And you need only to look at the stars to find that out. And it can be verrry disturbing, Sir Sark."

"Well?" said Sark. "If it should turn out to be such a 'verrry disturbing' experience, why do you so vehemently recommend it?"

"So you will understand!" said Elbon.

"Then I shall have to consider it sometime," said Sark, almost ready to surrender.

"Lost Trok tink moppy Olbont iss right, Sok."

"Oh! That is just fine, Lost Track," said Sark. "You, too, now. His disease is contagious, I see."

"Noh. Noh, Sok. Lost Trok tink moppy that iss da food foh tawt. Yew see?"

"Lost Track," said the mastodon, "Sark thinks maybe you have been eating too much willow bark."

"Well, I agree with Elbon, too," said Number Two.

"Me, too," said Number One.

"You really must listen to Lost Track, dear."

"And to Elbon, dear."

"An unfurled youthful frond of fern's thy nose."

"Elbon is the expert in this matter, dear."

"Dear, you really don't know where you are. Now do you?"

"When was the last time you looked at the stars, dear?"

"They have the clues, dear."

"Maybe you need a sycamore log."

"Sark is more windy than wise."

"That's it. Hold tight to the tail in front."

"All right! All right!" said Sark, grinning and shaking his head. "I know when I'm whipped. I surrender. So, everybody listen closely: I don't know where I am! I don't know where I am! I don't know where I am! And that is precisely my present location in the matter."

"Excellent! Excellent! Excellent!" said Elbon, thumping in delight.

Suddenly, Lost Track came to a halt, creating yet another black-pachyderm collision in the rank.

"Sok! Da air! There iss somptink int da air! Somptink interestink!"

# 50

THE RAIN FELL in the chilled, fragrant dampness of the early morning. It had, so far, been gentle and soaking, and it seemed as if it would stay around for a while yet. The forest region, so long starved for moisture, was now being replenished. The red mastodons had just returned from their alternate wintering grounds by the lake; for the vicinity of the forest-prairie interface was their favorite, so long as there was water. Old Ok stood before a stunned and wide-eyed audience as he finished up recounting his tale.

"Now do you see how Moksoos and I thought we were finished? Well, we were! But it was just at that moment when that terrible storm struck, and we were able to escape. Everyone was knocked to the ground by those smashing thunderclaps, and the sky became so black and yellow and green. I tell you I am one old bear, but I have never seen anything like it before. Some peculiar storm that was. Was it not? And it came out of nowhere! But it was what saved Moksoos and me by giving us a chance to escape those awful sans-pelages of Mungo. Funny how things sometimes work out when you least expect them to.

"Well, that is why I called this meeting. So all of you could hear it at the same time and I won't need to go on repeating it over and over, though I'm sure I probably will anyway. But there you have it. You have it all. And all that the owl said to me, too. Every single word of it."

At those last words, he glanced at Moksoos, who was sitting nearby, and he winked. And he could hardly keep from breaking into a grin. A little stretching of the truth for the sake of the balance was, for Old Ok, a pleasurable enterprise.

"And now," Old Ok continued, "I believe it is time for us to gather ourselves for a hunt, a hunt for the Great Fire Spirit!"

"But why," asked the jag, "would the owl suggest that I lead this party? When the possum and I separated so long ago on the mastodon highway, I went south. I had simply directed him to go north into the forest when it appeared that in doing so he could safely skirt the sans-pelage population of the region. But where he went after that I could not guess. It would be only a blind search; I can assure you of that."

"Swrogah, dear," said Moksoos, "are you going to lead us, or would you rather disappoint this fine assemblage? Come now. Your little possum has become a hero. Let us rise to the occasion and bring him home."

Swrogah looked around at the audience and its many eyes that were fixed on her.

"Well," she said, "if a field trip is what you all want, then let us not tarry longer."

So the jag set out for the west; she was flanked by Moksoos, Old Ok, Sena, Opal, and Shinboo. And what followed them was a great gathering of forest-folk that included foxes, deer, raccoons, ringtails, elk, Big Tal and his red mastodon herd, a collection of bison and gray wolves, several bobcats, wolverines and cougars and armadillos and turkeys and on and on. Even a pair of possums joined the rear ranks.

Off they went toward the west along the mastodon trail in search of their hero. The grand convoy of animals, big and small, quick and slow, moved along to the rhythm of the happy dispositions of its membership; all were chattering and gossiping and asking one another how each had ridden out the terrific storm and had they ever seen anything like it before and could they believe that a possum (their own poet at that!) had actually killed Mungo and become a legend and where could he possibly be and how in the world was he going to manage the duties of possum and poet and fire spirit all at the same time and didn't Old Ok and Moksoos get lucky being saved from those mean and nasty sans-pelages and wasn't Moksoos on his best behavior and wasn't it nice how the jag had taken the fierceness out of him and how in the world did this owl know all that stuff and who would be getting married next when the poet was found and, now that the mastodons had returned, when would the rodents return and wasn't it nice to finally be getting this good rain.

Finally, they reached the spot where the jag had, so many months ago, said goodbye to Zak so that she could continue alone to find Moksoos. It was here on the mastodon highway that she had directed Zak to turn north into the great forest, and it was here that she had implanted his mind with those most bedeviling questions of identity. So, without hesitation, they turned to the right and headed north to soon enter another region. And if they stayed the direction, it would lead them straight to Elbon's sycamore log. Swrogah didn't waver.

# 51

W HEN HE LEFT the scene of the bonfire and the bodies of Mungo and the roasting general, Zak continued his northwesterly course. He was still hopelessly lost and had no idea what direction he was following. He was a little shaken from his fall from the red oak and into the bonfire, but he was neither scratched nor badly singed from the experience.

Zak's direction of flight seemed to him most serviceable because there had been a strange storm of thunder and yellow and green fireballs and lightning bolts that had battered the sky behind him. As he traveled on, leaving the storm and his region far on the horizon, he thought back over the events of that strange evening: *How peculiar. First, I was chased up that grand old tree by coyotes only to later fall out of it and into a fire. And to land on what? No. What on earth would one of them be doing in the middle of a fire? And what was that I accidentally ran over? I swear I believe it was a sans-pelage. Perhaps it was asleep. Or dead. Well, it was certainly a scene from which to make tracks. That I do know.*

One afternoon, to his happy surprise Zak heard a familiar voice that came from a low hickory limb. It was Pitsee, his little flying squirrel friend and historian for the Canopy Connection. And it was indeed a most pleasant reunion they had as he trotted along and she skipped through the air from tree trunk to tree trunk, but she had so many questions for him to answer that he never got the opportunity to ask her which way his home was.

\* \* \* \* \*

The events that soon came to be were, of course, accurately reported on the spot by Pitsee, but at the time, many important details were yet to be available to her, although, she knew more than Zak did. Actually, Zak had not much new to offer her as they traveled the forest together, nearing the end of his lonely adventure. The only new information he could share was that of his fall from the tree and the fire and the bodies, all of which she thought was quite interesting, but its true significance could not have been known to her at the time any more than it was known to Zak.

It was not until a little later that so much of this important information was delivered to the Canopy Connection by a great horned owl—information that brought Zak a much higher status than did the title of "the architect's lost talking possum." Of course, Pitsee's fame as a reporter of current historical events would grow immensely, too.

The best accounting of the events to follow on that last day came later, when it was documented in an interview Pitsee gave to another young flying squirrel historian-reporter, whom she had, most ceremoniously, married at the "party," which she briefly alluded to in the interview.

An excerpt of her statements from that interview, though not strictly translated due to certain rather cumbersome idioms of the Rodent language, goes like this:

"Of course I did not know many details of the events of that region at the time because I had few reports from its rodents. They were in the process of returning to their homes, for they had all temporarily migrated to another region farther south, and that, of course, was their salvation, or it seemed to be, for not a single rodent perished. The warning system was finally properly activated, and it worked perfectly.

"But what amazed me was that our possum hero had gone marching into that dangerous region in the first place. And that is, of course, when I lost him, for I was not about to follow. One must remain among the living to continue to be a successful historian, you know.

But I came to find out that he had not been warned himself, and it was for two good reasons.

"First: When he entered the region, there were no rodents left in it to tell him that there was an evacuation. And the other reason: He was not told of the evacuation before he went in. To this day, I feel a bit guilty for not telling him myself, but I simply assumed that he knew not to go in there. So it was truly a relief to see him again that day when he came up from the southeast. I had many, many questions for him as we continued for the good long while that we did. He was cheery and seemed quite happy that we were together again. But there toward the end of that last day, as he was walking along, suddenly, he stopped and began to look and sniff about, like he recognized something. He did. It was well-known territory to him.

"He said, 'I've been here before. I know this place. Yes. It was here that I first met Elbon. His favorite log is somewhere ahead as I recall.' I said, 'Now, who is this Elbon again?' Then he said, 'You know. Elbon, the spotted skunk who walks upside down. You told me about him following my trail all the way to the tundra, then turning around and going all the way back home.' 'Oh, so that was Elbon,' I said. 'I know who you are talking about now. You asked me to send out a bulletin for him and that black mastodon. I didn't recognize the name, but I remember your saying it now.' And he said, 'Well, we must find that log. How nice it would be to see him again.'

"You know, I wonder if it was Elbon who was the friend—the friend who helped our hero find the architect. I never got the name.

"Well. As I say, to this day I feel badly about the fact that I had some information that he didn't know about but surely would have loved to have known. But, you see, I didn't know that he didn't know, and he didn't know to ask, I suppose. But that's how things get crosswise. I mean, I certainly knew that there were two very large expeditions looking for him; the one from the south I had recently heard about from a chipmunk—so quickly was the Connection reestablishing itself. And, of course, the architect himself had informed us days earlier about the one that was coming down from the North. And I knew that skunk was with it. But I sure had forgotten his name.

"Did you know that I'm getting that interview with the architect about his famous spiral stairway?

"So, anyway, it was about then that our possum walked under a palmetto leaf—I think he was distracted by a beetle. And that's when I looked around and saw them coming. From both the north and the south. These two great caravans coming straight at us. It was grand.

"Well, now, I thought that possum was pulling wool over my eyes, you see—playing dumb like that amid this big encounter. But when I think back on it, I remember that he was on the ground under that palmetto leaf and I was on a limb at the time, a better vantage point. So he really didn't see them coming, and, as it turns out, he didn't even know they were supposed to be coming. He was lost, and I didn't even know it.

"But, you see, I thought he had been playing a trick on me, so I climbed down to where he was sitting, and I said, 'Well? Aren't you going to invite me to your party?' He gave me the strangest look. Then we both heard the noises, and he looked to the south. And he was completely startled. I was watching him. Then he looked to the north and saw them coming, too. If only you could have seen his expression. Then he turned and looked me right in the eye and said, 'Incomprehensible!' I'd heard him say that before, you know."

# The Meeting of
# the Forest Committee

The carnivores ate catfish lips; the herbs had saw briar soup.
Chair Owl then rapped the gavel as the foreman of the group.

And the meeting came to order as all good meetings should.
But mission tends to vaporize in the shadow of the wood.

The squirrels complained of sour nuts brought on by a rainy spring.
The turtles clammed up from the start and never said a thing.

A scorpion scooped up gossip on the widow, Mrs. Black.
A possum was indignant that his tail had too much slack.

A beetle bugged a butterfly. The snakes went underground.
A 'dillo showed up fully armed. The bats just hung around.

The fire ants stoked the powwow fire 'til the powwow fuel was burned.
So, there not being further biz, the meeting was adjourned.

And the primrose wilted laughing, and the old pines shook their scales.
The privets all privately chuckled, and the dogwoods wagged their tails.

# Acknowledgments

My deepest thanks to Elizabeth Betsy Gilbert for her remarkably valuable role in the editing of *Shadowshine*.

Many thanks to Michael Mirolla and Guernica Editions for their support and publication of *Shadowshine*.

Some of us are fortunate to have had a childhood hero who has remained a hero throughout life, thus withstanding the test of time. Mine is the great American artist Charles M. Russell, from whom came my inspiration for the Shadow World and two of my characters, the great horned owl and the medicine man.

# About the Author

Conservationist and retired medical doctor (pathology), Johnny and his wife Karen and Opal (k-nine) live within a Nature Conservancy protected old-growth forest and woodland near Ruston, Louisiana.